SAFE
AT
HOME

LAUREN NORTH

CORGI BOOKS

TRANSWORLD PUBLISHERS
Penguin Random House, One Embassy Gardens,
8 Viaduct Gardens, London SW11 7BW
www.penguin.co.uk

Transworld is part of the Penguin Random House group of companies
whose addresses can be found at global.penguinrandomhouse.com

First published in Great Britain in 2021 by Corgi Books
an imprint of Transworld Publishers

A CIP catalogue record for this book
is available from the British Library.

ISBN
9780552177955

Typeset in 11/13.5pt Sabon by Jouve (UK), Milton Keynes.
Printed and bound in Great Britain by Clays Ltd, Elcograf S.p.A.

The authorized representative in the EEA is Penguin Random House
Ireland, Morrison Chambers, 32 Nassau Street, Dublin D02 YH68.

Penguin Random House is committed to a sustainable future
for our business, our readers and our planet. This book is made
from Forest Stewardship Council® certified paper.

To the ladies in my village; this one is for you.

Halloween

Village Girlies' Group Chat
Saturday 31 October, 18.45

Me: Has anyone got Harrie with them? She hasn't come back from trick-or-treating yet. @SandraBriggs she said she was meeting you at 5 p.m. Have you seen her?

Tracy Campbell: Sorry, no.

Gina Walker: She's not here. Clarissa says Harrie wasn't with them.

Me: Really? Are you sure?

Sandra Briggs: I kept an eye on all of them and Harrie definitely wasn't there. What costume was she wearing?

Me: A werewolf. Same as last year. If anyone sees her, please call me!

Gina Walker: Will do. Let us know when she's home safe x

Village Girlies' Secret Group Chat
Saturday 31 October, 19.58

Tracy Campbell: Has Harrie been found yet? I didn't want to ask in the other group.

Sandra Briggs: I don't think so.

Bev Pritchett: Anyone know what's going on?

Tracy Campbell: I thought I heard a siren a minute ago.

Bev Pritchett: OMG! Poor Anna. I hope she's OK!!

Tracy Campbell: Oh come on! I feel sorry for Anna, but, like I've said before, she brought this on herself!!!!

Sandra Briggs: True.

Bev Pritchett: Should one of us call Anna?

Tracy Campbell: Kat will know what's going on. Kat, are you reading this?

Bev Pritchett: Give your babies an extra kiss and cuddle tonight, ladies. Too precious for words!

Tracy Campbell: xx

Ten days earlier

Chapter 1

Wednesday, ten days until Halloween

Anna

The very thought of what I'm about to do scratches at the wall of my stomach as I shove the dinner plates haphazardly into the dishwasher. I slam the door shut, sending a silent prayer to the dishwasher gods that the machine will work today.

Excuses leap across my mind as I drag a cloth over the kitchen worktops.

It's dark outside.

It's too late.

What if you get scared?

What if you choke on something?

They keep coming, but I bite them back, squish them down.

We agreed, and that's all there is to it. Well, they did – Rob, Elise and Harrie. The three of them sounding so reasonable, as though it's utter madness we've not done it sooner. I can't blame Molly for this one. She's only seven and idolizes her big sisters.

'They're eleven now, Anna,' Rob said to me three weeks ago on his regular seven p.m. call. His face jolted and froze every few seconds as the image bounced across time zones and satellites. His voice was out of sync with the movement of his lips, his smile, the slight lift of his eyebrows, but at least we got to see him. 'In less than a year Elise and Harrie will be at secondary school. They'll have to get the bus on their own, they'll have to be responsible. Don't you think we should start getting them ready for that?'

'I guess,' had been my weary response.

'How about letting Harrie stay home on her own while you and Molly collect Elise from gymnastics on Wednesdays?' Rob continued. 'It's only twenty minutes and only once a week. And Elise can be left on Saturdays when you drop Harrie at football practice. When Elise doesn't have gymnastics, that is.'

'Everyone else in our class is doing it,' Elise chipped in. 'Everyone' was said with a slight pause between the syllables so it sounded like ev-re-one.

'Kat's been leaving Ben on his own since he was nine,' Harrie added, her tone as indignant as her twin's.

That was true. Kat is my best friend. I love her dearly, but how she's been able to leave Ben alone while she pops to the shops or goes to the gym is beyond my comprehension.

'But June next door doesn't mind popping in when we need her,' I replied. 'And anyway, it's nice to drive together and have a chat in the car.'

'For you, maybe,' Harrie said with an eye-roll.

'It's time, Anna. This isn't London,' Rob laughed then. 'They're safe at home. Barton St Martin has won Best Village Neighbourhood Watch in the county two years running. Come on, don't be a worrywart,' he added with a teasing smile.

I hate that name almost as much as I hate the phrase that usually accompanies it. *You never used to worry so much.* He's right, I didn't. But look where that got me.

Resentment courses through me. A bitterness I can taste in the back of my throat. *It's always on me, isn't it, Rob? Every sodding thing is down to me because you're not here.*

I turn my attention back to the dishwasher. There is no hum of the electrics. No *shhh* of water spilling into the machine. 'You piece of junk,' I hiss, opening the door and slamming it shut again before kicking the base, because in the history of broken kitchen appliances a swift kick in the electrical goolies always works. Not this time, it seems.

I glance at my phone, swallowing down the disappointment at the blank screen. No reply from Dean. I catch sight of the time. 7.27 p.m. already. 'Shit!' I abandon my battle with the dishwasher and dash into the hall.

'Molly,' I shout up the stairs. 'Time to get out of the bath. We've got to leave in twenty minutes.'

'OK, Mummy,' comes an echoey reply.

I poke my head into the living room and the first thing I see is the mess – a Barbie explosion on the rug. Dozens of tiny outfits – dresses, shoes, bags, tiaras – laid out before a pile of naked, messy-haired dolls. The riot of colour is almost enough to distract me from one of Elise's wireless headphones left on the floor. God knows where the other earpiece is. I'll be furious if she's lost it. They're the cheap imitations, but still we can't afford to replace them. I should be glad. There was one point after Christmas when I thought she'd never take them out.

Even after all this time, it's hard not to feel the sting of disappointment when I look in this room. Hard not to compare it to the long sitting room of our London house. The big leather sofas, the huge stripy rug on the oak floorboards, the crystal vase above the fireplace – all the things we couldn't take with us when we ran.

The second thing I see is Harrie, lying across the length of an ancient sofa – a beige monstrosity which despite being hideous is at least comfortable. Her long legs are stretched out and she's watching some screeching US TV show that looks like a remake of *Saved by the Bell*. Her shoulder-length black hair is loose and scooped behind her ears. She glances at me with her usual wide smile, and I light up inside.

All three of our daughters have Rob's dark features and what he calls Disney princess faces – large eyes, button noses and rosebud lips. Although only Molly likes to hear that now. Harrie and Elise roll their eyes at anything Disney. Twincesses, we used to call them. Their hair is thick like Rob's too, nothing like my wispy blonde hair that never seems to grow longer than a bob before breaking – brittle and dry.

A memory pushes to the surface. The twins aged four or five, disappearing into the bathroom together, returning ten minutes later wearing each other's clothes. They did it all the time. At pre-school and at home, confusing the staff, confusing Rob. Not me though. I can always tell them apart.

Harrie is still wearing her school uniform. Trousers not skirt, and no frill to her white shirt collar. She's throwing an orange football in the air and catching it. I've given up trying to stop her bringing the balls into the house. Harrie without a football in her hands or rolling at her feet doesn't look right somehow.

'Why are your sisters such messy creatures?' I ask, nodding to the rug.

Harrie raises one eyebrow in a Rob-like way. 'Have you seen the state of your bedroom this week?'

'Oi.' We both laugh as I pick up a nearby cushion and fling it at her. She knocks it to one side with her hand and offers me a triumphant grin. 'We're leaving soon, OK?'

'Sure,' Harrie replies.

'You can come with us, you know? If you don't want to be on your own?'

She gives a huffing laugh. 'I'll stay here, thanks.'

The light inside me fizzles.

'Oh Mum,' Harrie gasps. 'I forgot to tell you. Clarissa is getting a puppy and she said I can walk it with her and help her look after it whenever I want, and when they go on holiday, we can take care of it.'

'That's great.'

I can tell there's more Harrie wants to say. There are always more words with Harrie, my chatterbox of a girl, but I pull a face and point at my watch. I can't get dragged into another conversation about getting a dog. Instead, I race up the stairs to Molly, who is still in the bath playing with a soggy collection of My Little Ponies.

'Molly, I've asked already,' I say, my voice betraying my frustration. 'Get out please. We need to get Elise.'

Why is it always such a rush? No matter how early I cook dinner, listen to reading, run the bath, why are we always one breath away from being late on Wednesdays?

'I didn't hear you.' Her bottom lip quivers.

Yes you did. I keep the reply in and curse Elise's gymnastics coach for offering another two hours on top of the six Elise already does. Because six hours of gymnastics a week isn't enough any more. Not if she wants to stay in the elite squad, which she does, desperately, and so I've shoehorned another thing into our week that really doesn't fit.

'Come on,' I say, softening my voice and reaching for Molly's towel. I hold it up and she hops out before jumping into my arms for a soggy hug that soothes my frustration. 'Go get your onesie on and then I'll brush your hair.'

'Mummy, how many days until Daddy calls?'

'Four days, baby. He'll call on Sunday like always.'

More numbers run through my head. Rob has been gone thirty-four days and it's another fifty-six days before he comes home, but I don't tell Molly that. All the girls have their own countdown calendars in their bedrooms to look at.

'Can Bunny come with us to collect Elise?' She stuffs the worn fur of her bunny to her face and breathes in its smell – a magical heal-all act.

'Of course. As long as he doesn't snore this time.' I smile, kissing the top of her head.

Molly scuttles down the hall to her bedroom, the towel wrapped around her like a mantle.

My eyes move to my watch. 7.36 p.m.

The pressure returns – a bear hug of worry about being late for Elise and leaving Harrie. It squeezes me oh-so-tight. It's worse tonight than it was last week and the one before that. Thoughts of what happened on Monday with Dean threaten to break free and I wish for the hundredth time that I could take it all back. I don't trust my judgement any more and it makes leaving Harrie even harder.

'Nothing will go wrong.' It's what Rob would say if he was here right now.

Harrie is sensible. She's not like Gina and Martin's girl, Clarissa, who used marker pens to draw over her bedroom walls because she wasn't allowed to play at the park, or Kat's Ben who punched a hole in his door when he lost at a game on the Xbox. And Barton St Martin is the very definition of a sleepy village. 'Nothing will go wrong,' I whisper to myself again.

But of course it does.

Chapter 2

Anna

The gymnastics car park is bedlam as usual. Half the cars are trying to get out, the other half are trying to get in, and by the time I've waited my turn, and weaved my way through, it's 8.02 p.m. and Elise is walking out of the doors in her purple leotard and matching leggings, looking exhausted in the beams of the passing headlights.

I glance at Elise as she settles in the seat beside me. Her cheeks are flushed red and wisps of dark hair have fallen from her ponytail and hang around her heart-shaped face.

'How was it?' I ask her.

'Good.' She yawns, arching her back and stretching her arms up to the top of her head. She throws a glance to the back seats where Molly is doing the hundred-mile stare and stroking Bunny's ear to her cheek. 'Is Harrie at home?'

'Yes. We'll be back in ten minutes. Don't fall asleep, Molly,' I say, loud and sing-song-y.

'When can I be left on my own?' Elise asks. 'I'm the oldest.'

14

'Only by three minutes.'

'Dad said I could stay home when you take Harrie to football.'

'Only when you don't have gymnastics on a Saturday. When was the last Saturday you didn't have gymnastics?'

Elise exhales in the huffing way she does any time I say or do something she doesn't agree with. I think she's going to argue her point, but then she sits up straight, glancing back towards the gymnastics centre. 'I've left my jumper by the beams. Can we go back?'

'Not tonight,' I reply as we pull out of the car park and pick up speed. 'You'll be back there on Friday. You can get it then.'

A sudden heat creeps over my face and I'm grateful for the darkness of the car. Last time Elise left her jumper behind, it ended up in the lost-property bin – a huge plastic tub that stank of cheesy feet and sweat. I dug through it and found Elise's jumper, but I also found a leotard the perfect size for Molly. There was no name in it, so I took it – stole it – because I didn't have £32 to spend on the club leotard they all have to wear and I wouldn't have it next month either. I washed it and pretended it was new and Molly was so happy. Nobody knows I did that, but still the humiliation burns.

'But Mum—'

'Elise, no.' The words are more snappish than I intend and Elise turns her head away in a sulk, staring into the pitch-black night.

Sometimes I wish she would be more grateful for these journeys and the hundred ways our lives are stretched and bent around her gymnastics. I want to tell her for the millionth time how lucky she is and how my own mother never let me do gymnastics, or drama like Molly or football like Harrie. 'It's down to the school,' my mother used to say. 'Ask them.' I want to tell Elise how deprived my childhood was, not just of activities – of board games and bedtime stories – but of love, and how I have always vowed not to give my girls the same experience I had. I keep the words in. Elise will roll her eyes and I know she'll be thinking of all the things her friends have that she doesn't. The things we could have given her if we hadn't had to run away.

The familiar slap of resentment hits me again.

This is your fault, Rob, I want to scream. *You are the reason we had to leave London. You are the reason Harrie is alone right now. You shouldn't be a million miles away on an oil rig off the coast of Nigeria. You should be here with me, with us.*

I take a breath and remind myself that this is what I signed up for. We've been doing this dance of three months away, two weeks at home, for nearly four years. It's not Rob who has changed things recently, it's me. Fifty-six days until he is home. Eight weeks to find the words for my confession.

Thoughts of Monday leap into my head again and with them comes Dean. My skin feels clammy beneath my cardigan. The what-the-hell-have-I-done? question fizzes in my stomach like the white powdery sherbet the girls love so much.

I itch to check my phone again. Why hasn't Dean replied to my text? I wonder if his silence is about the line we crossed on Monday, or something else. Dean's mood has been plummeting for weeks. He's been edgy, distracted, but never tells me why. I know he sees me as an escape. Precious moments of forgetting the world. And so I've never pressed him, never forced him to talk.

16

He leaves his problems by the door, dumping them next to my own as he kicks off his shoes.

I pull on to the A12 with its two lanes of traffic running each side of a thick metal barrier and a no man's land of weeds and grass. I check my mirror. Molly's head is slumped forward, Bunny's too – his floppy body strangled in her tight grasp. I'll have to carry her up to bed and she hasn't done her teeth or gone to the bathroom.

What if she has an accident in the night? What if she tells a friend and the whole class finds out and she's bullied?

I force myself to focus on the road and a container lorry trundling slowly up the hill on the inside lane ahead of us. There's a row of ten or so cars behind it and I join the queue. Vehicles pull out and we creep closer to the lorry.

The signpost for Barton St Martin comes into view and from my wing mirror I catch sight of a car speeding in the outside lane, racing towards us doing at least a hundred miles an hour. A second later and it whooshes by. 'Idiot,' I say to myself.

Then it happens. There's a noise – a bang like a gun. The speeding car skids, weaving across the road towards the lorry, and suddenly I'm slamming on the brakes, jolting us forwards, eyes scrunching shut, waiting for the smack of impact.

Chapter 3

Anna

As my twelve-year-old Nissan judders to a halt, I open my eyes, my gaze flying to the rear-view mirror, bracing myself for the car behind to hit us, but it stops in time.

I look to the front again just in time to see the skidding estate car suddenly launch into the air. The lorry up ahead tries to veer away, crashing into the barriers. The screech of metal on metal fills the night. A split second later the car hits the tarmac, landing upside down, the roof collapsing like it's made of tin foil, and still it skids towards the central reservation and the line of traffic heading the other way.

The lorry is still moving too and a moment after the car stops, it seems to sway – a branch jostling in the wind – before it topples, landing on its side, the sound jackhammer loud. It misses the upturned car by a metre.

'Oh my God,' Elise says. Her mouth is hanging open and I realize mine is too, as though neither of us can believe our eyes. There's an eerie stillness to the crash and for a moment it seems like time has paused, but then people leap out of their cars and jog towards the wreck. Others hang back and I spot three people with phones pressed to their ears. Hazard lights go on, adding an orange strobe-like feel to the scene.

I'm relieved when the lorry driver pulls himself out of the cab. I think about getting out too and offering to help, but already I can see people milling around. What good would I be? My first aid doesn't stretch beyond cleaning grazes, applying plasters and kissing away tears.

'It's OK,' I say to myself as much as to Elise.

I turn to check on Molly. She's still fast asleep.

I squeeze Elise's arm. 'We're OK.'

'Is the driver of the car dead?' she asks in a loud whisper.

'I don't know.'

The panic returns – a fireball in my chest. We witnessed a crash. We're fine, but the road ahead is blocked. I check the time. It feels like hours have passed since I last looked.

It's 8.11 p.m.

Harrie has been on her own for twenty-three minutes. She'll be expecting us home any second. My heart starts to race so fast it feels like it's going to explode.

What if we're stuck here for hours?

What if something happens to Harrie while she's alone?

No, no, no, no, no. I can't let that happen!

I grab my bag from the footwell by Elise's feet. My hands shake as I dig through the pockets and for a horrifying second I think I've left my mobile on the worktop in the kitchen, but then my fingers knock against the hard plastic and I pull it free.

'Mum, what's wrong?' Elise asks.

'I need to phone home and tell Harrie we're stuck.'

'Are we going to be here all night?' Elise asks, looking from me to the wreckage and back again.

I give what I hope is a reassuring smile as I press the phone to my ear. 'I'm sure they'll clear the road quite quickly.' *Please please please let that be true.*

The answering machine clicks on. An electronic voice tells me no one is available to take my call. But Harrie is there. My daughter is home.

The desire to scream grabs hold of my throat. I'm not this person. I'm not a mother who leaves her child alone in the house. I'm the mother who always makes sure they look both ways before crossing the road. Every road. Even in Barton St Martin where the cars stop to let us pass. I'm the mother who won't let my children knock for their friends and go to the village playground without me. I'm the kind of mother who plans everything. General Mummy, Rob likes to call me with a twinkle in his eye and a cheeky grin. *Sir, yes, sir, General Mummy.* Organized. It's another thing I never used to be.

'Harrie?' I say into the silence as my message begins to record. 'Harrie, it's Mum. Pick up the phone, please.' I pause, expecting a click and to hear her voice, too breathy where she holds the mouthpiece so close. The silence stretches out. 'Harrie, I know you're there. There's been a car accident ahead of us on the road. We're fine. We've not crashed, but we're stuck and I don't know how long it's going to be before we get home. Can you pick up, please? Or call me back? My number is written on the Post-it by the phone.'

I stare at my screen and try to calculate how long it will take her to dial my number. Minutes pass and nothing. I call again and leave another message. And then I call June, our neighbour. She's always offering to help and has been a godsend on the occasions when one of the girls has been ill and I've not wanted to drag them with me, but I don't like to ask too often. June is in her eighties and the girls run rings around her.

The phone is a constant hum in my ear, but no one answers. I hear June's voice in my head. *Why do I want the hassle of an answering machine? If they can't get hold of me, they can try again later.*

'Harrie's probably gone to bed,' Elise says from beside me when I eventually give up.

'I hope so.' Could Harrie already be in bed, none the wiser as to the events unravelling before us? Harrie has always been a deep sleeper, out like a light the moment her head hits the pillow.

There was a spell after London, when we were living on top of each other in a one-bedroom flat on the edge of Ipswich, when Harrie had night terrors. Harrie and Elise were five – Molly just one – and all three had been ripped from everything they'd ever known. Night after night Harrie would sit up in bed, eyes open but unseeing, breathing fast, screaming, trapped in a place where I couldn't reach her. It was unbearable to see her like that and a huge relief when they passed and she started to sleep normally again.

'What do we do now?' Elise asks.

I shrug. 'Sit and wait.'

Elise pulls a face.

'Tell me about gymnastics, what did you do tonight?'

'It was conditioning,' she says with a sigh. 'I'm so hungry. Have you got anything to eat?'

I dig through my bag and find a squashed granola bar, floppy and more crumbs than bar by the feel of it. I hand it to Elise and unwind the deep-purple scarf

21

June knitted me for Christmas last year before looping it around her neck.

'Thanks.'

'Have you done all of your homework this week?' I ask Elise.

'Yeah, I did it all on Sunday,' she says through a mouthful of food and I try not to look surprised. From day one, Harrie was the worker and Elise the one who coasted through primary school, putting just enough effort into her schoolwork to get a 'meets expectations' mark on every report. But over the summer she sat me down, looking nervous and excited all in one go, and told me that she didn't want to go to the high school in the next village where Harrie and the rest of her class will go the following year. She wanted to go to a private school forty minutes away by bus. 'It's got one of the best gymnastics programmes in the country, and I'll get a fantastic education,' she said, sounding so confident. 'And there are scholarships and bursaries,' she added quickly, seeing the look of horror dawning on my face. 'If I work hard and do well in their entrance exam then I can get all my fees paid.'

I'm proud of her for applying herself, for the homework she does on time, and the extra tuition she's having with Mr Pritchett, the head teacher. And I want it for her desperately, as much as she wants it for herself.

When I first found out I was pregnant with Harrie and Elise, I promised myself that I'd be the kind of mother who always listened, always made time for my children. I promised I'd be there for them in a way my own mother never had been for me. I promised myself I'd give them everything they wanted and it kills me that we can't give this to Elise.

It's on the tip of my tongue to say something. A little

speech that straddles the line between encouraging Elise to strive for what she wants and managing her expectations, softening the blow if it should come. She needs a perfect school record and top grades. She needs to do well in the entrance exam and wow a panel of three staff members during a thirty-minute interview in January. And even if she does all those things, they still might choose to give the scholarship to someone else. She's only eleven. There is no manual for this stuff.

'You know—' The lights around us change and I fall silent. Blinking orange becomes strobing blue. A siren whoops then squeals, making me jump. I pull the car over to the barrier at the side of the road, making space for the emergency vehicles to reach the crash, and then I turn off the engine.

Within what feels like seconds three police cars, two ambulances and one fire engine have parked just ahead of us and there are more lights flashing behind us where I guess they're closing the road. Molly sleeps on. Elise and I watch the scene and on my lap my phone sits silent.

My eyes draw to the clock on the dashboard. 8.35 p.m. My stomach lurches. Harrie has been home alone for forty-seven minutes. Why hasn't she called back?

Chapter 4

Anna

'You do realize,' Elise says, twisting the empty granola-bar wrapper into a tight ball, 'that if you'd let us have phones like everyone else our age, you could text Harrie right now.'

'Not everyone else your age has a mobile. Besides, you have an iPod.' A second-hand reconditioned one which we still couldn't really afford.

'They do. And you won't let me use the message app on it, so it's just games and music.'

'Well, you can wait until next year when you go to high school for a proper phone, which by the way is still a lot younger than I was. I didn't get a mobile until I was in my late teens.'

'Only because they weren't invented before then.' Elise flashes me a smile, letting me know she's teasing me, and I laugh. I wonder what she'd make of the brick-like Nokia I had when I was a teenager, long before apps and Wi-Fi and predictive text, when the only game was a slow-moving snake chasing itself around the screen.

The laughter dies in my throat and ends with an exhaled 'ha'. The driver of the car could be dead. Someone's family could be missing a loved one. Harrie is all by herself and I can't get to her. There is nothing funny about this situation.

We watch in silence as the police officers talk to the driver of the lorry. Someone has wrapped a silver blanket around his shoulders. Even from this distance I can see he's shouting, hands gesticulating in the air. The paramedics and firemen are kneeling by the car, talking to whoever is inside.

'Are you going to get out and talk to the police?' Elise asks me, her voice suddenly grumpy. Tired. 'How long are we going to be here for?'

'I don't know.' I sound so patient. Calm and collected. Nothing like how I feel – trapped. I stare at the police officers and fight the urge to leap out and race over to them, to shake them, beg them to find a way to let me through. 'They've got more important things to do right now than talking to me.'

I look at Molly. Her head has dropped back against her car seat and her mouth is slack. Bunny has fallen to the floor and I scoop him up, brushing his worn fur with my fingers before placing him gently on her lap for when she wakes. Then I call the home phone two more times and June once. The calls go unanswered and I feel the worry claw at every piece of me from the inside out. A hundred what-ifs race through my mind.

The minutes tick by.

Five minutes.

Ten minutes.

Just when I don't think I can stand it any more, two police officers break away from the others and begin walking towards the cars.

'It's going to be fine. I'll just be a minute,' I tell Elise as one of the officers approaches us. I open the door and step out into the cold October night.

'Hi,' I say, wrapping my cardigan tight around my body. The officer is young. A twenty-something wearing a yellow fluorescent jacket over his black uniform. He has a prominent nose and a sharp goatee.

'I'm PC Jeremy Ross. Have you or anyone in your vehicle sustained any injuries?' He bends down and peers into the car, looking at Molly and waving a gloved hand at Elise.

'No. We're fine,' I reply. 'Are the people in the car OK?'

PC Ross glances back to the crash and I follow his gaze and watch as a fireman yanks open the car door with a giant pair of metal pliers. A shiver runs down my spine. 'It's only one person, thankfully. The paramedics are doing everything they can to treat his injuries. Can I take your name and address?' the police officer asks, already opening a notebook and jotting down my licence plate.

'Anna James. Four Middle Road, Barton St Martin.'

'Thank you. And would you mind talking me through what you saw?'

I replay the crash in my mind and explain as best I can – the speeding car, the gunshot-like pop.

'It's looking like a rear tyre blew,' PC Ross says when I'm finished. 'One of the cars ahead of you has a dash cam so we have the footage.'

'How long will it take to clear? I've got two children in the car,' I say, stating the obvious. *And one at home.*

The panic rises up. Tears form in my eyes.

'It's going to take some time. We're waiting on the arrival of a recovery vehicle to remove the car, and then

26

we'll clear the road of debris and get a lane open. The lorry is going to take longer to move. Try to be patient and make sure you stay warm. Have you got any water?'

'I think there's some in the boot. So how long?' I press. My tone has ebbed from polite to pushy.

'I can't give you an exact time. Ball park – three hours or so.' He makes a move, a step towards the car behind me.

Three hours? I can't leave Harrie for that long.

A frenzied terror grips so tight it's a fight to draw breath. 'I've left my daughter home alone,' I sob. 'We were only supposed to be twenty minutes. I don't know what to do.'

The officer moves back. I've caught his attention.

'How old is your daughter?' PC Ross asks.

'Eleven. I know she's young, but she's really sensible. I've tried calling a neighbour but she didn't answer. I don't know what to do,' I say, my voice cracking. 'I can't be here. I can't be stuck here with my daughter at home.'

Another sob escapes and then another. Fear is whipping up a tornado inside me. I have to get to Harrie.

'Calm down,' PC Ross says, voice firm, and suddenly he doesn't seem so young any more. 'Getting upset isn't going to help your children in the car or your daughter at home. Is there a friend you could call? Anyone with a spare key?' he asks.

I instantly think of Kat and want to kick myself for not remembering her before. Kat has a spare key to the house. She only lives a few minutes' walk away. And I know she'll check on Harrie if I ask her to. We'd do anything for each other.

'Yes, I'll try.'

'We'll get you out of here as soon as we can.'

The officer moves on to the next car and I slide into the driver's seat and close the door. I'm breathing too fast. It's OK, I tell myself. I can't get to Harrie, but Kat can.

'What did he say?' Elise asks.

'It's going to be a few hours.'

She groans and flops her head against the window. 'Can I play on your phone?'

'I need it in case Harrie tries to call. I'm going to ring Kat now and ask her to pop round.'

'Harrie's asleep,' Elise says with a long yawn and the same conviction, as though she's in their bedroom standing over her bed.

What if she's not?

What if she's had an accident?

What if she's fighting for her life this very second and I'm not there to save her?

Suddenly, Harrie being scared and alone doesn't feel like the worst thing any more. I close my eyes and a single tear rolls on to my cheek. I'm losing control again.

'Mum?' Elise's one word jolts me and I turn to see her wide eyes and the confusion creasing her forehead. I don't blame her. I rarely cry. I'm a doer not a crier. Except there's nothing I can do right now but wait for the crash to be cleared and hope Harrie is OK. Hope Kat answers her phone, something she rarely does. Whereas my phone feels permanently glued to my hand, Kat is always leaving hers in her coat pocket or in the car, the bottom of a handbag, finding it a day or two later and laughing at her carelessness.

But PC Ross is right. I must keep it together.

'Why don't you try and get some sleep too?' I say to Elise. 'The time will pass a lot quicker that way.'

'Will you wake me when we start to move?'

'Sure.'

Elise snuggles into my scarf, shimmying her body down the seat and leaning against the edge of the door where the window starts.

Kat's number is right at the top of my favourites list and I press it quickly and hold the phone to my ear. It rings and rings but she doesn't pick up.

Damn it! What now?

I hang up and fire off a text explaining what's happened, asking her to call, to help.

The minutes pass slowly. Two. Then three, then five. Only when another ten minutes have passed and there's no little white tick in the bottom corner of the message telling me Kat has seen it, do I turn to Elise. 'I'm just going to get some air.'

She gives me a puzzled look but snuggles deeper into my scarf as I open the car door and stand in the chill of the autumn night. My hands shake as I find Dean's name in my contacts. *Please answer. Please, please, please. I need to hear your voice. I need you to tell me everything will be OK.*

The ringing hum gives way to a recorded message and I feel the tears build in my eyes as I hang up.

Only when I'm back in the car do I open up the village girlies' message group. There are already a dozen unread messages talking about some vandalism in the village I know nothing about. I ignore them and scroll to the end.

My stomach tightens another notch. I don't want to do it. I don't want to post a message on this group for all the mums to see, to judge. Despite the years we've lived in this village, I've only really made friends with Kat, and that's because Elise and Harrie have always got on so well with Ben. I talk to the other mums in the playground and when we pass on the street, and I share a table with them at the summer fete, drinking sticky white wine from a plastic cup, but I've never clicked with any of them like I have with Kat.

They're nice people. Everyone in Barton St Martin is nice. But it's hard to drop my guard, the barrier I put up to keep our secret – our humiliation – safe.

I click on the comment box of the messenger group and swallow down my reservations. I may not be bosom buddies with these women, but I know that one of them will go to my house and knock on the door and check on Harrie, and that's all that matters right now. Harrie is all that matters.

Me: Hey, there's been a crash and I'm stuck on the A12. I've left Harrie by herself and she's not answering the phone. I'm sorry to ask this, but would anyone mind going to my house and knocking on the door to check on her please? Thanks!

Gina Walker: OMG poor you! I heard the sirens. Sorry, Martin is out and it's just me at home with the kids.

Sandra Briggs: Just spoken to Jack and he says it's bad. You're going to be there for hours. I've got my dinner on the table. Give me ten minutes and I'll go.

Tracy Campbell: I'm out walking the dog. I'll do it now. Hang on.

Me: Thanks Tracy!!!

No more messages appear. Everyone is waiting for Tracy's reply and I wonder if I should've phoned Tracy after Kat instead of asking for help in the group. In the last few months Tracy has started to join Kat and me for cups of tea and stands with us at the school gates for a chat long after the kids have gone in. Tracy's daughter, Olivia, is in Molly's class and the pair have become good friends. But my friendship with Tracy feels tentative somehow. Like it only exists if Kat is with us.

The message from Tracy comes five minutes later.

Tracy Campbell: I knocked on the door, but Harrie didn't answer. There's a light on in the living room and I tried calling through the letterbox, but she didn't appear. Is the back door open? I could pop in and check.

Tears spill on to my face and I try to breathe through the lump digging into my throat. Everyone I know in the village leaves their back doors unlocked. Gina tells everyone who'll listen that she's not carried a door key around with her for a decade because there's no need. I understand the logic. Barton St Martin is a peaceful place. Nothing bad ever happens, and yet I've never been able to shake my London thinking. Our doors are always locked, whether we're there or not.

My phone buzzes in my hand.

Tracy Campbell: ???

Me: Thanks so much for trying, Tracy! I'm sure she's asleep. Kat has a spare key. I'll call her again now. Thanks xx

Tracy Campbell: No worries.

Gina Walker: Hope you get home soon!! X

I close the app and place my phone in my lap, staring at the blank screen, trying not to feel judged.

It could've happened to any of us, but it didn't. It happened to me. The only mum in the village with kids Harrie and Elise's age who won't let them walk to and from school on their own, even on the afternoons that Molly stays for an after-school club and it's just Elise and Harrie I'm waiting for in the playground.

Time drags. The driver is pulled from the car and placed on a stretcher. Both ambulances leave. The fire engine too, and then a breakdown truck arrives, yellow lights flashing. It's got a long flatbed and a thick metal winch cable. I sit up straighter and wipe the condensation from the windscreen as hope balloons inside me. We'll be moving soon.

Except we're not.

It takes another hour for the road to be cleared. By the time we arrive home, it's nearly midnight. I shake Elise awake and lift Molly from the car, laying her on the sofa before dashing through the house.

'Harrie?'

No answer.

The house feels cold and empty. Goosebumps travel down the length of my body as I run upstairs and into the darkness.

'Harriet?' Her name is a hoarse whisper. It's all I can manage over the fear strangling me.

I flick on the hall light and open her bedroom door so fast I almost fall through it.

The room is empty.

No. Oh my God. No.

Tears blur my vision and when I blink them away, my gaze lands on Harrie's bed and the lump of what I first thought was just a duvet. I step closer, trying to hear over the thundering of my heart in my ears.

I reach out a trembling hand and feel the firm warmth of Harrie's sleeping body. A gasp escapes my throat. Then a sob. She's here. She's safe. My head spins, airy and light. More tears roll down my cheeks. Relief this time.

'I'll never leave you again,' I whisper, kissing the top of her head.

I carry Molly to bed and tuck her in.

'Is Harrie OK?' Elise asks in a voice groggy with sleep as she follows me up the stairs.

'She's fine, darling. She's asleep just like you said she would be.'

Elise nods before wriggling out of her leotard and pulling on one of Rob's old T-shirts she wears as a nightdress. I don't have the heart or the energy to tell her to brush her teeth as she snuggles under her covers.

When I'm back downstairs, I reach once more for my phone and feel the sharp tug of disappointment at yet another blank screen. I know Monday was weird, I know it's changed everything between us, but Dean's silence still hurts.

That night I fold all the clothes. I pair the socks. I creep into bedrooms and slide open drawers, putting everything away. I tidy the Barbie dolls and locate

Elise's missing wireless headphone under the sofa. Finding comfort in the order I create. Then I wash up, lifting each plate, each cup, each bowl one at time from the dishwasher so as not to make a sound.

It's two a.m. and I'm about to switch off the kitchen light when my eyes fall on the phone on the sideboard and the solid red light that tells me the messages I've left have been listened to. But if Harrie heard them, why didn't she call me back?

Out of habit I check the back door is locked. My hand jiggles the handle, expecting resistance, but instead the door flies open and I'm hit by the cold of the night. I slam the door shut as though a monster is about to leap over the threshold. I turn fast, back to the kitchen, and that's when I see the mud by the door. A trail of dark-brown clumps and a partial outline of a footprint, as though someone has walked in the back door with muddy shoes. As though someone has been in this house tonight.

Chapter 5

Harrie

Harrie blinks in the darkness of her bedroom, her eyelids heavy with the sleep she so desperately wants. If
only she could catch her breath and calm the thundering beat of her heart. It's deafening her. But every time
her mind drifts and her breathing slows, the events of
the night punch into her thoughts and she's right back
there, the terror pinning her down.

She rubs her hands against the duvet cover. They're
clean now, and dry, but she can still feel the slick wet-
ness of the blood they were coated in only a short
while ago. She presses her lips together, a hard pinch,
trapping in the scream threatening to escape.

Her bladder aches, but she's too scared to move.
From across the room, Elise sighs in her sleep. The noise
should be comforting, but it's not. Everything has
changed.

Minutes pass. The silence feels like it's humming all
around her.

Everyone is asleep now. Everyone is OK. Everyone
except her.

Fresh tears burn her eyes before rolling down the side of her face and on to her pillow.

It had taken everything in Harrie to pretend to sleep when her mum had rushed into the room at midnight, panicked and gasping for breath just as Harrie had been moments earlier. How she'd wanted to throw off the covers and leap into her mum's arms, allowing the words, the horrors of the evening, to spill out.

But she couldn't do it.

She'll never tell. Never, never, never.

What is she going to do?

The question churns in her stomach until she's sure she's going to be sick. Did her mum notice the unlocked back door? Harrie only remembered it when she was in the bathroom. She should have gone back to lock it, but her hands were shaking so violently that it took ages to wash away the blood. Her skin feels raw in places where she had to scrape at the dried bits.

Harrie thinks of her ruined clothes, stuffed in the bottom of an unused toy box beneath the bed. How is she going to explain them to her mum? She'll have to throw them away tomorrow. Today. Her head spins with exhaustion. Sleep is coming at last. Harrie draws in a ragged breath and that's when she feels it – the hand grabbing her in the darkness, the night looming over her again – but this time she can't stay awake. The claws of a nightmare dig into her and there's nothing she can do. Nothing, nothing, nothing.

**Interview with Mike Pritchett,
head teacher of Barton St Martin
Primary School
Interview conducted by Melissa Hart,
The Daily Gazette, 2 November**

Mike: Is that thing on? Is it recording?

MH: Yes. Is that a problem?

Mike: No, not at all. Just checking. So you want to talk about what happened?

MH: Yes I do, but first of all can I get some details from you for my notes? You live in the village, I take it?

Mike: Yes, my wife and I moved from Berkshire in 1992 when the kids were still little. They're all grown up now. Flown the nest as they say. So it's just me and Bev at home.

MH: And you're the head teacher at the school here?

Mike: That's right. I've been at the helm, so to speak, for . . . crikey, about fifteen years. Although I'm retiring now.

MH: And how did you feel when you heard about what happened?

Mike: We felt sick, as you can imagine. Bev and I both did. We couldn't believe it. Barton St Martin really is a safe place to raise a family. I can testify to that. It makes it more shocking, doesn't it? This kind of thing – well, you expect it in the bigger towns, the cities, but not here.

MH: Why not here?

Mike: Because Barton St Martin has an award-winning Neighbourhood Watch. We look out for each other.

MH: But not this time.

Mike: No. Evidently not.

MH: Why do you think that is?

Mike: I don't know. It's the question I've been asking myself.

MH: But it's not the first time something has slipped past the Neighbourhood Watch recently, is it?

Mike: I assume you're referring to the recent vandalism. Who told you about that? It was nothing. I honestly don't know why the women got themselves so worked up about it and I definitely don't see how there is a connection between some silly vandalism and murder. Do you?

Interview with Bev Pritchett, member of Barton St Martin Parish Council Interview conducted by Melissa Hart, ***The Daily Gazette*****, 2 November**

MH: Are you OK, Mrs Pritchett?

Bev: [Silence]

MH: Can I get you a glass of water or a cup of tea? Something for the shock?

Bev: I'm sorry, but I don't think I can do this today. It's just too upsetting. You have to understand how close we all are. We're a tight community and now . . . two of our own are dead. Two precious souls gone, and practically on my doorstep. Such a waste of life, isn't it?

MH: Would it be better if I came back tomorrow, Mrs Pritchett?

Bev: Yes. Yes please. I think that would be for the best.

MH: You've got my card. If you change your mind and want to talk to me before then, please give me a call.

Bev: I just wish I knew how Harrie and Anna got involved in all this. Have you spoken to Kat and Steve Morris yet? Kat was best friends with Anna James. Did you know that?

Chapter 6

Thursday, nine days until Halloween

Anna

Even before I open my eyes the exhaustion crowds me like children around a birthday cake. There is no escape from it. My eyelids are sticky, hard to open. I long for sleep but the alarm is beeping, drilling into my head.

I fumble for my phone and silence the alarm before dragging myself out of bed and throwing on my tattered grey dressing gown. It used to have a colour. White, I think. Or pale pink. I've had it forever, since before the kids anyway, which feels like a different lifetime. One of the things I remembered to shove into a suitcase on that sticky August night. The towelling material is rough in places and worn to nothing in others, but I only wear it for this one task and it does its job – keeps the worst of the cold at bay while I fix myself a coffee and gather myself for the day.

On the stairs I move left, then right, skip a step, then left, avoiding the creaking floorboards, a dance I've done a thousand times before. I doubt a trained assassin could scale these stairs with the same silence as I can. Molly is the one most likely to wake and hear me moving around. She's always been an early bird, galloping into our bedroom at four a.m. the moment she could climb out of her cot. Wide awake. Ready for the day. In desperation, I bought her one of the clocks with the stars that count down until it's time to wake up. It helped, but not as much as the routine and exhaustion of school.

My reason for the silence is simple. I need this hour. It is mine and it is more precious to me than the extra sleep, even after last night when I climbed into bed and lay there for hours reliving the anxiety, the raw horror I felt sitting helpless in the car while Harrie was alone. I tossed and turned and kept telling myself that it was OK, I was home and Harrie was safe, but the fear stuck – chewing gum in my mind.

The kitchen is dark. The waking sun has yet to reach the windows and I close the door and turn on the light. My eyes draw to a smear of mud by the back door that I missed last night when I cleaned up. I bite the inside of my lip as yesterday's anxiety presses down on me, flooding my mind with the same what-if questions.

I reach for the kettle and push the questions aside, reminding myself again that Harrie is fast asleep in her bed.

I spot a smudge of pasta sauce on one of the blue and white wall tiles and scrape it away with my finger. The Tangier pattern looks too busy, too squashed, in our cramped little kitchen with the table and chairs that someone had stacked outside their house five years ago, just after we moved to the village for our fresh start – the one I'm still waiting for. The table had a note stuck on the top – *Free to a good home*. So we took it and Rob sanded it down and painted it a glossy white. One of the

42

legs is a fraction shorter than the rest and it wobbles if we don't keep a piece of cardboard pushed underneath it, but we told ourselves it was temporary.

'Just until I've got a few months of pay under my belt and your website design company is up and running. Then we'll buy a new one,' Rob said, planting a kiss on my neck.

I grit my teeth as I stare at the faded paint, the pen marks from the kids, and wonder if we'll ever buy that new table. I know we won't repaint it. That would be admitting defeat and Rob would never do that. *Far easier to run away to Nigeria, eh Rob? Leave me and the kids to live day after day after day in our squashed little house with our shitty second-, third-, fourth-hand furniture.*

It has felt endless at times – the scrimping and the payments. We've not climbed out of debt, we've crawled on our hands and knees through a sewer of shit, slipping sideways and backwards as much as forwards. It got easier when Rob took the job in Nigeria, but that has come with its own price, and there's still nothing spare at the end of the month. Not with the debts and three sets of school uniform, three sets of school shoes, three sets of trainers and clothes and birthdays and Christmases, and a new washing machine when the old one broke down.

I swallow down my resentment as a long yawn coils around my body. I fill the kettle and listen to it rattle and bubble before moving to the fridge in the corner. It's a white monstrosity. Fridge on the top. Freezer on the bottom. Both are covered with Molly's drawings, and the latest certificates from the school. Molly's star reader, Harrie's handwriting improvements, Elise's maths. One for each. Always fair.

Dead centre, in the middle of the fridge door, is one of my printouts. It's just a single piece of A4, like all the rest I've got dotted around the house. Meals for the week. Bath and shower days. Homework schedules. Order and plans keeping me sane. Nothing feels as scary if it's in an Excel spreadsheet.

I press down the bottom corner of the paper where it's curling up. The Blu-Tack is starting to dry. This one is the kids' week planner. I stuck it up at the beginning of the new term and already it is a tattoo on my brain as we zigzag from one club, one day, to another.

Saturdays are the worst. Football training for Harrie, gymnastics for Elise, and drama club for Molly. The frantic driving between clubs, the dodging of traffic in and out of town. Three hours when anxiety flutters in my chest as I rush to drop off and collect one child then another. It's lunchtime before we're home, usually with a killer headache in tow.

Only on Sundays do I feel like we draw breath. Harrie still has a football match most weeks, and Elise has her extra studying. Sometimes she pops over the road to Mike Pritchett's house to drop off extra work he's set her or ask a question. It's one of the benefits of living opposite the head teacher. Although most of the time tutoring takes place during lunch break once or twice a week.

I try to fit in family time – a walk, a film night. I say family time, but it's not really, not without Rob. Fifty-five days until he's home.

And then what?

I'm here for you, Anna. Always. Dean's voice pushes through my thoughts along with yesterday's disappointment. I don't know what I'm doing any more. I don't know how I became this person.

The thought is a dead weight inside me as I turn to the counter to make my coffee, splashing in extra milk so I won't have to wait for it to cool. Coffee is the answer. At this time in the morning, it is always the answer. Nothing too strong. Just a little kick up the bum to get me in the shower before I have to wake the kids.

The shower, the coffee, the make-up – they all help. The exhaustion is still there, like invisible weights pulling down my muscles, but it's no longer a fog, more a fine mist across my eyes.

At seven a.m. my hour is up. It's time to wake the children. I normally start with Molly. She is the one most likely to faff with her socks and her hair, the one who needs the longest to get ready, but today I am pulled towards Harrie.

It's dark in the twins' bedroom and smells of sleep and the lingering sickly sweet scent of the body spray Elise loves to wear.

I push open the curtains. One then the other. Elise is still fast asleep, her face to the wall, buried in her duvet, but Harrie is awake. Her eyes are wide open but vacant and glazed as though she's not really here at all. Her body is shaking and her face is deathly pale.

'Harrie?'

My voice doesn't register. It's like I'm not here.

I step close and hear her then – a barely there whisper. 'What do I do?' she says over and over, hardly drawing breath between each 'do' and 'what' so it's like a tune rather than words. The anxiety I felt in bed last night returns – needles prickling everywhere, inside and out – but this time it isn't for an imagined what-if, it's real. Something is wrong with Harrie.

Chapter 7

Anna

'Harrie?'

She doesn't respond. Her eyes are watery, the skin around them puffy. She's been crying.

From across the room Elise lets out a groan and turns over to face us. She scrunches her face up. 'What's going on?'

I don't answer. My focus is on Harrie. I sing-song her name again.

I sit on the bed, scooping Harrie into my arms, holding her tight against me. Her body remains limp, her head drooping back as though she's still asleep, and I cup my hand around it and hold her closer.

'What's wrong with Harrie?' Elise asks, her voice no longer sleepy, but worried, scared.

'I don't know,' I reply, before pressing my mouth to Harrie's ear and saying her name again. She moves at last, her hands flying up and pushing against me, shoving me back. She wriggles up the bed and out of my arms.

'Are you OK?' I ask.

She doesn't answer.

I look at her face, desperate for reassurance and finding none.

My fingers reach to smooth down her hair at the back where it's knotted and lumpy, but she slaps them away, shrinking into herself. She looks younger all of a sudden. Eleven years old. Still a child. Anger burns, a lit flare inside my body. Anger at myself, and at Rob for talking me into leaving Harrie alone. What was I thinking? Why did I let him convince me it was a good idea? He's a million miles away. He doesn't know what it's like for me day after day. What it's like for us. He sees his children on a screen once a week when they're excited and happy and bubbling over with things to tell him. He doesn't see the tantrums they have, the times they're scared or forget to brush their teeth even though I tell them every day, twice a day. They are still so young.

I push my anger aside. It's clouding my head and I need to think straight and find out what's wrong with Harrie.

I try again to touch her, resting a hand on her shoulder. She yelps, flinching away so fast that her top moves, showing the bare skin where her neck reaches her shoulder. And that's when I see it – the dark smudge of a bruise. It's wide – the width of my palm – and blotchy, darker in places than in others.

'Harrie, your neck!' I cry out. 'What happened?'

She shakes her head but still she says nothing.

'Harrie, please, talk to me? What's going on? What happened last night? The back door was unlocked. Did someone . . ,' It's a fight to finish the question I know I have to ask. 'Did someone come into the house?'

47

Another side-to-side movement. I don't know if she's answering me or telling me she can't talk.

'Elise,' I say. 'Would you get Molly up, please? And get some breakfast?'

Elise doesn't complain as she throws off her duvet and walks out of the bedroom.

'It's just us now, Harrie. I need you to talk to me. Tell me what happened last night,' I say, trying to soften the edge of desperation in my voice.

I gnaw at my bottom lip and pull out my phone from my pocket. Should I call someone? The police? A doctor? *Fuck! I wish Rob were here.*

'Why didn't you call me back?'

Still nothing. It's a fight now not to grab her arms and shake the words right out of her.

There's a clang from the kitchen that sounds distinctly like a bowl dropping to the floor, followed by Elise's bickering tone. 'Because I said so.'

'I want Mummy.' Molly's whine reaches my ears and I feel myself being pulled away. There's a small thud and I imagine her little foot stamping to the floor in the way it always does when Elise winds her up.

'I'll be just a minute,' I say to Harrie before running down the stairs to sort out Elise and Molly. In the time it takes for tempers to be soothed and for them both to be sat at the table eating their breakfast, Harrie has dressed in her school uniform. She appears from her bedroom just as I'm climbing the stairs back to her.

She looks a ghostly form of herself against the navy school jumper.

'Baby? You don't have to go to school today.' I'm not sure what's going on, I'm not sure of anything right now, but the urge to keep her close to me is so strong – an innate force.

'I'll go,' she says. Her words are too soft, just a whisper of her usual voice.

'What happened last night?'

'Nothing.' She shrugs before moving past me on the stairs. 'I had a bad dream, that's all.'

And now it's me who is shaking my head and struggling to find the words. 'The bruise on your neck—'

'I got that playing football at school yesterday.'

'Oh.'

Harrie disappears into the kitchen and I stay where I am. Rooted to the middle stair, torn between wanting to believe what Harrie has told me and wanting to keep pushing. The latter wins and I follow Harrie into the kitchen.

'So nothing happened last night?' I ask again.

Elise and Molly look up from their bowls of cereal, their eyes on me and then Harrie, who is shaking her head again.

'Were you scared on your own? Why didn't you call me back?'

'I couldn't remember how to work the phone.' Her voice doesn't sound right. It's too robotic and nothing like the up-and-down tones I'm used to from Harrie. 'I just went to bed.'

'Did you press the green button first and then dial the number?'

Harrie shrugs and a wave of hot frustration floods my body. If it were an iPhone, they'd be fine, even Molly. It's as though they're born with some innate knowledge of Apple technology, but the old black phone with the built-in answering machine, which time and again I've shown them how to use, is too archaic for them to grasp.

'There was mud on the kitchen floor when I got

back last night, Harrie, and the back door was open. Did you go out?' The atmosphere in the kitchen is charged. I wish it didn't feel like an interrogation, but I don't know how else to play this. The other questions teeter on my lips but I hold them back and roll them around my mind instead. *Did someone come in? Did someone hurt you?*

'I thought I saw an injured cat in the garden,' Harrie says. 'I went out to help it but it ran off.'

'And nothing else happened? You don't seem yourself.'

She spins towards me then, milk slopping from the bowl of cereal in her hands. 'I'M FINE,' she yells, her voice as sharp as it is loud.

Molly scurries from her chair and pushes up against my side. Elise is frozen, as stunned as I am by Harrie's outburst. The kitchen falls silent and I stare at Harrie and wish I could ignore the pale skin, the tired eyes, and believe her words, but I can't. Harrie is my daughter, she's part of me. And even though she isn't as easy to read as she used to be when she was five or six and needed a wee but didn't want to say anything, I still know her. I know how her gaze drops down when she lies, like it's doing right now.

Chapter 8

The night of the crash, 7.48–7.52 p.m.

Harrie

Harrie drops her head back on the sofa cushion, her eyes fixed on the TV show she's supposed to be watching. She listens to the slam of the front door, the start of the engine. An energy pumps around her body, willing her to move, to act, but she doesn't. It's fifty-fifty her mum forgets something and runs back into the house, a hurricane of frustration and muttered swear words she thinks no one else can hear. Harrie smirks thinking of Elise's impression of their mum when she can't find the car keys – arms flapping, hissing swear words under her breath.

The smile drops and for a second Harrie wishes they could swap places – Harrie at gymnastics and Elise here – just like they did when they were little, but this isn't a silly game, this is real.

Harrie mutes the TV and listens to the silence, half expecting her mum to open the front door and yell at her to get in the car after all.

She looks at her watch and forces herself to wait some more. It will take her mum two minutes to drive out of the village and on to the dual carriageway. No turning back after that. Harrie waits three just to be sure. That gives her seventeen minutes, more if Elise faffs about and has to go back for something like she almost always does.

Time to move.

Harrie leaps up and turns off the TV. She reaches the front door in seconds, shoving her bare feet into her school shoes. She doesn't have time for the laces of her trainers.

She grabs Elise's black winter coat from the hook. The zip is broken on Harrie's red one. She hasn't told her mum yet. It will only stress her out. Elise won't mind if Harrie borrows her coat, and anyway, it's black so she'll be less visible.

Harrie reaches for the key hanging on the hook by the door, but her hand hovers mid-air in a sudden moment of doubt. Is she really doing this?

Harrie bites her lip and thinks of her mum. She will be so angry if she finds out Harrie has left the house. There will be no more staying home alone.

Is it worth the risk?

The answer doesn't matter, Harrie realizes. She has to do this. And anyway, if everything goes to plan, her mum will never find out. But using the front door is risky. Mr Pritchett, their head teacher, lives just across the road. If he or his wife spots Harrie leaving, they're bound to tell her mum.

Better to use the back door and the gate at the side. She can stick to the shadows of the house that way.

Harrie darts through the kitchen to the back door. She'll leave it unlocked. Easier to get back in. It isn't like anyone is going to walk in and steal stuff. What would they take? The tablet with the crack in the corner where Molly dropped it on the floor? The TV that's half the size of all her friends' ones? Mum used to have some nice jewellery. Harrie can remember standing in her PJs, barefoot on the bouncy carpet in their old house. Her mum getting ready for a night out, sweet perfume hanging in the air, her ears and neck sparkling with jewels. Harrie hasn't seen that jewellery in forever.

With the back door open, Harrie hesitates again. The darkness is like a wall she isn't sure she can walk through. She thinks through the plan one more time, picturing each step like she's done every night before bed this week. It sounded so easy in her mind, but now she's here and actually doing it, it feels impossible.

A sudden fear grips her. A babyish kind of fear, like when she was little and scared of the dark and her dad would read her stories until she fell asleep, Elise pushed up against her, protecting her from the night.

Harrie swallows hard and pushes the fear down. The only thing she has to be scared of is what happens if she doesn't walk out the door right now.

With a final glance at the house, her home, the place she feels safe, Harrie zips up her coat and runs.

Chapter 9

Anna

The routine of the morning unfolds. Breakfast, then teeth brushed, bags packed, lunches made, and all the while I watch Harrie. I see the way her hands shake as she reaches for her school shoes.

Before we leave the house, I crouch on the floor beside her and ask one more time if she wants to stay home, if she's all right, if anything happened. The questions come out in a whispered flood. I touch her arm and she freezes, her body tensing beneath my hand, but she doesn't pull away. I can see her thinking now, weighing up both sides. Elise is the hothead, the dive-right-in child. Act now, think later. Harrie is logical, like Rob, as though she has a crystal ball inside her mind and can see one step into the future. Then she moves her head from side to side and stands without another word, and I'm left with no choice but to open the front door and bundle us out – winter coats, bags and water bottles.

A pale sun is fighting to break through the clouds, but the day is bright and there's a chill in the air that pushes through my thick padded coat – the cheap kind that looks cosy and warm but isn't.

Our neighbour, June, is halfway up a ladder in her front garden and trimming a laurel bush. I bite back an offer to help after the school drop-off. June will only laugh and shoo me away with the same wave of her arms as she gives to the cat on the street who tries to crap in her flower beds.

'Good morning, James family,' she calls in her usual cheerful tone, looking down on us from her position on the ladder.

'Good morning, June,' I reply, adding extra vigour to my voice to make up for the children's mumbled greeting. Molly slips a warm hand into mine and I give it a gentle I-love-you squeeze. She tugs at my arm and I glance down and see the worry on her face, the 'what if we're late and the bell has already gone and I get in trouble?' question in her eyes.

'We've got plenty of time,' I whisper. 'We're never late.'

'I saw you were back very late last night.' June steps cautiously to the ground and leans a supportive hand on the gate.

I nod. 'We got stuck in traffic. I hope my car didn't wake you.'

'Oh no,' she smiles. 'I'm often up in the small hours. One of the benefits of living alone. I can do as I please, when I please.'

She glances up the road to where Elise and Harrie are standing. 'I thought I heard something last night from your garden. But then I saw you were out.'

'Really? Like what?' I think of the mud on the kitchen floor and Harrie's strange behaviour this morning and feel my gut twist into a tight knot.

'I don't know, dear. The gate was banging. Perhaps

have a check later, just to be sure it's all secure. It could just as easily have been a senile moment on my part.' She laughs.

'I will. Thank you.'

'You know, I'm always here if you need a hand with the kids,' she says, like she always does.

'That's very kind, thank you,' I reply, not wanting to mention how much I needed her last night. June has one of the old-fashioned landline phones. No caller ID. No answerphone. She has no idea I called her and I don't want her to feel bad for not answering. 'But I would hate to be a bother.'

I look ahead to where Harrie and Elise are now huddled together. Elise is talking furiously but Harrie is silent.

'Why not? Bother away, Anna. My social calendar isn't exactly rammed to the hilt.'

I smile as she laughs again. 'OK. I will ask more. Thank you.'

June leans in then, narrowing her grey eyes at me. 'Are you all right, Anna?'

The question startles me and I'm not prepared for the dam of emotions that threatens to break free. My pulse quickens and I think of Monday, of Dean, and I think of Rob and my confession. I think of Harrie too and the feeling that something isn't right, and it all pushes forward like the coin-pusher machines at the arcade. Everything is teetering on the edge and June's question is the final coin in the slot that will bring it all crashing down.

I swallow and give a furtive nod. 'All good, thanks,' I add, plastering on a smile that I'm sure is not fooling June. 'We'd better go. Don't want to be late.'

'Of course. Bye for now.'

June returns to her ladder and Molly and I jog, bags jumping on shoulders, to catch up with the twins. It's a ten-minute walk to the school, or five if it's just me and I'm walking fast, keen to be in the playground before the bell rings.

The school is at the edge of the village, built at the same time as an estate of detached houses – the big kind with five or six bedrooms, four bathrooms, long gardens, double garages and sweeping driveways.

We head for the alleyway that connects our road of ex-social housing to the estate, saving the long walk down the main road with its grand Tudor houses and quaint thatched cottages interspersed with grazing fields for horses and sheep sometimes too.

'What day is it today?' Molly asks, skipping along beside me, her hand in mine, her weight tugging at my arm with every skip.

'It's Thursday, sweetheart.'

'Yessssss,' she says with a little wiggle. 'Cookery club tonight. Mrs Waller said we're making pizza.'

'That sounds nice.'

Molly chats away to me about Mrs Waller and pizza toppings as my gaze travels between the twins. They're walking separately now. Elise is lagging behind, tired after her late night. Harrie is in front. Head down, shoulders slumped. It takes me a moment to realize there isn't a football at her feet. She is still Harrie, still my beautiful daughter, yet something has changed or shifted and I hate myself for thinking it, but it's the truth. This is not the bright cheeky girl I left on the sofa yesterday.

I don't know what's happened to Harrie, but I do know that this is my fault. I was the one distracted this week, so distracted by Monday, by Dean, that I didn't even try to convince Harrie to come with me last night.

Chapter 10

Anna

The school playground is a buzzing hive of activity. Parents huddle by brightly coloured fences while kids tear across the tarmac, jumping over discarded bags, some chasing each other, others racing after a ball.

Harrie and Elise head straight to the corner where the older children stand. It feels like only yesterday that they were the little ones. The thought sends a pang of something shooting through me. Longing? Sadness? I don't know, but it's there all the same.

Molly pulls me towards her class line and her best friend Olivia, who is standing beside Tracy and the other mums. I watch them together, Tracy, Sandra, Kat and Gina, and for a moment I feel overwhelmed, like it's five years ago and we're the new family, and I'm struggling to remember everyone's names, let alone the names of their husbands. Struggling to keep my shit together, too.

It was embarrassing how many times I got their names mixed up – calling Sandra Tracy and thinking Gina was married to Jack, not Martin. They laughed at first, but it soon stopped being funny. In the end I made little rhymes to help me. They still run through my head when I look at them.

Kat spots me at the edge of the group and beckons me with a grin. There are strands falling out of her blonde ponytail and a lump at the front as though she's slept with it in and hasn't bothered to brush it yet. Mascara is smudged under her eyelids too and yet she still manages to look like Cameron Diaz in that film with Jude Law. Or any film actually. Slim and strikingly beautiful.

One hour to get ready in the morning. Two. Three. It makes no difference. I resist the urge to touch the wispy ends of my own hair, so dull compared to Kat's. I used to be so much prettier. I catch my reflection in the mirror sometimes and almost do a double take as I wonder if it's really me. It's the same face – clear blue eyes, small nose, the same shape to my lips as the girls'. Thirty-seven years old and I've aged well, even with the pinched lines between my eyes, but I've lost something in the years since London – an inner glow or an energy, something that changes beautiful to plain.

Kat wraps her long knitted cardigan around herself and I smile when I see the fluffy Ugg slippers on her feet.

She follows my gaze and laughs. 'Running late as usual. At least I'm dressed. That's got to count for something,' she says as though she knows the words that were about to leave my mouth before I've even thought to say them.

'We're just talking about the vandalism,' she says, nodding to the others.

'I heard from Bev that Mike thinks it was that supply teacher,' Sandra says with a sniff.

'What supply teacher?' Kat asks.

'Mr Dudley, the one who taught Year Two for half a term and then Mike complained he was incompetent.'

'*I* complained he was incompetent,' Tracy hisses, adjusting the headband that keeps her braids away from her face.

'You complain everyone is incompetent,' Gina quips and they all laugh. The conversation makes a sudden U-turn to a cleaner Tracy hired once and I force a smile and stare between them.

There's Sandra Briggs, married to Jack. Sandra is in her mid-forties with shoulder-length auburn hair and a sharp nose. She's wearing her usual high-heeled boots and skinny jeans. Kat told me once that Sandra has Botox every four months, but I'm not sure if that's true or just Kat's suspicions. It would fit with the rhyme I made up, I suppose.

> *PC Jack, not so tall,*
> *And his wife, Sandra, the fairest of them all.*

Jack Briggs isn't actually a police constable. He's high up in the local force and also head of Barton St Martin's Neighbourhood Watch, but it helped me remember who Sandra is married to.

Then there's Tracy in her activewear and muddy trainers, ready to disappear across the fields on a run. Tracy is black and has an elegant way about her. She used to be a ballet dancer, she told me once, narrowly missing out on a place with the Royal Ballet. She's married to Anthony Campbell. Their rhyme is stupid. They're all stupid, but it makes me smile when I think of it now.

> *Anthony Campbell has lost his hair,*
> *Run, Tracy, run and find him a spare.*

Her husband, Anthony, works with Dean at Dean's building firm, and has the shiniest head I've ever seen. Anthony is in charge of the Parish Council that looks after the village affairs. They keep the benches painted and the footpaths from overgrowing. Dean is on it. And Gina's husband Martin and Jack Briggs. Kat and Tracy.

Gina tips her head back and laughs at something Kat has said. It's a loud raucous laugh. The kind that makes people turn and stare, and typical of Gina.

Gina is always smiling. So is her husband, Martin.

> Gina and Martin Walker,
> Non-stop talkers.

They're a pair, Gina and Martin. When they're not laughing, they're talking. Gina will tell anyone who listens that she has an allergy to exercise. 'Anything more than a walk and I'm covered in hives. I'm stuck this way and always will be,' she always says with a nod to her round waist. 'Martin isn't allergic but he is sympathy fat so I don't feel like I'm the only one.' They are both lovely people and their daughter Clarissa is good friends with Harrie and Elise.

Only Bev Pritchett is missing from the group. She and Mike have two sons, but I don't know their names. She always refers to them as 'the boys'. *We're off to visit the boys at university. The boys have got a summer internship at IBM. The boys did well in their exams.* I'm not sure she's ever mentioned them individually.

There are other ladies in the village of course, other mums who join the message group sometimes, but these are the core, the ones who message every day. All except Gina run their own small businesses. They like pamper and Prosecco evenings, little events they all take it in turns to host, where everyone gets drunk and spends money on tat they don't need. Kat hosts them for the beauty products she sells, Tracy for the jewellery she makes and Sandra for candles. For Bev, it's gel nails. They visit her every few weeks for a bottle of wine and a fresh colour or a glittery design. I sometimes think the nails are a branding, like they're part of a club. They all have them. All but me.

I've lost count of how many times Kat has begged me to get June to babysit so I can join them in the pub on a Friday. Each time I nod and tell her I'll think about it, when we both know I'll text her with some excuse. Kat tries to understand that things are tight for us, but she doesn't get it. No one with money can really understand the day-to-day struggles we face. We don't have the spare money for a bottle of wine a week, let alone an £80 round of gin and tonics at the overpriced village pub.

My unwillingness to socialize makes me an outsider still, even after five years here. Rob has done a better job of fitting in than I have. Although it's different for men. Easier. They don't ask so many questions.

In the brief intervals Rob is home, he's managed to become part of the dad crowd. Of course he has. Rob is always happy to lend a hand, helping with the electrics for the band at the fete that's held on the playing field every summer, letting Anthony Campbell convince him to join the Parish Council. It's a token seat, a vote by proxy when they need him to swing a decision. How can it be anything more? He's never here. I should know.

The conversation turns back to the vandalism and I wish I'd read the messages about it last night. I nudge Kat, and when she turns I keep my voice low and ask, 'What vandalism?'

She shakes her head, ponytail swishing from side to side. 'Do you live in a different world to me, Anna? How can you not know about it? Someone kicked down the fence at the back of the school playing field on Saturday, and threw toilet rolls all over the trees. It took hours to clean up and the fence needs to be replaced. The whole village is up in arms about it. The Neighbourhood Watch have had a special meeting.' Kat's voice dances with amusement but I can't tell if she thinks this is an over-reaction or not. Kat is fiercely protective of the village and is always the first to organize a team of volunteers to repaint the playground fence or plant more daffodil bulbs on the verges.

'And they think it's a disgruntled supply teacher?'

'Well, Bev says Mike does too, but—'

'I think it was that new boy,' Tracy butts in, lowering her voice and throwing a furtive glance around her. I look too, glad to see Molly and Olivia have gone to play and aren't listening to their mothers gossip.

'Which new boy?' Gina asks, her eyes widening with excitement. She pushes her short brown hair behind her ears and leans closer.

'Kai, the boy in Year Five who joined last summer. They live in town and his mum only moved him here because he was going to be expelled from his last school. How does a nine-year-old get expelled? That's what I want to know. His mum is always dropping him off in the village and leaving him to his own devices. He came and knocked for Freya the other day to see if she wanted to play out. Honestly, the look she gave him was hilarious. Why would a thirteen-year-old want to hang out with a nine-year-old?'

'Oh my God,' Kat laughs. 'That must have been the same day he came to ours. He spent all day playing

Xbox with Ben. I assumed Ben invited him and forgot to tell me.'

'I had to complain to Mike about him last week,' Tracy adds. 'He's been teaching Olivia and some of the younger kids swear words.'

'For crying out loud.' Sandra shakes her head. 'This is a village school for this village. Children from out of catchment shouldn't be allowed to attend.'

'But if they have the space—' Gina starts to say before stopping when Sandra shoots her a sharp look. I know it well. It's the same disparaging glare I received when I first moved here, when it felt like Sandra was assessing me for my worthiness to live in Barton St Martin. Rob thought I was being ridiculous, letting my own insecurities cloud my judgement, but he never saw that look.

> PC Jack, not so tall,
> And his wife, Sandra, the fairest of them all.

It's not Snow White I think of when the rhyme runs through my head, it's the wicked queen.

'Did you make it home in the end last night?' Sandra asks me then, her face now full of sympathy, and I remind myself that I made up the rhyme before I knew her properly. Sandra is fiercely loyal and will do anything for her friends. 'Jack said it was an overturned lorry.'

I nod. 'Yes, and a car crashed. It was horrible but we got home about midnight.'

'And Harrie was OK?' Tracy looks from me to Kat and I follow her eyes. Kat has a sheepish look on her face.

'Sorry,' Kat groans. 'You know I'm terrible with my

phone. I left it in the car last night. Only saw the messages this morning.'

'Don't worry about it. Harrie's fine. She was sound asleep when I got home.' It's the truth and it's not, but I can't tell these women – my friends – about Harrie's strange behaviour this morning when I've not had a moment to process it myself.

The bell rings and I breathe a sigh of relief, stepping away from the other mums to say goodbye to the girls. Elise and Harrie are standing at the back of their line beside Ben. He's grown taller, I think as I step closer. He used to be a head shorter than the girls but now they're almost the same height. With Kat's features and his dad's dusty-blond hair, Ben is going to be a heartbreaker one day.

Kat likes to joke about which of the twins will date Ben when they're older, but I can't see it. Dating and boys are just too far into the future for me to contemplate.

I bend down to kiss Elise and then Harrie goodbye, and when I do, I'm sure I feel Harrie flinch away from me again. The thought turns something in the pit of my stomach. I'm about to pull her aside and check again if she's really OK, but then the line starts moving and I've missed my chance.

Molly wraps herself around my legs and hugs me tight before skipping into school, hand in hand with Olivia, and then I hurry out of the gates, the loneliness closing in, the emptiness of the day unfolding before me as my phone sits silent in my pocket.

Chapter 11

Anna

Kat catches me when I'm halfway down the road. 'Anna, wait up.' I turn to see her jogging towards me.

She steers me to the side of the pavement to let a group of mums stride by with their Bugaboo and iCandy pushchairs. The mums are walking fast and chatting over each other. They'll do five loops of the village like that before pouring into the baby and toddler group at the church for tea and biscuits.

Kat nudges my arm. 'What is the collective noun for a group of pushchair mums?'

'A gaggle?' I suggest.

'A flock?'

'A cackle?'

We laugh and I'm glad it's just Kat now and not the others. Standing with Kat makes me feel more like myself than I have done since Monday. Since Dean stood in my kitchen and looked at me with knowing in his eyes, undoing me as easily as a zip on a jacket, buttons on a blouse.

What have I done? The question rises with the bile

in the back of my throat and I swallow hard, pushing them both away.

'I'm so sorry about last night,' Kat says. 'Are you OK?'

'I'm fine.' There's a wobble to my voice and we both know I'm not.

'Of course you are,' she says, raising a knowing eyebrow. 'Come on, let's go to yours for a cuppa. You look like you need it.'

'Yours is closer.' I nod across the road to Kat's house. It's one of the bigger detached properties on the estate, set back from the road. There's a bushy magnolia tree in the front garden that blooms a stunning pink in the spring.

'Yours is tidier. And I bet you ten pounds you've got milk in your fridge.'

I roll my eyes. 'Come on then.'

We walk together, Kat still in her slippers, and I feel grateful to have her in my life. Kat is a fiendish lover of memes that she sends me in flurries. Two, three, four at a time before she puts her phone down and forgets about it. They always make me laugh out loud. She's forever buying me little things too – a plant for the garden, a notebook with butterflies on it because she knows they're my favourite – plus the free samples she gives me from the range of beauty products she sells that are far too expensive for me to buy. I know she never means for it to feel like charity.

Ten minutes later we're sat at my kitchen table, two mugs of tea in front of us. Kat listens without interruption as I relive the events of last night and this morning.

'It feels like something happened to Harrie,' I finish, wrestling to control my emotions, to breathe normally.

'Has she said anything?' Kat asks.

67

I shake my head. 'No, but she's not herself. Nowhere close. I know you think I'm nuts sometimes, but I can feel it.' I press a hand to my chest. 'The bruise on her neck, the mud on the floor, the open back door.'

'What do you think happened though?' Kat says. 'You're not in London any more, Anna. And for the record, I don't think you're nuts. You just worry too much, that's all.'

'I can't explain it, I just have this feeling. Maybe I'm overreacting,' I say with a long sigh.

'You need to relax a bit and give yourself a break, OK? I'm sure Harrie is telling you the truth. The bruise will be something she got at school, messing around with the boys playing football no doubt, and she left the back door unlocked because she went into the garden to look for a cat. She probably got a bit scared on her own in the house and that's why she was acting weird this morning. I'm sure she'll be absolutely fine later. You always get like this when Rob has been away for a while.'

'Do I?' I look up, surprised by Kat's revelation.

She nods. 'Yes. You start to worry over everything. It's only when you reach the halfway point and can start counting down the days until Rob comes home that you unwind again. Not that anyone would blame you for how you feel. It can't be easy doing this all on your own. I struggle a lot of the time and I've only got Ben. Well, and Steve too, who is a big kid mostly. You've got three girls and no one to share the burden with.'

I nod and drop my head, hiding my face. Inside, my chest aches. I always avoid talking about Rob's job. Even with Kat, it's something I brush over. It's not because I don't want to talk. I do.

I want to tell Kat that when Rob showed me the job

advert for an engineer on an offshore oil rig in Nigeria four years ago, I laughed at the absurdity of it. Of course Rob, my husband, the father of my children, couldn't take a job working away for three-month stints. He couldn't put his life in danger and work in one of the few places in the world that still have pirates – actual pirates – and gangs of men in trucks who kidnap anyone who has a government willing to pay to have them returned and kill those who don't.

'It's the only way, Anna. The pay is more than triple what I can make here,' he said.

'Because it's so dangerous,' I replied. 'It says so right there in the job description. I know we're in debt—'

'A debt I don't want to spend the next twenty years paying off, knowing that you're worrying about how we'll afford food at the end of the month. We're a team and we've always been a team and I won't go unless you agree, but please, Anna, I'm begging you to let me do this. I've made mistakes,' he said, his voice cracking with the emotion I could see swimming in his eyes. 'So many stupid mistakes. I got us into this mess; I lost our home, our friends, our lives. Let me make it right,' he continued. 'I know it will be hard for you and the kids. But I'll be back every three months. And it won't be forever. I've run the numbers. Things will still be tight but we'll be able to afford to buy more while I pay off the debt. Five years, maybe six, and we'll be back on our feet. Imagine it, Anna.'

And I did. I imagined what it would be like not to worry. Not to fear every phone call, every knock at the door, every letter. Not to feel my heart skip and flutter in my chest when I checked the bank balance before buying food. So I nodded. Shocked. Dumbfounded. Stricken with the weight of it all, but in the back of my mind I thought he'd come to his senses. Rob is his own man, his own boss. It was impossible to see him working for a big company. An employee. Grunt work, he always called it. And he wouldn't, he couldn't really leave us, could he? I should've known it was already a done deal. That's Rob all over. He had the job offer before he even mentioned it and left a week later.

I want to tell Kat how precious those fourteen days are when Rob is home. Fourteen days when my bitterness melts – ice in a heatwave – and we cling to him, the kids climbing all over him, me waiting until the evenings before he pulls me into his arms. And then he's gone again.

But how can I say any of that without talking about London and the little flat that followed? Sometimes I wonder why I bother hiding our dirty secret. Isn't it obvious that we're in debt up to our eyeballs? Why else would we choose to live our lives like this? But I say nothing. The humiliation is too raw.

Kat reaches a hand across the table, laying it over mine. 'You must get so lonely,' she says.

I jolt at Kat's words. The heat of her touch is travelling up my arm and it's all I can do not to snatch my hand back and leap away. For a single second I wonder if she knows. Is it written on my face? Did Dean tell someone? No, of course not. Dean wouldn't do that.

There have been times over the last few months when I've almost told Kat about Dean, but something has always stopped me. I might trust Kat with my life, but I don't trust her with my secrets. It's a horrible thing to think about a best friend, but she has known Tracy, Gina, Sandra and Bev for a lot longer than me and I can imagine it happening so easily. A tiny little

70

slip on a Friday night when the gin has been flowing. Gossip is part of village life and we all do it.

I know the truth will come out, but Rob has to hear it from me and it's not a conversation we can have on a video call.

The buzz of a phone cuts through the silence and saves me from answering. Kat withdraws her hand, but the heat remains in my cheeks as she pulls out her iPhone and grimaces at the screen. 'Oops. Is that the time already? I forgot the gardener was coming today. I'd better go.'

Kat stands and collects her mug from the table, taking it to the dishwasher.

'Just leave it on the side,' I say. 'The dishwasher is broken.'

Her soft brown eyes dance with mischief. 'Oh no, Anna. How will your OCD tidying cope with the mess?'

I laugh and shake my head. 'I'm not OCD, I just like things to be organized.'

'Yeah right! Actually, you won't believe this, but we've got a spare dishwasher in the garage. Steve's mum asked him to take it to the tip for her and he's not got round to it yet. It's in good condition. Less than a year old.'

'You're joking? Why did she get a new one?'

Kat rolls her eyes. 'Something to do with the light at the bottom or the noise. I don't really know. I never pay attention to a word that woman says, but I know it works and it's built-in like you've got and I'm pretty sure they all come in the same size.'

I couldn't possibly. These are the first words that come to mind. I can't accept a dishwasher. It's too much. And when this all began six years ago, when we did our midnight dash, that is what I would have said. My pride was still strong then – it hadn't been pummelled by a daily grind of counting pennies, by choosing whether to pay the electricity or the water – but while things are better now, we are a long way from winning this fight and I know I won't be calling a repairman. I either accept this from Kat or we go without and wash up the dishes.

'Are you sure?' I say. 'Can I give you some money for it?'

She makes a face. 'Anna, we're throwing it away. You'd be doing me a favour by taking it.'

'Well, OK. Thanks. That would be great. I could drive over at the weekend and—'

'Don't be ridiculous, I'll send Steve with it in the van tonight when he gets back from work. He's fitting bathrooms in those new-builds going up on the edge of town.'

'Won't he mind?'

'What's that got to do with anything?' She laughs before moving to the front door. 'He'll be around before seven,' she calls over her shoulder as she hurries down the road.

I close the front door and feel the silence, the loneliness, pushing into me. My phone is in my hands before I even realize and I'm texting Dean again, asking him to meet me. I hold my breath as I wait for the three little dots to appear below my message, but they don't come, and only then do I allow the worry to creep in.

What if Monday changed things between us for good?

What if he told someone?

What if the truth comes out before I'm ready?

**Interview with Kat Morris, member of
Barton St Martin Parish Council
Interview conducted by Melissa Hart,
The Daily Gazette, 2 November**

MH: Mrs Morris, are you OK to answer a few questions?

Kat: I'm not sure I'm the right person to speak to but I'll try.

MH: What can you tell me about Harriet James?

Kat: I can tell you everything about Harrie James. Harrie's mum, Anna, is . . . was my best friend. I was probably the only one in the village who was close to her. What you need to understand about Anna is that she's always been really protective of the kids. So when she started getting worried about Harrie, I thought - actually all of us thought – that it was just Anna being Anna, but then on Halloween . . . well, you know the rest.

MH: And Harrie?

Kat: [Crying] She and Elise were best friends with my son, Ben. I'm sorry. This has all been such a shock.

[Phone ringing]

Kat: Would you mind pausing that, please? I need to take this. You're better off speaking to Gina Walker. She's the one who knows everything that goes on in this village.

Chapter 12

Harrie

The noise of the school hall pounds into Harrie's head; every scrape of knives and forks on the plates screeches in her ears. For a moment she wishes she could fast-forward the lunch break and the afternoon history lesson. As if she cares about Ancient Greece right now. But fast-forward to when? Her body tenses. It doesn't matter if she's at school or at home, awake or asleep, there's nothing she can do to stop her mind replaying what happened.

Harrie looks down at her lunch bag and the uneaten food. Her stomach rumbles, but the tiny bites she tried to eat have left her feeling sick. How can she swallow it when there's a constant lump in her throat? She zips up her lunch bag and stands up to leave with the others.

Across the hall, Elise catches her eye and raises her eyebrows in a silent 'you OK?' question which Harrie pretends not to see.

Rufus weaves his way through the group until he's beside her. He scoops a wave of brown hair behind his ear and nudges her side as they leave the lunch hall.

She jumps at his touch, feeling instantly stupid. Rufus is loads shorter than Harrie and definitely not someone to be scared of, but fear lingers like the images of last night. 'Do you wanna go in goal today?' he asks.

She nods. Not because she wants to or even because she wants to play football, but because nodding is the easiest thing. At least in goal she can be alone.

Miss Holloway appears in the classroom as they reach the coat pegs. 'Are you feeling all right, Harrie?' she asks, lines appearing on her forehead. 'You're awfully quiet today.'

Harrie nods again, too scared to open her mouth now. Too scared of the words that might fly out, the truth, the confession that is swirling in her head. Images of the man's body crash through her thoughts.

Laughter breaks out from the boys around her. Tyler jumps out of the line forming by the door. He throws his body one way and another, singing a stupid song.

'Found this on TikTok,' he laughs as Ben joins in, the two of them pushing against the line.

A second later, Tyler is next to Harrie. He crosses his legs back and forth, flossing at the same time, before losing his balance and barging into Harrie. She stumbles back, unable to right herself. The feeling of helplessness drags her back to that room and with it comes the terror – an all-consuming tidal wave of fear.

No, no, no. Let me go.

Her body reacts before she can stop it. Her hands reach out, shoving Tyler with such force that he flies across the room, his back hitting the side of a table.

He yells in pain but Harrie doesn't hear it.

'Harrie,' Miss Holloway cries out.

Harrie ignores that too and without waiting for

permission, she runs to the door. With every step she waits for the hand to grab her, the hot breath on her face.

The day is bright and grey, the air cool on her flaming cheeks. A sob catches in her throat as she races across the playing field, only stopping when she reaches the fence and Elise and Rufus catch up with her. Their faces are a mix of admiration and worry.

'He totally deserved it,' Rufus says first.

'Yeah.' Elise is staring into Harrie's eyes in a way that makes Harrie want to tell her everything.

Chapter 13

Anna

The day drags – a void of emptiness. I leave to collect the girls from school early, desperate to escape the house and myself. The day is mild but the wind, whipping at the autumn leaves, is biting.

I walk slowly, but I'm still the first one in the playground, which is where Harrie and Elise's teacher, Miss Holloway, finds me.

'Mrs James, may I have a word?' she says, hurrying over to me.

'Of course, and please call me Anna.'

She nods but I know she never will. 'It's about Harrie. She's not been herself today.'

'Oh.'

'We had . . .' She pauses as though searching for the right word. 'An incident at lunch. Harrie became quite upset when waiting to go outside and she pushed another child over and ran away without apologizing. Obviously I feel as though I know Harrie very well and that's not the kind of behaviour I've ever seen from her before.'

'No. Definitely not. She's the peacekeeper at home, always stopping Elise and Molly from bickering.'

'That sounds more like Harrie. She was incredibly quiet throughout the day. As you know, it's normally an effort to get her to stop talking in class, but today was the opposite. To be honest, Mrs James, it was like she was a different child.'

I nod, hugging my arms to my body. Hearing Miss Holloway echo my own fears from this morning feels like a gut punch. I should never have let her go to school. 'I'll speak to Harrie tonight and see if I can get to the bottom of it.'

'Thank you. While I'm not condoning the pushing, right now my main concern is for Harrie as it's so out of character for her.'

'I'll speak to her,' I say again.

Miss Holloway nods before striding back to the classroom.

A moment later, the playground fills up with parents and the children pour out. I scan the groups, searching only for Harrie. When our eyes lock, it's an effort not to shout out, to rush over and pull her into my arms. Her face is hauntingly sad and I wonder again if something happened last night. Whatever the answer, I'm going to find out, and I'm going to find out now.

I wait until we're out of the gates and walking home before trying to talk to Harrie.

'I just spoke to Miss Holloway,' I say, keeping my tone conversational. 'She said you pushed another kid today.'

Silence.

'Harrie?'

She shrugs.

'Mum, where's Molly?' Elise asks from the other side of me.

'Cookery club,' I reply, my gaze still on Harrie.

'What's for tea?'

'Not now, Elise. I need to chat to Harrie for a moment.'

'It wasn't Harrie's fault,' Elise huffs. 'Tyler was acting like an idiot. He was pushing everyone in the line. Harrie pushed him back, that's all. He fell over and made a massive fuss about it, but we all knew he deserved it.'

'Just because someone deserves something doesn't mean you do it. You should have told one of the teachers if he was pushing.'

Elise looks at me like I've just suggested she shaves off all her hair. 'We're not in Reception any more, Mum. Teachers don't want us telling on each other. Tyler was acting like a baby.'

'I get that, but I really want to hear it from Harrie. Harrie? Miss Holloway is worried about you and so am I. I wish you would talk to me. Are you sure nothing happened last night to upset you?'

Harrie mumbles something I don't catch.

'I didn't hear that.'

'Anna?' A voice calls from behind me. I groan inwardly and ignore it.

Elise tugs my arm. 'Tyler's mum is calling you.'

I glance around and spot Sandra striding towards us. She has five-year-old Imogen on her hip and Tyler lagging behind. With a sinking dread, I lift my hand in a wave and mouth 'Just a sec,' before turning back to Harrie.

'What did you say?' I touch her arm, desperate for an answer.

Harrie glares at me, eyes stony. 'I said, why can't you leave me alone.' And then she's gone, sprinting down the road, almost colliding with a toddler on a scooter.

'Harrie?' I yell her name at the top of my voice, but she doesn't stop. A dozen eyes look my way.

'I'll go after her,' Elise says, already jogging ahead. I'm about to run too. All I want to do is take Harrie in my arms and hold her tight, beg her to tell me what's going on inside her head. But then Sandra is by my side, her auburn hair shimmering like she's just walked out of a salon.

'Anna,' she says.

'Hi Sandra, before you say anything, I'm going to speak to Harrie tonight and make sure she apologizes to Tyler.'

I wait for Sandra's wrath, but instead she waves her hand in the air. 'Don't worry about it. Sounds like they were only messing around. I actually only wanted to ask if anyone on your street has a CCTV camera?'

'I don't think so.'

'That's what I thought. I just wondered because with Rob away, I thought you might have the extra security. More and more people have cameras these days. The Neighbourhood Watch are asking for anyone with footage of last Saturday. Jack's hoping to spot the vandals walking around the village.'

'That's good.' I look down the road, wishing Elise and Harrie had waited for me. 'I'd better—'

'Can you do anything with these cooking apples?' she asks, thrusting a carrier bag at me. 'Our tree has been crazy this year and I don't think my family can cope with another apple pie this week.' Her laugh is tinkling.

'Thank you,' I say, taking the bag and already

moving away. 'Anyway, I'd better catch up with the twins or we'll be turning straight back around to collect Molly. Thanks so much for the apples.'

'Any time. Oh, and Anna?'

'Yes?'

'I'm hosting a Scented Life party for my candles next month. They make such lovely stocking fillers. You will come this year, won't you?'

'Thanks. I'd love to.' My stomach tenses as I rifle through a dozen excuses and try to remember which one I gave for the last party I missed. A migraine? A tummy bug?

I hurry away, only slowing when I reach the end of the alley that leads on to Middle Road and see the top of our house and the girls on the street. It's another few steps before I notice the silver car pulled up beside them. The passenger window is down and the driver is leaning across the seat.

Harrie is holding on to Elise and they're both stepping away from the car. My heart thuds in my chest. What is the driver saying to my girls?

I start to run, flat out sprint, and at the same time June's front door opens and she's shouting something. Before I can get another step closer, get a better look at the driver, the car pulls away and disappears on to the main road.

By the time I reach the house, I can see Elise is crying and Harrie is still clinging to her.

'What happened? Who was that?' I gasp for breath.

'We don't know,' Harrie says.

'Everything all right, Anna?' June asks as she reaches her gate. 'I saw that car pulled up by the girls and thought I should come check they're OK.'

'Thank you,' I sigh. 'Did you see who it was?'

She shakes her head. 'Sorry, no. What did he say?' she asks, looking from me to Harrie and Elise.

'He was . . .' Elise starts to say, but it's Harrie who picks up the thread.

'. . . asking for directions.'

I shake my head. They're lying. 'Why are you both upset?'

'He was rude,' Harrie says.

'I'm fine,' Elise adds. 'He was an idiot.'

'Can we go inside?' they ask in unison.

'Not until you tell me what's going on. Harrie?'

Silence again.

Frustration rises up, tearing at my insides. A scream catches in my throat. 'TELL ME!' I shout the words so loud both girls jump.

Harrie lifts her face, her eyes meeting mine. 'Nothing is going on.' Her voice sounds so little next to mine. 'Please can we go inside?'

I hand over my keys and nod towards the house before they see me cry. Hot, embittered tears.

'Are you all right, Anna?' June reaches an arm around me, pulling me close, and I catch the smell of patchouli oil and aloe vera.

'I don't know,' I say, wiping my eyes. 'I'm sorry I'm a mess. I don't normally shout like that.'

'Of course you don't,' she says. 'I live next door, remember? I would hear you. And my dear, the last thing you are is a mess.' June's smile is kind and it makes me want to cry all over again.

'Harrie hasn't been herself today, but she won't tell me why. And Elise is upset. I think they're lying to me.'

'Someone is lying,' June says. 'What kind of person asks for directions from two school children on a road like this?' She tuts. 'Even from my bedroom window I knew he was scaring them. One of those perverts, I expect, cruising around trying to grab an innocent child.'

A shiver races over my skin and I shudder. 'I hope not.'

'You must report it to the police,' June says.

'But the girls say he was asking for directions. I don't think the police will do anything.'

She raises her eyebrows but says nothing.

'I'll tell the Neighbourhood Watch,' I say. 'Jack Briggs is a police officer. He'll know whether we should report it.'

'Good.' June nods before catching sight of the bag in my hands. 'Oh, cooking apples. How lovely. My tree has had a terrible year.'

I look down at the bag. The handles are stretched and digging into my fingers. I should bake a cake or a crumble, something for pudding for the weekend, but my mind is stuck on Harrie and now Elise. 'Do you want them?' I ask. 'One of the mums just gave them to me. I don't have time to do anything with them.'

'Only if you don't mind,' June beams. 'Thank you. But expect a crumble in return at some point in the next few days.'

We say our goodbyes before June turns back to the house and I walk around the hedge to my front door. I'm not sure what it is that makes me look back towards the main road, but I do, and that's when I see the silver car. It's passing slowly. I narrow my eyes, desperate to make out the driver or the licence plate, but the car is too far away. For a moment I think there's something familiar about it, but I shrug the feeling off. I don't even know the make or model. It could be a completely different car to the one that pulled up beside Harrie and Elise, but still I shudder again as I step inside.

Chapter 14

The night of the crash, 7.52–8.01 p.m.

Harrie

Harrie's eyes adjust quickly to the dark of her garden. The black wall of night she didn't want to step through is now a multitude of shadows. The smell of chimney smoke is heavy in the air, reminding Harrie of bonfires and eating sticky toffee apples on Fireworks Night. There's an almost full moon in the sky and a million stars. On any other night Harrie would try to spot the constellations her dad has shown her. Orion and Scorpius and the saucepan with the proper name that Harrie always forgets. But there is no time to stop and look up, no time to notice the cold of the night.

Sixteen minutes left.

Harrie pulls out the little torch from her pocket. It's the first time she's used it this year and the battery is weak, the circular light a dull yellow, but it's enough to guide her around the side of the house and to the gate with the stiff metal bolts that creak in her hand. She pulls the top one first and for a moment it won't budge.

She grits her teeth, trying harder until it moves, sliding open with a clonk that echoes through the stillness.

She pauses. Just for a second. Just to listen. She holds her breath, straining to hear above the thumping of her heart in her ears, but the only sound is the distant hum of traffic a world away from where she's standing.

The bottom bolt is easier and moves silently. Harrie is about to lift the handle and open the gate when a light flicks on, illuminating the garden beyond her house. Panic seizes Harrie's body. Her first thought is her mum. She can't be back from collecting Elise already. Harrie fumbles to switch off her torch as lies race through her head. Could she say she saw an injured cat?

A door opens somewhere. Footsteps outside. The surprise of the light subsides and Harrie can see the source. It isn't her mum. It's June.

Harrie likes June. She makes the best hot chocolates on earth. Better than anything Harrie has ever tasted from a shop. June used to have a dog called Walter. An old black Labrador that would roll over and let Harrie stroke his tummy any time she saw him. June is a dog person, just like Harrie. At least, Harrie would be a dog person, if her mum and dad would let her have a dog.

But however much Harrie likes June, she wishes she would turn around and go back into the house. Harrie ducks down, crouching in the corner by the gate. She watches the top of June's head – a hat of grey hair – shining in the light.

'Is someone there?' June calls out, her voice directed straight at Harrie. 'Anna, is that you?'

Footsteps tap on the paving stones. June is going to look over the fence.

Move, a voice that sounds like Elise's shouts in Harrie's head. *Now!* She pulls her hood up and jumps up, throwing open the gate and running, legs pounding the pavement, arms pumping like she's chasing after a striker on the football pitch. Behind her, the gate slams against the wall of the house with a shudder of wood, but Harrie is already across the road, keeping close to the hedges and away from the streetlights.

The village is deadly quiet, like a ghost town from a film. Only the occasional flickering glow of a television through a window makes Harrie feel like she's not completely alone in the world. She takes the shortcut, ducking down the alley that connects the two sides of the village. She walks this route every day to school and back, but it feels different now. There is no streetlight in the alley, no moon shining through the canopy of trees either, only the pathetic glow of her torch to show her the way. *Always check the batteries before you go out,* her dad's voice echoes in her thoughts.

A sudden longing hits Harrie as she runs. Their dad took Harrie and Elise camping last summer. It was only in the empty horse field a hundred metres from their house, only one night, but it was just the three of them and it was perfect. The field is huge and stretches far back from the road with trees bordering the edges – a woodland so thick with brambles that no one ever walks through it. When their dad chose a spot right at the back, it felt like they weren't in the village any more. They stayed up until long after midnight, their dad telling them stories about his job and the pranks his co-workers play on each other. Harrie sat in her sleeping bag, staring up at the sky, listening to her dad's voice boom through her, silent tears falling from her eyes because she was so happy and so sad too. He left again the following week.

Something rustles in the undergrowth, dragging

Harrie's thoughts back to the alley. She jumps, almost tripping over her feet as the torch flickers again and dies. Fear chases her through the darkness, nipping at her heels and skipping through her body until she reaches the road and the streetlights.

A silver car passes through the housing estate as Harrie leaves the alley. She slows to a walk, her chest heaving as she drags in breath after breath. Clarissa's mum drives a car like that. If she sees Harrie, she'll pull over to ask why she is out at night alone.

Harrie keeps to the inside edge of the pavement, her head down, her hood pulled low, and the car passes. She waits another ten seconds, counting them out in her head, before running again. This time she doesn't stop until she reaches the house.

There's a gate at the side with a latch but no bolts. She slips into the garden and around the edge of the house.

Her heart is still racing from the running, from the realization that she's here, that she's doing this. It's no longer a plan in her head – imagined steps. It's real.

The back door is just ahead and Harrie knows if she reaches out her hand that it will be unlocked, that it will open into a kitchen. She hopes it will be empty. She hopes the TV will be on and the living room door shut. The room she has to get to is up the stairs, first door on the right, and she has to do it without being seen.

Village Girlies' Group Chat
Thursday 22 October, 17.28

Tracy Campbell: Have you heard about Dean?

Gina Walker: No???

Kat Morris: What's happened?

Bev Pritchett: I just heard too.

Kat Morris: What?

Tracy Campbell: He's missing. Apparently, he didn't come home last night. Sue phoned Anthony this morning to ask if he's seen him, but Dean didn't go into the office today.

Sandra Briggs: She just phoned Jack too and asked if she should report it to the police. Jack's gone round there to talk to her.

Kat Morris: He's probably got a cheap flight to Spain for a few days. He did that a few years ago, remember? @TracyCampbell didn't Anthony have a hissy fit about it?

Tracy Campbell: YES! Anthony's raging now too.

Kat Morris: I'm not surprised. I know it's Dean's company but it's so unprofessional and Anthony's the one running the day-to-day stuff.

Tracy Campbell: Exactly!

Bev Pritchett: Has someone called the hospitals?

Sandra Briggs: Yes, Jack did.

Gina Walker: OMG! Hope Dean's OK. Poor Sue. Is anyone thinking of popping round there?

Sandra Briggs: I don't think we should. Sue is the one who stepped away from us. She knows where we are if she needs us.

Gina Walker: True.

Bev Pritchett: I saw Dean driving into the village last night. I remember because he was doing over thirty!

Kat Morris: Are you sure it was him? Seems weird that he'd come into the village but not go home.

Bev Pritchett: I thought it was him, but I didn't have my glasses on. Could've been anyone in a blue BMW I suppose.

Tracy Campbell: @AnnaJames do you know anything? I saw you and Dean together on Monday.

Village Girlies' Secret Group Chat
Thursday 22 October, 17.52

Bev Pritchett: OK, spill @TracyCampbell! What did you see?

Sandra Briggs: I was just wondering that too. Have I missed something?

Tracy Campbell: Oh, I just happened to be walking the dog on Monday afternoon and saw Dean leaving Anna's house. Anna looked pretty flustered. It's not the first time I've seen him stopping by. His car is parked outside her house at least once a week.

Kat Morris: To be fair, Anna is redeveloping Dean's website for Stockton's, which you know @TracyCampbell. FYI – the window cleaner popped inside the other day to clean the inside windows. I wouldn't want anyone thinking there's something going on because I let a man who isn't my husband into my house.

Tracy Campbell: Fair enough @KatMorris, but how long does a website take to build?

Bev Pritchett: OMG do you think they're having an affair?

Sandra Briggs: Rob is away A LOT! And Dean is rather lush.

Tracy Campbell: #Silverfox

Kat Morris: #Suchgossips

Bev Pritchett: Do you think it has anything to do with Dean going AWOL?

Tracy Campbell: Not unless Sue found out and he's buried under their patio, LOL.

Bev Pritchett: BTW it wasn't the supply teacher who vandalized the school. Mike called the agency to ask about him and it turns out he's teaching English in St Lucia.

Sandra Briggs: No surprise it wasn't the supply teacher. Jack and the Neighbourhood Watch are all over it. They'll find who did it. Someone will have seen something. Do you all know what your kids were doing last Saturday?

Tracy Campbell: Freya was at home with us all afternoon. So was Olivia but I don't think we need to worry about the little ones, ha ha.

Kat Morris: Ben was home too. The James twins came over. So it can't have been them either.

Sandra Briggs: And Tyler was at football camp all day so at least we know it wasn't any of our lot.

Bev Pritchett: What's Jack going to do about the vandalism @SandraBriggs?

Sandra Briggs: You'll see.

Chapter 15

Anna

I'm in the kitchen cooking dinner when the messages *ping ping ping* on to my phone. The air is thick with steam from the potatoes bubbling and boiling on the hob and the smell of the roast chicken which will give us the meat for three meals. I glance at the screen, spoon in hand, hoping it's Dean replying to my earlier message.

I scan the messages, already turning my focus back to the dinner when I see it's the village mums, but then I spot Dean's name in the text.

Have you heard about Dean?

He's missing.

The spoon drops with a clatter of metal on the worktop. A trail of starchy water spills down the side of the cupboard as I snatch up my phone and call Dean. They're wrong, I tell myself as I hold my breath and wait for him to answer. He'll be at home right now with Sue, his wife, and he'll laugh when I tell him what they're saying.

The ringing stops. Voicemail starts. I hang up without leaving a message.

I know he hasn't replied to my texts or returned my calls but that doesn't mean he's missing. I saw him on Monday. If I close my eyes I can still feel the heat of his body against mine. I can see the deep sadness etched across his face, the dark anxiousness that hovered around him. He wouldn't tell me what was wrong, but there was something. I'm sure of it.

The words I spoke circle my head and I remember the alarm on his face, the sense of something changing between us. But for the first time, I wonder if there is another reason for his silence.

I press a hand to the counter, steadying myself as I wait for the next message to come through, but it's silent now. Tracy's final message sits unanswered. Everyone is waiting for my reply. Annoyance pulses through me. This village, these women, can feel stifling at times. Times like now, when it feels like they are all crammed into my kitchen, breathing down my neck, whispering in my ear. It doesn't matter how beautiful the landscape is, how picturesque, how safe the village is, I'll never feel comfortable with the 'everyone knows everything' ethos that comes with living in Barton St Martin. We can't be the only family in this village with a horrid little secret, can we? Two secrets now, I remind myself.

I scroll through the messages again, my gaze resting on the final one.

```
@AnnaJames do you know anything? I saw
you and Dean together on Monday.
```

Am I imagining the passive-aggressive tone to Tracy's comment? Yes, I tell myself. Tracy is a friend. Her husband, Anthony, works with Dean. She's just worried about him, that's all.

'Mummy.' Molly's hand tugs at my sleeve.

My eyes are dragged from my phone by Molly's voice. I push away the dread building inside me, the memories of Monday, the truth I will soon have to face.

'How long until dinner?' Molly asks. 'I'm hungry.'

'Soon. Two minutes. I've just got to make the mash.'

'Can I help?'

'Of course. One sec. Let me reply to a message quickly.'

I tap out a reply, delete and try again. On the fourth attempt I press send.

```
Hope Dean is OK! We chatted Monday about
Stockton's website and he seemed fine.
```

'I've got the masher.' Molly holds up the utensil like a flaming torch and swirls and skips over to the counter as I tuck my phone into the back pocket of my jeans.

'Great.' I smile as I drain the potatoes, letting everything go except Molly and this moment together.

The potatoes are overcooked and soggy lumps, half mash already. 'Be careful, the pan's hot,' I say to Molly. 'I'll hold it, you mash.'

Even under Molly's seven-year-old strength, the potatoes give easily. They'll taste watery, the texture a slop. Elise will pull her face. She's always been a fussy eater. There was a period soon after being weaned when all she'd eat was toast. Toast and butter. Toast and jam. Toast and Marmite. Toast and honey. Toast. I'd park the high chairs side by side and watch Harrie scoff back the entire contents of Annabel Karmel's cookbook, all the food I'd spent hours chopping, grating and cooking, and in one sweep Elise would push it to the floor with the back of her hand and cry and cry until I gave in and made her toast.

Gravy will help. I'll do extra.

My phone buzzes from my pocket as I serve the dinner on to four plates. 'Go wash your hands,' I say to Molly. 'And tell your sisters it's time for dinner.'

No one has replied to my message on the village girlies' chat, but there's a message from Kat on my lock screen.

```
Steve will be round in a bit with the
dishwasher. Can I ask a favour? X
```

I reply straight away:

```
Of course!! Anything x
```

The three bubbles roll across the bottom of the screen. Above my head Molly, Elise and Harrie squabble for their turn in the bathroom.

```
Kat: Our Parish Council clerk has just
resigned and we need a new one. Before
you say no, it's paid not voluntary! 5
hours a week. Good hourly rate!!! We're
desperate. PLEASE xx
```

My heart sinks. I need to use my time to build my business and be both parents to the girls while Rob is away.

But how can I say no? Kat is giving me a dishwasher for free. And now she's offering me paid work.

```
Me: What do I need to do?
```

Kat: Not much! Attend the meetings and take the minutes. Keep the records in order. Answer email enquiries and send them on to the relevant member of the council. It's boring stuff. Overgrowing hedges and cars parked in the wrong places, but we need your organization skills. Honestly, it's a breeze and most weeks it probably won't even take an hour and it'll be money for nothing!

Me: OK. Count me in xx

Money for nothing. If only there was such a thing. But the idea of extra income is impossible to turn down. Already, I'm lying awake at night worrying about the cost of another Christmas. We save a little every month for the presents and we try to get everything on the lists the girls make, but it's getting harder with the twins. Molly is still at that age of wanting the plastic crap – a new Barbie, a Lego set – but Elise is desperate for technology, and all Harrie wants is a dog. It's all she talks about some days. Which breed would be best, how she'll walk it every day, twice a day. 'It doesn't have to be a puppy,' she said last week. 'We could get a rescue dog. That wouldn't be expensive, would it?'

I said I'd think about it but I already know the answer. Insurance. Dog food. Vet bills. I can't do it. I can't add another burden to this family.

Footsteps thud – a herd of elephants – on the stairs and Elise and Molly rush into the kitchen, laughing and jostling playfully with each other for who gets to sit where.

'Where's Harrie?'

The smile drops from Elise's face. 'She's coming.' Her tone is defiant. Protective. It's a reminder that however much I want to drag the truth out of Harrie, now is not the time.

Harrie slides into a chair as I place the plates on the table. She's tense, her face set in a scowl.

Only when I jolly the conversation along over dinner, talking about gymnastics and school and our plans for the weekend, do Harrie and Elise relax a little.

Molly delights in Harrie's silence. Her voice is usually the first to be drowned out, ignored by her sisters, but she takes centre stage over dinner telling us all about the new girl in her class and why Molly thinks she's going to be best friends with Alice. 'They both like horses and they both have red hair,' she explains.

'Why do you keep looking at Harrie?' Elise asks me when Molly is done with her story.

'I'm not,' I lie.

'Yes you are.'

'I'm worried about her. Are you OK, Harrie?' I ask, trying to draw her into the conversation so she's not listening to us talk about her like she's not here.

'Fine,' she says, the one word bitten off and short. 'Can I get down now please?'

My gaze falls to her plate. She's barely touched her food. One piece of chicken and one mouthful of mash. No peas.

'Not hungry?'

She shakes her head.

'There's nothing else. No cereal or toast.'

'I KNOW,' she shouts, the words so loud Molly squeaks. 'You always say that. We're not babies, Mum. We get it.'

I stare open-mouthed at Harrie. I know I should tell her off, but I still can't wrap my head around who this child in front of me is. Harrie's face is tilted up, she's waiting for my response, but her eyes swim with tears that break my heart.

It's the doorbell that shatters the silence. My eyes are still on Harrie and so I see her freeze. I see her body tense, her eyes grow wide, and a terror draw across her features. She leaps up so suddenly that her arm knocks the place mat, and I watch helplessly as her plate flips to the floor in a clatter of broken china.

Chapter 16

Anna

The air in the kitchen electrifies as Harrie's fear zips around us. Elise jumps up too, chair scraping against the floor, sensing her sister's terror. Molly is silent, staring between me and Harrie. It's only a beat, a second when we all stand there, gravy seeping into the grout between the tiles.

Harrie moves. Two quick strides to the back door, a shaking hand already on the handle when I find my voice.

'It's all right,' I say. 'It's just Steve with a new dishwasher.'

'Why is he bringing a dishwasher?' Molly asks.

'Our one has broken and they had a spare,' I reply, my focus still on Harrie. 'Who did you think was at the door?' I ask her. *Who are you so scared of?*

Silence.

The doorbell rings a second time. Elise steps to her sister and pushes her towards the stairs.

'Can I watch TV please, Mummy?' Molly asks.

'You know the rules,' I tell her, dropping a kiss on

to the top of her head. 'No more technology. You've got half an hour until it's time to get ready for bed. Go and play.'

'All right, Anna,' Steve says with a friendly smile as I open the front door.

'Steve, hi. Thank you for doing this.'

Steve wheels the dishwasher into the kitchen on a trolley, bumping it carefully over the lip of the door frame.

'As if I had a choice,' he says, but he's smiling his crooked smile, letting me know he doesn't mind.

Steve Morris is every bit as handsome as Kat is beautiful. He isn't broad like Rob, but his face is boyish despite being in his forties. He has a Jaime Lannister from *Game of Thrones* look about him, but maybe that's just the sandy colour of his hair. Steve is also the most easy-going person I've ever met. A go-with-the-flow type who'll leap out of bed in the middle of the night to fix a leak and who never seems to complain when Kat announces there's no dinner that night because she's been drinking wine in the garden with me and can't be arsed. Steve does as he's told, and they both seem content with the balance in their relationship.

'What happened to the old dishwasher?' he asks, opening the door and peering into the empty racks

'It's been temperamental for a while now. But yesterday it gave up altogether.'

'Do you know how old it is?'

'Five years old. We got it when we moved in.'

'You've done well then. They pretty much have a three-year lifespan now. Same as washing machines. Cost as much to fix as they do to replace most of the time, but it shouldn't take long to swap these around.'

I do a quick calculation in my head and feel queasy

at the realization that our washing machine is three and a half years old.

'Do you want a cup of tea?' I ask.

'You're all right thanks, Anna. Been drinking the stuff all day. I swear I piss tea most evenings. I should be out of your hair in five minutes.'

Steve sets to work and I clean away the dinner plates, the mess, feeling the drag of another job that I have no one to share with. If Steve notices the broken plate, the spilt dinner, he doesn't comment.

'Did you hear about Dean?' I say, my tone casual. Just gossip. Nothing more here.

'Yep, Kat just told me. I'm sure he'll turn up, though. It's not the first time he's done a runner.'

'Oh really? Do you know him well?'

Steve laughs. 'Everyone knows Dean well. He's the Alan Sugar of the village. Got his fingers in all the pies, so to speak.' Steve chuckles, easy and relaxed, and I wonder if we're talking about the same person.

Fingers in all the pies.

I know about Stockton's Builders and Contractors of course, but Dean never speaks about the business. We talk about the films we like and music and . . . and me, I realize. We talk a lot about me and the girls and Rob sometimes too. My life. My troubles.

As I cut the last of the chicken for tomorrow's dinner, I think about how little I really know about Dean. The thought is unnerving.

'All done,' Steve announces a minute later, clambering to his feet. 'Any problems, give me a shout.'

'Thank you. Thank you so much.'

'It's what friends are for.' He smiles and pushes the old dishwasher on to the trolley. 'Did Kat tell you her news, by the way?'

I frown, thinking back to my conversation with Kat this morning. Did she tell me anything new? 'No, I don't think so.'

'She's been promoted to a sales manager.'

'Oh wow, that's great.' I make a mental note to dig out a congratulations card for her. 'She's really good at selling those beauty products.'

'She really is.' Steve rubs his hands over his dirty overalls. 'You know, when she first told me about it, I thought it was a scam. One of those pyramid-scheme things, but we've taken Ben on two amazing holidays this year thanks to her earnings. If you're short of a few bob, you could sell the stuff too. I'm sure Kat could help you get started.'

I tell him I'll think about it as I walk him to the door, hiding the sharp smart of humiliation. Short of a few bob? That's an understatement, but I've not got Kat's selling sparkle, her ease. I'm too desperate.

When the kitchen is clean again and the new dishwasher is humming in the silence, I head upstairs, my heart in my throat, preparing myself to talk to Harrie again. This can't go on.

Chapter 17

Friday, eight days until Halloween

Harrie

'This isn't going to—' Elise starts to say, staring at her reflection in their bedroom mirror and pinching the silky material of Harrie's football shirt.

'It will,' Harrie cuts in. 'It has to.'

Their school clothes are piled on the floor by their feet beside a scattering of other clothes and two of Harrie's footballs. Their beds are on either side of the room. Elise by the wall, Harrie by the window. They have their separate sides, their separate drawers and bedside tables, half a wardrobe each, but still their things seem to drift towards each other – like magnets – the same way they do. One of Elise's gymnastics trophies is nestled next to a football medal of Harrie's. *Man of the Match* is inscribed on the front. Their mum said it should say woman, but Harrie doesn't care.

'Can you at least tell me why we're doing this?' Elise asks. 'Where are you going?'

'I told you.' Harrie steps beside her twin, catching

sight of the pink jumper she's wearing and frowning at the sight of it. How does Elise wear this colour? Harrie feels like a tub of candyfloss. 'I have to leave the house. I won't be long. Ten minutes max. You're the only one allowed out on your own and only to go across the road to see Mr Pritchett. So I have to be you.'

'But Mr Pritchett gave me my work for the weekend at school today. What if Mum asks him about it?'

'She won't,' Harrie replies with more conviction than she feels. She stuffs her hands in her pockets so Elise can't see them shaking.

'But why do you need to go out? Where are you going?'

'I can't tell you.' Harrie shakes her head, wishing she could. They don't keep secrets from each other, but this is so much bigger than them. So much bigger.

Elise sighs, flopping on to her bed so hard it wobbles. Her leg brushes against the cluttered bedside table, knocking a snow globe to the floor with a small thud. There are dozens of them around the room. Big and small, all filled with different scenes – Christmas trees, and the Eiffel Tower, a car, a house, a tabby cat. Elise used to have more, but she gave the babyish ones to Molly last year.

Elise lies flat, then pushes her body up into a perfect bridge. 'You know we're leaving for gymnastics in like an hour, right? You can't be me for that.'

'I know. Don't do that,' Harrie hisses. Their bedroom door is closed, their mum downstairs making dinner, but if she walks in right now, everything will be ruined and Harrie will be stuck here and that can't happen. Ten minutes, that's all she needs, just to see, just to check.

The thought makes her heart race and her breath catch as though she's running.

Elise drops the bridge and hops across the floor to Harrie's bed. 'Better?' she asks.

Harrie nods.

'It's weird being on this side of the room,' Elise says, pulling a face. 'I wish you'd tell me why we're doing this. Is it because of—'

'No,' Harrie shakes her head. Elise is talking about yesterday and the car. It has everything to do with that, but it's better Elise doesn't know.

'He was an idiot,' Elise says.

'Yeah. He thought you were me because of—'

'My coat. I get that, but why did he want to talk to you?'

Harrie? She can still hear the growl of his voice, his anger in her head, and the way his eyes had narrowed as he'd looked between them. That strong hand reaching for Elise – even now the thought of it makes Harrie's heart pound with a fear that steals her breath.

'Nothing,' Harrie mumbles.

'Something happened the other night.' Elise crosses her arms and looks at Harrie, her face a mix of pleading and knowing. 'I know it did. You totally freaked out when Tyler pushed you yesterday. You looked really scared.'

'I can't talk about it.' She wants to. So badly. But the threat still has its nails dug deep inside her. She has to keep quiet.

'Are you ready?' Harrie asks.

'It's not going to work though. Mum has never ever been fooled by a swap and she isn't going to buy this. You do realize that?'

'She will. We just need—'

'A distraction,' Elise finishes.

'Molly,' they say at the same time.

Harrie opens the bedroom door and shouts for their little sister. A second later her head pops out of her bedroom.

'What is it?' she asks.

'Quick.' Harrie beckons. 'We need you in here. It's top secret.'

A wide smile spreads across Molly's face and she scurries across the landing.

Elise stands up. 'We need your help.'

Molly's eyes narrow. Her gaze moves from Elise to Harrie and back again. 'Why are you wearing Harrie's football kit?' she asks Elise.

'I told you.' Elise rolls her eyes. 'This isn't going to work.'

'What isn't?' Molly asks.

'We're playing a joke on Mum,' Harrie says. Desperation grips tight. Elise is right. They can't even fool Molly. How are they going to trick their mum?

Molly giggles and claps her hands. 'Goody. Can I help?'

'Yes. You're the star,' Elise says, before telling Molly the plan.

Five minutes later they gather on the stairs. 'Ready?' Harrie whispers to Molly.

'Ready,' Molly nods.

'Go on then.' Elise gives Molly a gentle push and she moves, jumping the final step and rushing into the kitchen, a teddy bear squished in her arms.

'Mummy,' Molly wails. 'Arthur Le Blanc has a hole in his side. Can you sew him up?'

'Sure,' their mum says. 'I'll do it tonight when we're back from taking Elise to gymnastics.'

'Can you do it now? I think he's in pain.' Molly begins to cry. Perfect pitiful tears.

Elise looks at Harrie and they share a smile. It's now or never.

'Mum,' Elise calls out from the stairs. 'Mr Pritchett said I could pop over and collect some extra home-work tonight. Can I go now?'

'Now?' comes their mum's reply, her voice almost lost behind Molly's tears. 'All right, Molly,' she soothes. 'We'll sew him up now. Elise, can it wait until tomor-row? Dinner is almost ready and we're leaving for gymnastics after that.'

'But he said tonight and it will be too late when I get back,' Elise replies. 'Please?'

'Fine, but don't be long and look both ways before you cross the road.'

'I will,' Elise shouts.

'Where's Harrie?'

'Upstairs reading,' Elise replies, nudging Harrie to go.

Harrie moves, keeping her head down as she passes her mum. She holds her breath, expecting her name to be called, but Molly is still sniffling and their mum is digging in the drawer for the sewing kit. She glances up for a second just as Harrie reaches the front door and pulls on Elise's coat.

'Don't be long, Elise,' her mum says.

Harrie nods, not daring to speak. She shoots out the front door and into the early evening, feet hitting the pavement. The cold wind burns her lungs and whips her hair as the dark closes in around her.

The fear is almost choking as she draws near, like thick smoke she can't breathe through. Every part of her body wants her to turn around, to run away, but she can't, just like she couldn't two nights ago.

**Interview with Gina Walker, Chair
of Barton St Martin Primary School
Parent-Teacher Association
Interview conducted by Melissa Hart,
The Daily Gazette, 2 November**

Gina: None of it makes sense. I just wish I knew what happened. My daughter, Clarissa, is absolutely distraught. You just don't expect things like this to happen here. These were people we saw almost every day. Thank God it's half-term or she'd be missing school. I was going to speak to Mike Pritchett, the head teacher, about having a special parent-and-child assembly, but he's retiring so I don't know what will happen there.

MH: Where is Clarissa now? Do you think she'd mind having a quick word with me?

Gina: Oh no. I'm sorry but I don't want to upset her any more. She's at a friend's house right now.

MH: Could you give me a bit of background? You were in the same friendship group as Anna James. Is that correct?

Gina: Yes, I suppose so. The twins and Clarissa played together, but that stopped when Harrie went off the rails. You know she was violent, don't you? She got in trouble for hurting other kids. As for Anna, we weren't that close. She kept to herself. It's Kat or Tracy you should speak to. They were closer to Anna than I was, although I got the impression there might have been a falling out last week.

MH: Really? What about?

Gina: I've no idea. Probably something and nothing. We tried and tried to bring Anna into our circle, but she didn't make an effort to be part of the village. I know a lot of people found that annoying. We all volunteer for things and do our bit, all except Anna. I never minded. I've got my hands full with two kids, so I can only imagine how hard it must be with three, especially with Rob away. You know I was the one who texted her on

Halloween when Harrie went missing? We were all so worried. I wish I'd done more that night. Maybe things would be different now if I had.

Chapter 18

Anna

I wake with a jolt. It's late. Middle-of-the-night kind of late. There is no splinter of light creeping in from the curtains, no whisper of dawn. Only silence.

I'm sure something woke me but sleep is already pulling me back into its clutches. Then I hear it again. A whimper. A cry. A voice through the thin walls. In an instant I'm alert and throwing off the covers. I pull on my dressing gown and fumble to find the armholes. It will be Molly needing the toilet and being too scared to get up in the dark. Did I tell her to use the bathroom before bed? I can't remember. The list of things I have to remind my children to do seems to grow each day. Flush the toilet, wash your hands, brush your teeth, make your bed, wash your face, wash your face again with soap, brush your hair, pack your school bag. There are countless more. I feel like the words are etched into my brain somewhere, never to be forgotten, a robotic reminder I barely register saying any more.

It's only when I open my bedroom door and hear

the noise again that I realize it's not Molly. The whimper is coming from Harrie and Elise's room.

I turn on the landing light. The harshness of it stings my eyes and pushes the last of the drowsiness from my head, but it casts a soft glow over the twins' bedroom as I open the door and my gaze moves straight to Harrie. She's sitting up in bed, the covers thrown to the floor. Her face is wet with tears and she's crying softly, saying words I can't make out.

I know instantly that it's a night terror. It's been years since she had one, but I'll never forget.

'Harrie?' I say into the darkness.

'Mummy?' comes a reply, but it's not Harrie speaking, it's Elise.

'It's OK, Elise. Harrie is having a night terror.'

'I thought she didn't get them any more.'

'So did I. Go get into my bed and sleep in there.'

Elise slips out of the bed and with a pained glance at Harrie leaves the room.

'Go away, don't hurt me,' Harrie says, the words blending into each other as she cries, loud whining gasps.

I step closer to the bed and whisper Harrie's name, my voice soft and gentle. My hand reaches out to touch her shoulder but Harrie jerks away and cries out. 'Go away.'

'Harrie, you're having a night terror. You're OK.'

She can't hear me. It's as though she's trapped in a soundproof room, a locked door keeping us apart. I can't touch her. I can't wake her. All I can do is wait for it to pass and for Harrie to wake on her own.

I kneel beside Harrie's bed, tears pricking my eyes as I watch the terror on her face.

Minutes pass. My love for her swells up – an ache in

my chest – as I watch her cry and fight. I'm helpless. It's Wednesday night all over again. I'm stuck. I can't get to Harrie, but this time she's right in front of me.

Minutes pass like this before her cries soften. She gasps like she's been underwater, holding her breath for too long. Her hands fly up, protecting her face from some imaginary danger.

With slow movements I take one of her hands in mine and feel the tremor shaking her body. 'It's OK, baby. I'm here. You were having a night terror.' I switch on the bedside light so Harrie can see the safety of her bedroom. The dog posters on the walls, the footballs on the floor.

Harrie's eyes focus on my face and then she's in my arms, her body damp with sweat. She cries in a way I've not seen since she was a little girl.

She's *still* a little girl, I remind myself. It's so easy to look at them and see the adults they're becoming. The attitude they have, the intellect, how much they know about the world. But they're not adults or teenagers, not even tweens. Harrie is still a child and the fierce need to protect her burns through my body.

I wrap my arms around Harrie and hold her tight until her sobs become whimpers. My eyes fall to the bruise on her neck. The blotches have darkened into a deep purple. They look like finger marks. The realization sends an ice-cold horror charging through my body.

'What were you dreaming about?' I ask.

She pulls away and settles on to her pillows. 'I don't remember.'

'Harrie? I think you do. I think something happened on Wednesday night that's making you scared. I want to help you. Where did this bruise on your neck

116

come from? Please talk to me. There is nothing you can say to me that will make me mad or upset, I promise. I just want to help you.'

Another pause. This one longer. Harrie's breathing changes and I realize she's fallen asleep.

I turn off the lamp and climb into Elise's bed with my body facing Harrie. I stare into the darkness for a long time listening to her breathing, waiting for any sign of another night terror while the worry for her gnaws in the pit of my stomach.

Chapter 19

Harrie

Harrie crouches on the ground before lifting her head and peering into the window. Light is spilling in from the hallway, illuminating the empty kitchen and an open bottle of wine on the side. Harrie wrestles with the sleeve of her coat and checks her watch. She's already been ten minutes. Seven more than she thought it would take her to get here. She still has ten minutes to get in and get out without anyone seeing her. Then all she has to do is run home and get into bed before her mum gets back.

The enormity of what she's doing rises up again. Saliva builds in Harrie's mouth and she can't seem to swallow. She has never done anything like this before. Never will again, she's sure of it. Worry grips hold of her like the little boy being clenched in the giant's fist in one of Molly's fairy-tale books.

Run home. Go now, a voice shouts in her head. And she wants to. More than anything, she wants to go home. She thought this would be easy, but it's not. It's hard and she's scared. Maybe there's another way, something she didn't think of before. If only Harrie could ask for help, but she can't.

For a second, Harrie's feet are stuck fast, fixed in cement. This is the only way, she reminds herself.

Before she can talk herself out of it, Harrie opens the door and in one swift movement she steps inside.

The warmth of the house hits her and she's immediately too hot in Elise's coat. Even with the heating on full blast at home, which it never is, the house never gets this warm. Harrie pushes down her hood and takes a step to the table. Her heart is racing, thumping through her body so hard it's like it's jolting her, and she can't concentrate on listening to the unfamiliar noises of the house.

All Harrie has to do is walk down the hall and up the stairs, grab the phone and leave. Except she can hear voices. People. More than there should be – and it's not the TV.

No, no, no. This wasn't part of the plan.

Harrie steps towards the door that leads into the hall and holds her breath as she listens to hissed whispers. It sounds like two men arguing. They're angry. Harrie can see their shadows circling each other. The living room door is wide open. Whatever is going on, she'll never be able to sneak up the stairs unnoticed.

A long breath leaves Harrie's body, a sagging disappointment. What can she do? The answer is bitterly obvious. She has to leave. Give up. Go home.

The voices grow louder. 'Did you think you could get away with this?' one of them growls. The reply is muffled, pleading.

Harrie backs quickly away from the door, panic

rushing through her body. She turns to leave, ready to flee, but something catches her eye on the worktop. It's an iPhone. A black iPhone 8 with a white face, plugged into a charging cable.

She gasps. It's the phone. The very reason she's here. She hasn't failed.

A noise erupts from the hallway behind her and Harrie jumps.

'I can do what I like,' a man is saying, the noise so close Harrie swears they're right behind her, but the kitchen is still empty.

Someone laughs. It's mocking, like the laugh of Darcy, their football captain, when one of them falls over.

'No you can't.'

Harrie dashes across the kitchen and snatches up the phone, sliding it into her pocket, barely slowing as she heads to the back door, but there's a movement in the corner of her eye and she hears the scuffling of feet and the sound of a thwack, a thud. Something lands against the wall. The noises are moving this way fast. There's no time for Harrie to reach the back door and escape unseen. It's all she can do to drop to the floor and slide herself into the corner behind the table as the kitchen explodes with shouting and anger.

Chapter 20

Anna

'Am not.'

'You are.'

'Am NOT.'

'You so are.'

'Girls, please.' My hands tighten around the steering wheel and I glance in the mirror to the back seats where Elise and Molly are arguing. 'We'll be home in one minute.'

'But Mummy,' Molly says, her voice serious, as though the next words that will leave her mouth will be the most important she ever says. 'Elise is saying I'm a scaredy-cat because I wouldn't trick-or-treat at Olivia's house last year because of the ghosts hanging in the trees, but I'm seven now—'

'Still scared,' Elise jumps in. I don't need to look in the mirror to know Elise is smirking.

'Enough,' I snap and the car falls silent.

It's been like this since we left for the Saturday

121

medley of clubs and I wonder if they can sense the dark cloud hanging over Harrie like I can. I flick a glance to Harrie, sat beside me. She catches my gaze and dips her head, shrinking another layer into herself.

The desire to ask if she's OK bubbles inside me but I keep it in. Begging Harrie to talk to me hasn't helped. I need to give her space today and hope, pray she comes to me.

We pull into the village and drive slowly through the outskirts with their undulating landscape of fields, farmland and woodland, all lit by a bright beam of sunshine. Barton St Martin is the kind of beauty spot that people flock to in the summer to escape the towns. They all head for the river Barton, which cuts across the entire county and all the way out to sea. In the summer the riverbanks are steep, the current lazy, and it's filled with kayaks and paddleboards.

But as the summer fades into autumn, the current awakens – a gushing beast.

A few years before we moved to the village the river broke over the banks suddenly one morning, spilling on to the neighbouring fields and sweeping a dog walker into its depths. The dog was found alive five miles downstream, but the woman drowned. I've never forgotten that story, never taken the children near the river after summer.

I park outside the house and kill the engine. June is at her window, the net curtains pulled to one side as though she's waiting for someone. She waves when she sees me and I lift my hand in reply before she disappears.

We trudge inside, arms full of football boots and coats, gymnastics bags and water bottles. My handbag is heavy on my shoulder where I've stuffed it full of drink cartons and books – entertainment as each of the girls took their turn waiting for the others to finish. We dump it all down by the door and for once I don't complain.

I let the girls watch TV while I make lunch. I'm halfway through buttering the bread for sandwiches, hollow from hunger and drained, when the doorbell rings and I find Sandra's husband, Jack Briggs, standing on my doorstep, dressed in his black police uniform.

The rhyme runs through my head before I can stop it.

> PC Jack, not so tall,
> And his wife, Sandra, the fairest of them all.

There is something compact about Jack. He's around the same height as me – five foot eight, maybe a little more – and has a wiry physique, a 'don't mess with me' presence about his stance.

'Is this about Rob?' The words are a whisper. A torrent of fear hits me then – wild like the river – and I want to take it all back, all the anger, the bitterness I feel towards Rob so often now. Images flash through my mind. An explosion on the oil rig. Rob's body burned beyond recognition.

For the two seconds it takes Jack to reply I'm sure my heart doesn't beat.

'No.' He shakes his head and there's pity in his eyes when he looks at me, but I don't care because I can breathe again. 'I'm sorry for startling you, Anna. I was called to the station this morning, hence the uniform, but this is Neighbourhood Watch-related. It's about last week's vandalism. May I come in for a few minutes, please?'

'Oh, of course, yes.' I nudge Harrie's football boots

to one side and hang up Molly's coat that has fallen from the hook.

'I'm glad you're here actually,' I say, leading him into the kitchen. 'I've been meaning to call. I wanted to mention something to the Neighbourhood Watch that I saw the other day.'

'Oh?' Jack leans closer and I can smell the citrus scent of his aftershave.

'I'm sure it was nothing, but on Thursday after school the girls walked ahead of me and by the time I got home there was a silver car pulled up beside them, just outside, and the driver was talking to them.'

'What was he saying?'

'I don't know.' I shake my head. 'By the time I got there, he'd driven away and the girls say he was just asking for directions, but—'

'Something didn't feel right about it?' Jack nods.

'Exactly.'

'Leave it with me. I'll mention it to the Neighbourhood Watch and also check in at the station and see if there have been any similar reports.'

'Thank you.' I smile. Of all the husbands – the dad crowd – I like Jack the best. He's not overly friendly, a try-too-hard type like Tracy's husband, Anthony, or a joker like Martin, Gina's husband. Jack is watchful. He seems to know just the right thing to say or do. Once, a few years ago, a big snowstorm hit overnight. Jack went out early and cleared the doorsteps and paths of dozens of residents, mine and June's included. And last summer at the fete when Rob had too many beers watching the band, Jack helped us all home, carrying a sleeping Molly like she weighed as little as a kitten.

My stomach growls, an empty rattle that sends a

weariness through my body, but I push back the chopping board and the half-made sandwiches and offer Jack a tea or coffee.

'I'm all right for the moment, thanks,' Jack replies. 'I won't keep you long. I'm just taking a few minutes to talk to the families in the village about the vandalism we had at the school last week. We decided in a Neighbourhood Watch meeting this week that perhaps some personal chats might nip this in the bud before it goes any further. Vandalism is the type of crime that tends to escalate.'

'Oh, I see. Do you want to sit at the table, and I'll call the girls in?'

'How about we talk in the living room.'

I nod before leading Jack through to the living room where the girls are spread across the sofa. I turn off the TV and see all three girls stare wide-eyed and anxious at Jack's police uniform. 'This is Jack Briggs, he's the head of the Neighbourhood Watch and he just wants a quick chat with you all. There's nothing to worry about. You can trust him, he's a police officer.'

'We know. He came to the school and did an assembly last week,' Elise says.

'He's Tyler and Imogen's daddy,' Molly adds. 'Imogen's in Reception now. I'm her anti-bullying buddy.'

Only Harrie is silent, her eyes fixed on the old laminate floor. Seeing her side by side with Elise, the change in her is startling. Harrie's hair is limp and straggly, her cheekbones are more prominent, her body shrunken and looking suddenly smaller than her sister's. The same questions, the same desperation to know what happened to her, swirl through my mind.

'That's right.' Jack flashes Molly a wide reassuring smile. 'And as I mentioned in assembly, I'm the head of

125

the Neighbourhood Watch for the village and we're concerned about the vandalism at the school last Saturday.' Jack speaks slowly and clearly, his eyes moving to each of my children in turn.

'Someone threw toilet roll over the trees,' Molly says, looking up at me. 'It's true,' she adds as though I'm about to question her statement.

'I know.'

'Much more worrying,' Jack continues, 'is the wooden fence that was kicked down, allowing the vandals into the school playing field.'

'But you don't know who it was?' I ask, thinking back to last Saturday, feeling relieved to know the girls were at Kat's house all afternoon, and the guilt of considering for a second that it might have been them.

'Not yet, but I'm sure we'll know soon enough. I don't suppose I could have that cup of tea now, could I, Anna?'

'Of course.' I step back to the kitchen and listen to the rise and fall of Jack's voice from the living room. He has a commanding tone, a sit-up-and-listen voice. I click the kettle on to boil and wonder what more he has to say to the girls. It feels like overkill to be visiting every family with school-age kids in the village, especially after already talking to them in assembly, but then the damage to the school fence is the first bit of vandalism, the first crime of any kind we've seen in the village in the years we've lived here, so maybe overkill is the best course of action.

My phone buzzes on the worktop. A message from Tracy fills my screen.

Super excited to have you on board the Parish Council!!!! Meeting on Monday, noon,

126

at mine. Can you make it? Don't worry
about being up to speed. I've been on the
PC for years and I still don't have a clue
half the time, LOL xxxx

I reply with a thumbs-up and swallow back the niggling regret I feel. I'm doing this as a favour to Kat, and it's paid, I remind myself as I make a mug of tea for Jack.

'Here we are,' I say, holding out the mug as I step into the living room.

'How long until lunch, Mummy?' Molly asks and I could kiss her for it.

'I'll leave you to it,' Jack says, taking a sip of tea before handing it straight back to me. 'Thanks for that. Remember, girls, I'm always here if you want to talk about anything happening in the village.'

It's not until the afternoon when I'm folding yet another load of washing in the bedroom, when Elise is doing the extra work she collected from Mike last night and Molly is playing with her Barbie dolls, that Harrie comes to find me.

'Can I ask something?' She sits on my bed and picks up two socks to pair for me.

'Anything.' I give Harrie my best mum smile, my I'm-here-for-you smile. I think of the questions Harrie is forever asking. Like: what is your favourite continent and why? Or: how does electricity get from the power station to the house? Or: if you could be any wild animal, what would you be? Harrie questions, Rob and I call them.

The resentment burns through me. *You should sodding well be here, Rob.*

I swallow it back. A bitter pill.

'What age can people be sent to prison?' Harrie asks.

'Oh.' The question throws me. 'I'm not sure. I think it's sixteen. Why?' My stomach knots. Is this one of her normal questions, or something else? 'Is this about something Jack Briggs said to you? You don't need to worry about that. He knows you're good kids.'

'So children don't get sent to prison?' She keeps her eyes on her lap and it's hard to read her face, but I think she looks desperate and sad. I want to scoop her into my arms and open her up, find out what is making her act this way, what happened to change my daughter so much.

'Not really. Sometimes, if they're really bad, and I mean really, really bad, they might be sent to a detention centre, I think. Something a bit like prison but for kids. People don't get sent to prison for silly vandalism. When the Neighbourhood Watch find out who damaged the school, that person will get a telling-off and they'll probably be asked to do some litter-picking around the village, and that's it.'

'Right.'

'It wasn't you, was it, Harrie?'

'No.' She shakes her head.

'I didn't think it was. So why are you asking me about prison?'

'Nothing,' she says, her eyes fixed on the carpet. 'Just asking.'

'Mum?' Elise calls. 'Can we watch a film? I've done my homework.'

'Yesssss,' comes a cry from Molly.

My eyes rest on Harrie and the feeling returns that I'm missing something. Like the game Grandma's Footsteps that Molly loves to play. Every time I turn around something has changed, moved, but I don't see it happen. I can't be sure.

Chapter 21

Anna

Later, when all three of the girls are under their duvets watching a film they've seen a hundred times before, Kat pops in with the access codes for the Parish Council files and shows me how to open them on Google Drive. I ask her to stay for a cup of tea and when we've chatted for a while about nonsense stuff – Bev's new haircut and the holiday Kat and Steve have booked – I force a casual tone and ask if there's been any word from Dean.

Kat shakes her head. 'No, nothing, but Sue's reported it to the police officially now so I'm sure they'll track him down to a golf course in Spain.'

'Do you think so?'

Kat looks at me then with knowing in her eyes. 'Dean does what he wants, when he wants,' she says softly. 'He always has. If he wants to take off and not tell anyone, he will.'

My cheeks colour and I'm grateful when the doorbell rings. I stand quickly and open the door to find June outside holding a warm apple crumble and a tub of thick cream. 'I thought you and the girls deserved a proper treat.'

'Wow, thank you,' I gush before inviting her in.

'Oh God,' Kat says from behind us. 'Is that the time? I'm supposed to be at a yoga class in twenty minutes.' She kisses my cheek and with a wave to June she's gone.

'Did you report that car the other day?' June asks a few minutes later, wrapping her thin fingers around the fresh mug of tea I've made for her.

I nod. 'This morning actually. Jack Briggs popped by about the vandalism at the school and I mentioned it then.'

'Vandalism.' June cocks an eyebrow. 'A fallen-down fence and a bit of loo roll. They're treating it like the Crown jewels of Barton St Martin have been stolen. It's all the old biddies in the post office could talk about this week.'

I raise my eyebrows and June laughs, wagging a finger at me. 'Now Anna, I'm sure to you I may seem like an old biddy, but let me tell you something, eighty is the new sixty. It's those ones in their nineties you really need to watch out for.'

'I can believe it,' I laugh. 'You're more active than I am. And for what it's worth, I agree about the vandalism. It does feel a bit like overkill to go door to door.'

'A bit? More like a lot. Imagine what would happen if an actual crime were committed. They'd be getting their shotguns out.'

We laugh together and soon the girls join us for apple crumble and cream, begging June to stay for a game of Scrabble. Even Harrie joins in, teaming up with Molly and helping her with the spellings.

June keeps us all laughing with her jokes and her blatant attempts at cheating and I realize how lonely our weekends normally are. My weeks feel the same and I think with a pang that there are still fifty-three days until Rob is home. With that comes the unbidden thought: *I miss Dean.*

Kat's words from earlier jump into my thoughts. *Dean does what he wants, when he wants.*

That's not the Dean I know, the one who brings pastries filled with fresh cream from the bakery because he knows they're my favourite. Dean who is always there to listen when I need someone to talk to. Dean who took me in his arms on Monday and told me everything would be OK, even though we both knew it wouldn't.

**Interview with Kat Morris, member of
Barton St Martin Parish Council
Interview conducted by Melissa Hart,
The Daily Gazette, 3 November**

MH: Mrs Morris, have you got a moment
please? I thought we could finish our
interview.

Kat: I'm sorry but my son is upstairs.
He's quite upset about everything and I
don't want him disturbed.

MH: We can chat on your doorstep. It won't
take a moment.

Kat: I'm really not sure I feel comfortable
talking to you. This is such a difficult
time. Maybe you could come back in a few
weeks when everything has calmed down.

MH: Have the police been to see you, Mrs Morris? What questions did they ask you about Anna James?

Kat: They've been to see everyone. Look, I really don't have time—

MH: Can you tell me about the village girlies' message group?

Kat: What's there to tell? It was a group for friends in the village to chat about things going on.

MH: What about the secret group?

Kat: That was a stupid name for it. Tracy called it that years ago and no one bothered to change it. It wasn't meant to be exclusionary. We're all good friends and a few of us run our own businesses, so we made a separate group to chat about it. Lots of women in the village get invited to join the main village girlies' group, but I think they often leave or mute it, which is fine. Each to her own.

MH: I just want to check I've got my facts right. One group had you, Tracy Campbell, Bev Pritchett and Sandra Briggs in it - the secret group. And the main group had all the same people again plus Anna.

Kat: Gina wasn't in the secret group either.

MH: Why not?

Kat: I don't really know. Like I said, it was originally to chat about our businesses. Besides, Gina's crap with technology. She would hate being in two groups.

MH: So if it was for your friends with small businesses, why wasn't Anna in the secret group?

Kat: When you put it like that it does sound bad, but it really wasn't like that. We've had the 'secret' group, if you must call it that, since long before Anna moved here. I really need to go now.

MH: I just have one question. What do you know about the video footage?

Kat: Nothing. Absolutely nothing. I'm not answering any more questions. Please leave my doorstep or I'll call the police. Go speak to one of the others. Bev loves a gossip.

Chapter 22

Sunday, six days until Halloween

Anna

Time passes slowly on Sundays. I wake up and watch a minute tick by on the clock on my phone and wonder how we'll ever make it through to seven p.m. and Rob's call. I trudge through the detritus of jobs – the cleaning, the washing, the to-ing and fro-ing to Harrie's football match. The girls feel it too. That long wait. We fidget and clock-watch and bicker until the anticipation of seeing their father bubbles up like the fizz of lemonade.

Molly has drawn a picture of the five of us holding hands and watching fireworks. 'Because Daddy will miss the firework display,' she says with a sad smile that makes me ache deep inside. This is so much harder for Molly. Her time moves so much slower than mine. I remember when the months between one Christmas and the next felt like a lifetime and now it's little more than a blip, a sneeze and *oh, here we are again*. It's the same way they must feel from one Sunday to the next waiting to speak to their dad, let alone the months he is away.

Harrie is quiet again. Even football – one of her favourite things – couldn't shake her from her stupor. She stood shivering on the pitch, scuffing the grass with her boots. She didn't even move when the ball flew past her. Eventually the coach pulled her off and sent her back to me.

'What happened?' I asked her as we left the pitch.

A darkness clouded over Harrie's face. 'Headache,' is all she said. Another lie.

The twins stayed in their room and I spent the afternoon playing endless games of Guess Who? with Molly and pretending I didn't know that she always chooses one of three characters – Joe, Anna or Sarah.

It's only when I start to cook dinner that Harrie appears in the kitchen doorway, a football in her hands.

'Hey,' I say. 'Is your headache better?'

'A bit.'

'Dinner is in half an hour. It's pasta, your favourite,' I tell her as though she's forgotten what she likes.

'I'm not hungry.'

'Did you sleep better last night? No more nightmares?'

She shrugs.

'Harrie.' I take a step towards her. 'Please talk to me. Tell me what's going on with you. And don't say you're fine because you're not.'

'God,' she huffs suddenly, throwing the ball to the floor with a resounding thud.

'Harrie,' I chastise.

'You want to know what's wrong with me? Fine. It's *you*,' she shouts. 'You never let us do anything. You let us out for school and that's it. We can't go to the park

137

unless you come. You're like a prison guard. Everyone else our age in this village has phones and freedom and can do whatever they want and you just keep us trapped in here.'

My body reels back and I'm stunned, hurt, by the words and spite that fly from my daughter's mouth. 'Harrie, that's not fair. It's my job to protect you. I know we don't have the money to go out every weekend and do all the stuff your friends do, but we still have good times and you're definitely not prisoners.'

'Yeah right. If Dad were here, he'd let us go out.'

'That's not true,' I say before wondering if in fact it is. I know Rob thinks I worry too much, that I'm overprotective, but I'm the one here every day, I'm the one raising the girls. I'm being unfair. Rob is only working away to support us and he worries too, but not like I do. 'Your dad agrees with me, but he's calling in an hour and you can speak to him about it if you want to.'

'I will.' She moves suddenly, striding across the kitchen heading straight for the front door.

'Where are you going?'

'Argh,' she shouts, grabbing something from among the coats. 'Why are you trying to know everything about me? Can't you just leave me alone for once? I've told you the only thing wrong is you.'

And before I can stop her, the front door is slamming shut and she's gone.

'Where's Harrie going, Mummy?' Molly calls from the living room. 'Can I go too?'

'Shhh,' Elise says to her sister as I throw myself at the front door and yank it open in time to see Harrie sprinting around the corner.

'Harrie,' I shout. 'Come back.'

'Mum?' Elise says and I turn around.

'Elise, Harrie has just run off. I'm going to call June to come over and I'll go after her.'

Sudden tears well in Elise's eyes. 'She'll be back in a minute, won't she? She always cools down quickly.'

I take a moment to breathe, to think, and I realize Elise is right. Elise will harbour her anger for days. She'll build it into a pyre, her eyes forever ablaze as though waiting for one of us, Molly usually, to strike the match. Harrie though, and Molly too – there is something more of me in them. A quick-to-anger, quick-to-forgive response that I understand far better than the slow burn.

Elise steps close and wraps her arms around me. I breathe her in and hold her tight. Molly rushes over, joining in too.

'Just give her ten minutes to come home,' Elise pleads. 'She'll be OK.'

'Do you know what's going on with Harrie?' I ask.

Elise shakes her head. 'She won't tell me either.'

I look at the clock in the kitchen and bite my lip so hard I taste blood in my mouth. Ten minutes. I'll give her that. There is still a little light in the sky after all.

It doesn't feel right but it's what Rob would say, and there's a part of me that doesn't want to pick up the phone and ask June to come over. I don't want her to know about my fight with Harrie. I don't want her to think I'm a bad mother.

So I return to chopping peppers, my eyes on the kitchen clock as much as the chopping board. This isn't London any more, I tell myself. Harrie knows how to cross the road safely. She'll come back.

But as I count down the minutes, the what-if questions whir like sirens in my thoughts.

What if something happens to Harrie?
What if I can't protect her?

139

Village Girlies' Secret Group Chat
Sunday 25 October, 17.37

Tracy Campbell: OMG! Just walking the dog
and saw Harrie running down the road and
Anna shouting after her.

Bev Pritchett: I'm not surprised. She's too
protective of those girls. Never lets them
out on their own. It makes kids rebel if
they have no freedom.

Tracy Campbell: So true!

Kat Morris: You are such a gossip
@TracyCampbell! Don't tell me Freya never
did the same.

Tracy Campbell: Also true! LOL.

Bev Pritchett. Must be hard for Anna without Rob around though. No way I could

have raised the boys on my own. Why does Rob work away? Does anyone know?

Sandra Briggs: For the money! Rob told Jack once that they're in a load of debt.

Bev Pritchett: Has anyone else noticed how Anna never talks about her past?

Tracy Campbell: Something is up there, I bet.

Bev Pritchett: @SandraBriggs what's going on with the Neighbourhood Watch and the vandalism?

Sandra Briggs: Jack's been out all weekend asking people if they saw anything.

Kat Morris: @SandraBriggs tell Jack to come our way. Steve is happy to be questioned over a few beers, LOL!

Chapter 23

Harrie

The moment she's out of sight, Harrie stops. She takes a breath and waits, watching for any sign of her mum.

It's quiet. There's no traffic on the main road. No one about. It's dead. The thought makes Harrie's chest tighten, her breathing come quick. Puffs of smoky breath drift into the cold air. Droplets of rain patter on to her coat and the top of her head.

She wishes she was at home. She wishes she didn't have to go to that place again.

Headlights appear in the distance. The silver car leaps into her thoughts. Those rushed threats thrown at Elise. The threats meant for her. She should never have worn Elise's coat that night.

Harrie's stomach flips and she sprints across the road, only slowing when she's climbed the metal gate into the empty field.

The earth beneath her feet is bumpy and she stumbles as she moves towards the back of the field, but she doesn't fish the torch from her pocket. Not yet. She can't risk anyone seeing her from the road.

Harrie keeps moving, treading carefully, trying to avoid the mud. The air smells musky like the cow shed up at the farm where they walk sometimes at the weekend, when their mum tells them it'll do them good to be out in the fresh air, instead of what she really means – they can't afford the cinema or the swimming pool. They can't afford anything. Molly is clueless but Harrie and Elise talk about it sometimes when it's just the two of them. They talk about the old house in London. Big rooms and toys. It's more a feeling than a memory. A feeling of having stuff.

But Harrie would rather have Elise than a hundred toys, or all-inclusive holidays to the Caribbean. Australia. The Maldives. The places her friends go. Nothing matters more to her than Elise.

The darkness intensifies the closer Harrie gets to the stable. She's a few metres away when she smells it. A foul stench that makes her feet stop dead and a surge of wild panic rise up from the tips of her toes all the way to the top of her head. Only then does she fumble for the torch, hands shaking as the orange beam hits the ground. New batteries this time. Harrie won't make that mistake again.

There's a movement from inside – a shuffling noise – and for a moment it feels like Harrie's entire body is frozen and she'll never be able to move again.

'Who's there?' a voice shouts.

Harrie takes a final deep breath and steps into the stable without a word, shining the torch straight on to the old dog cage in the corner that she and Elise found last summer when they camped in the field with their dad.

The cage is too small for the man. He can't stand up or lie down flat.

He cries out when he sees her, the noise strangled and ending in a fit of coughing. 'Please help me.'

Harrie can't speak. It's like she's swallowed some cardboard and it's stuck in her throat, blocking the air, blocking her words. The desire to be outside, away from this place, is so intense that she throws the bag within reach of the cage and she runs. His pleading shouts chase her across the field. She moves fast, no longer caring how the mud is squelching against the edges of her shoes or how she'll explain it to her mum. By the time she reaches the gate, she hears nothing except the drumming of her heart pounding in her ears.

Chapter 24

Anna

It's nine minutes before Harrie returns. Nine minutes when darkness swallows the day. Nine minutes of replaying Harrie's words over and over, feeling the sting of her spite. My phone is clammy from where I've been gripping it. I've opened up my contacts to call June three times, and the police five times, but each time I stopped myself.

The front door opens and crashes shut and a moment later Harrie is standing in the doorway of the kitchen, red cheeks, breathless from running, and staring at my face as though waiting for me to react. When I say nothing she rushes towards me, pushes herself into my arms and sobs against my chest.

'I'm sorry,' she cries. 'I didn't mean any of it. I don't know why I said it.'

'I understand,' I say as I stroke the back of her hair, pulling out a stray leaf and smoothing down the bumps, and for a moment it feels like I'm holding the old Harrie. 'It's OK for us to argue sometimes and it's OK for you to get mad, but you can't run out of the house like that again. I was so worried about you.'

She nods and wipes her eyes. 'I won't.'

'Where did you go?'

Something in Harrie's face changes and just like that the barrier is up.

Desperation digs its sharp claws into me. I want to shout. To swear. To scream at her to talk to me, but I can't risk her turning around and running out of that door again.

'Take your shoes off and go wash your hands for dinner,' I say eventually.

She turns away and I catch a sudden whiff of something pungent and rotten. I look down at the kitchen floor and see the smears of thick black mud her trainers have left. It looks like the same mud I found on the kitchen floor four nights ago when I left Harrie alone.

All three girls stay close to the kitchen after dinner, hovering around me, Molly's and Elise's voices high and quick. Even Harrie seems to brighten at the prospect of speaking to her dad.

At 6.50 p.m. I open the tablet and place it on the kitchen table, moving the chairs so all four of us can see the screen. Harrie sits down first, then Elise, then Molly on my lap. The minutes pass slowly but no one fidgets or gets up. None of us wants to miss even one precious second of time with him.

Our calls always follow the same format – talking as a family first and listening to Rob tell us about his week. Then he talks to all the children without me, together at first and then individually. The hour he spends with us is gone in the blink of an eye and it's time to say goodbye. At the end of each call the girls give him a riddle to solve during the week. Something silly that he'll pretend he doesn't know and will make us laugh by giving the wrong answers to. Last week he had to answer what has hands but doesn't clap.

'I've been really thinking about this one and I've got it,' Rob grinned, pinning his arms to his side and roaring at us through the screen. 'It's a T-Rex, isn't it? Little hands that can't clap.'

The girls howled with laughter.

'Noooo,' Harrie all but shouted, loud and boisterous. Was that only a week ago? 'It's a clock, Dad. A clock.'

'A clock and a T-Rex, right?'

My turn with Rob comes later when the girls are in bed. I've never told them that Rob and I speak privately. They'd want to stay up and see him again but this time is ours, it's all I have.

Earlier this week, I didn't know how I would be able to talk to him, to see his face and not blurt out what happened on Monday. But this thing with Harrie trumps anything going on with us.

The resentment towards him for not being here melts away and I'm desperate to share the burden with him. He'll have a solution. Something I've not thought of that will get through to Harrie, and it'll work because it always does and then Harrie will be herself again and I can stop this worry from eating me up.

'What was the riddle we asked him last week?' Molly asks, looking between us as we wait out the final minutes.

'What gets wetter the more it dries?' Elise answers.

'I can't remember the answer.' Molly's voice has a whine to it. Tiredness and excitement coalescing.

'A towel,' Elise whispers as though Rob might hear.

The clock changes. It's seven p.m. My finger is poised

to swipe the screen and accept his call, but nothing happens. Not at seven p.m., or 7.01 p.m., or 7.02 p.m.

Only after another minute passes do we look away from the blank screen.

'What's happened, Mummy?' Molly asks, twisting herself around to look up at me. 'Why hasn't Daddy called yet?'

'It's only five past,' Elise says before I get the chance.

'He'll call in a minute,' Harrie whispers.

By ten past seven the excitement seeps out of the room like air from a punctured paddling pool, slow and drooping.

'Shall we try to call him?' Elise asks.

'Good idea.' I unlock the screen and tap Rob's name. The rhythmic hum of the outgoing call is the only sound as we wait for him to answer.

He doesn't.

The girls look at me. Even Harrie, who has barely spoken since our argument, is staring at me with a quiet expectancy, but I'm flailing, lost at sea. In the years Rob has been working in Nigeria, he has never missed a seven p.m. Sunday call. He's never been late. He's never forgotten. Never. Until today. When I need him more than ever.

I close my eyes and picture a motorboat filled with men, guns slung over their shoulders, bandanas covering their faces. I know from my late-night Google searches how easily these criminal gangs can board the rigs and take control. A quick pay-off to the right guard is all it takes and my husband is theirs to ransom back to the British government.

What if he's hurt?

What if he's dead?

Molly moves on my lap, her shoulders shaking, her

hands covering her face. 'I miss Daddy,' she wails. The sound, the pain of my daughter, snaps me out of my own anxiety and I paste on my cheeriest smile and hug her tight with one hand, and reach the other one out to Elise, who isn't crying but looks as though she might.

'Hey, hey, hey,' I coo. 'There's nothing to be upset about. It's probably a storm messing with their internet connection or he's been called into an emergency. We'll take the iPad upstairs with us and read some stories and maybe he'll call later, or tomorrow.'

'Is Dad OK?' Harrie asks.

I search my daughter's face for any sign of her earlier anger, the hate I saw flashing in her eyes, but it's gone and she is frowning and rubbing her hands up and down her knees as though she's bruised them.

'Yes, I'm sure he is,' I say, hoping it's not a lie. 'There are a hundred simple explanations for why he's not called.'

'Maybe he dropped his phone down the toilet,' Molly says. Her tears have stopped as quickly as they started and she gives me a watery smile. 'Our teacher, Mrs Cole, did that last week.'

'Exactly.' I squeeze her tight. 'Come on, let's get ready for bed and we'll see if Daddy calls later.'

'You have to promise to wake us up if he calls when we're asleep.' Elise looks at me, wide puppy eyes.

'Of course. I promise.'

We traipse upstairs, the bounce gone from our steps. Molly dives on to my bed and snuggles into Rob's side. Elise lies across the bottom and Harrie takes the floor, pushing herself against the wall and rolling a football around with her bare feet. My shared disappointment for the girls, the worry for Rob, eases a little as I sit on the bed and open the book we're reading.

I used to read to the girls every night when they were little. Beautiful picture books with rhyming stories I knew off by heart and back to front, but Elise and Harrie have grown up so much. They read their own books and no longer want to listen to the picture books, the three-minute reads, and with the greatest will in the world, I cannot find the time in our evenings to squeeze in chapters and chapters of books.

But when Rob started working in Nigeria and the Sunday calls became part of our lives, the girls needed something afterwards to calm their excitement, to distract them from the blow they felt when their elation died and they remembered that their dad was thousands of miles away and it would be another week before they saw his face again. Listening to a story together has become part of our ritual.

It was Dean who suggested I read the girls *The Famous Five*, and as I open the book at the right page, I cast my mind back to last week's chapter.

'So, George has just been kidnapped by the man in the caravan,' I say.

'And Timmy is on their trail,' Molly says, her words mumbled against the fabric of Bunny, pushed against her face.

I take a breath and start to read, remembering to add the voices and not to go too fast, but even as I read aloud I feel the anxiety twisting and coiling in my mind.

First there was the accident on the road, leaving Harrie and whatever happened to her that night. Then Dean disappeared. He's been a rock these past months and his disappearance has left a gaping hole. And now Rob hasn't called. I know these three events aren't connected. Harrie has never met Dean. Rob is thousands of miles away. But still they knot together in the pit of my stomach.

Chapter 25

Anna

It's late. Two a.m. The nothing hours of the night when the only sound is the rustle of my duvet as I fidget from one position to another.

Why didn't Rob call?

The question turns over and over in my thoughts like a spin wash that won't end.

Rob is a good dad. Even three thousand miles away from his children, he is still better than most. He is present in their lives. Always. He writes notes for the children – one each for each day he is away. It could be something silly – a 'knock knock' joke; it could be a reminder – *help Mum with the tidying*; or something profound – *in a world where you can be anything, be kind*.

Something must be wrong. Rob knows how desperate the girls are to speak to him.

I wish I knew what he was doing out there. I wish I could picture it in my mind the way I can the memories of our relationship. The day we met fourteen years ago. It sounds like a long time, but it doesn't feel like it.

We've been married twelve years. Eight years longer than my parents were married for before my dad got sick of Mum's bitterness and moved to Edinburgh. A new life for him. A new family. Leaving my mother with a child she didn't want.

Fourteen years have gone by in a flash of babies and toddlers and a baby again, moving, scraping by, school and routines. When I look back at our marriage it feels like we've not drawn breath, not stopped to chink our glasses, to look at the beautiful children we've made, to enjoy the moment, any moment.

Even our first date – in our pre-marriage, pre-baby days – seems rushed when I look back. Rob and I met on a blind date in London.

My friend Tina was dating Rob's friend Nicholas and the two cooked up a match. Of course I didn't know it was a blind date at the time. I was single, living in a shared flat in Soho, a five-minute walk from the boutique website-design agency I worked for. I spent my weekends exploring London and drinking with my friends. Marriage, children, even a boyfriend were not on my horizons, and yet within three years of meeting Rob I had the lot.

I twist the covers around me and turn on to my back, trying to remember the first things we said to each other, but it's a blur. All I have of the memory is the sitcom-style cheesy way we were brought together, the comedy of our friends cancelling at the very last second and the horror of discovering what Tina and Nicholas had done. I remember laughing a lot that night. I remember the way my stomach flipped when Rob smiled at me and the broad slope of his shoulders, his thick dark hair, eyes that danced with mischief.

Tina and Nicholas emigrated to Australia the year

after our wedding. We email back and forth a few times a year and send Christmas cards. I miss Tina but I'm glad she left before our downfall. I never told her what happened to us and I'm glad my humiliation didn't stretch across the world.

I close my eyes and try to stop thinking, try to sleep. I'm just dozing off when a scream shatters the silence, piercing my thoughts. I leap out of bed and rush into Harrie and Elise's room.

'Stop,' Harrie shouts. 'Stop, stop, stop.' She whimpers like an injured animal before sitting up and rubbing her hands on her knees. Her words are incoherent mumbles at first, but then they change. She says a name and it's crystal clear. 'Dean,' she whispers.

My blood runs cold and it hits me – hard and fast. The night of the crash, the night I was stuck on the road and Harrie was alone, is the same night Dean went missing.

Chapter 26

The night of the crash, 8.06–8.14 p.m.

Harrie

Harrie covers her ears with the sleeves of her coat and pushes herself further into the corner. The noise of the two men is deafening. Grunting. Hitting. Shouting. She cowers, wishing she could shrink down, down, down like Alice in Wonderland, wishing she'd taken a chance and run out the back door the second the phone was in her pocket.

Too late. She's stuck. Trapped. Not even hidden. If either of the men turns towards the corner where she's hiding, they'll see her.

She thinks of Molly and how only a few years ago she would hide by closing her eyes. *I can't see you, so you can't see me.*

But Harrie's eyes are open. Wide and frightened. She can only see legs, dancing around each other, kicking out. There is no escape from the sounds they're making – the punches, the shouts of triumph and pain – like the tennis players on TV when they hit the ball, but louder, so much louder.

She moves her hands from her ears to her mouth, stopping herself from crying out.

For a minute she wonders if it will ever end and then something changes. Something red and wet splats across the floor and Harrie has to bite back a scream as she realizes what it is. Blood.

One of the men starts to shout something. 'I've already texted my brother. He's—' But there's a crash against the worktop and the rest of the words are gone. Harrie doesn't think he's fighting back any more, but she can still hear the smack of someone being hit and the grunts of pain that follow.

The sound that comes next makes Harrie's stomach flip like she's on a rollercoaster. It's not a punch. It's louder. Harder. A thwack of a noise. It's only as the wine bottle drops to the floor with a crack, sending thick shards of glass sliding across the tiles, that Harrie realizes the man didn't cry out with pain when the bottle hit him.

And then one of them is on the floor. Two metres away from her. She can see his whole body now through the gaps in the chair legs. His face is covered in blood. More blood than Harrie has ever seen and it's pouring out of him and into a puddle on the floor.

He's dead.

Someone is screaming.

She is screaming.

Chapter 27

Monday, five days until Halloween

Anna

The school playground seems noisier today. More shouting, more parents cramming in around me. It's a fight to wait for the bell to ring and say goodbye to the girls before turning for home.

Maybe it's me. My lack of sleep after Harrie's night terror. Hearing Dean's name on her lips and lying awake for the rest of the night trying to understand why.

Ben races past me with a breathless, 'Hi Anna,' followed a moment later by Kat.

'Hey you,' she says, appearing beside me and nudging her shoulder against mine. 'Check me out. I'm here before the bell again. I deserve a medal.'

I smile as I look down at her feet. 'And no slippers this morning either.'

'Ah, well, I wore them to the shops the other day by accident and they need a wash. Sometimes I don't know what's wrong with me.'

'Ben looks like he's shot up recently,' I say, and we

look across the playground to the group of Year Six boys. Ben is jumping on Tyler's shoulders as though trying to dunk him in a swimming pool.

'Tell me about it. I feel like I've ordered the entire collection of boys' wear from Next recently, but at least he's growing at last,' she adds, humour carrying in her voice. 'Are you looking forward to today's meeting?'

I frown, my head so filled with Dean, with Harrie and Rob, that there is nothing else. 'What meeting?'

Kat tips back her head and laughs. 'Anna James, is that you in there?' She taps my forehead as though knocking on a door. 'The Parish Council meeting at Tracy and Anthony's house at lunchtime.'

'Of course. I hadn't forgotten,' I lie.

'I should think not,' she grins. 'There's only room for one forgetful person in this friendship. Anyway, how's Rob? Are you feeling better now you've spoken to him?'

My mouth opens but no words come out.

'Anna, what is it?' Kat frowns and touches my arm.

'He didn't call,' I say at last.

'Really?'

I nod. 'He always calls, but not last night.'

'Oh honey, that can't have been fun for you and the girls, but I'm sure there's a good reason. He's bound to call tonight instead.'

I nod and wish Kat's reassurance could sink in past the worry and the unanswered questions.

The bell rings and I steer Molly into her line, before kissing her cheek and heading to the twins. They're standing at the back of the line and stop talking as I approach. Something is different. It takes another step before I realize – they've swapped coats. Elise is wearing Harrie's red one, and Harrie is wearing Elise's black one.

'What's going on?' I ask, my voice quiet. I don't want the rest of the class to hear me.

'Nothing.' Elise shrugs.

'Why have you swapped coats? You know how the school feel about you trying to trick them.'

'We're not,' Harrie hisses. 'I was cold—'

'And I was hot,' Elise adds.

'My zip is broken on my coat,' Harrie admits, her head dropping as though she's in trouble.

'What?' I step to Elise and pull at the zip. It moves easily. Too easily. The metal claws split open the moment the zip has pushed them together. 'Why didn't you tell me?'

'We didn't want—'

'To worry you,' Elise finishes.

I shake my head, angry at them for not telling me about the zip, angry at myself that I've done such a bad job hiding my anxiety, angry at Rob for not calling, for being away when he should be here, for making me into this handwringing woman who counts every penny.

If they couldn't tell me about a broken zip, is it any wonder Harrie won't tell me what happened last week? Is this my fault? It's been five days now and I'm no closer to knowing what went on that night.

Harrie might be talking more, but not like she used to. It's mumbled words, it's snapped remarks. Then there are the night terrors, the running off, the jumping out of her skin when the doorbell goes.

'It doesn't matter,' I say, tone as breezy as I can muster. 'I'm sure it can be fixed and if not, we'll have to get you a new one.'

They eye me with suspicion and I keep my smile in place as they follow their class into the school.

*

159

The moment I'm home I take the stairs two at a time and head straight into Harrie and Elise's room. It isn't messy in the same way that Molly's is. They no longer leave their toys piled across the floor, a sea of pink plastic. Instead it's clothes and empty glasses, a plate with toast crumbs on it and footballs. So many footballs. There is an imperceptible line down the middle of the room, a divide that shows the different personalities of Harrie and Elise. Harrie's bed covers are the colours of her favourite football team: pale blue and yellow. The wall beside her bed is covered with action shots of football players and pictures of dogs – puppies in baskets and Labradors jumping over fences – posters that she's torn out of magazines.

Elise's side of the room is more cluttered. Her bedside table is covered with knick-knacks, magnets, snow globes, a Rubik's cube I've never seen either of them use. Bits of string, Blu-Tack and paperclips are scattered around the surfaces like confetti. There are two long bookshelves on the wall, double-stacked with books. *Malory Towers*, *The Twins at St Clare's*, *Harry Potter*, and a long line of Jacqueline Wilson books. The window ledge is their shared space and it is crammed with medals and trophies they've won over the years.

The urge to cry pulses through my body as I scan the room. I have the Parish Council meeting in a few hours and I haven't even opened the links to the files Kat gave me, not to mention three website enquiries to answer.

And yet here I am, in Harrie and Elise's bedroom, hoping to find something, anything, that can tell me why my beautiful daughter is fading away before my eyes, waking in the night terrified that someone is trying to hurt her, saying the name of a man who no one has seen or heard from since the night of the crash.

I start with the drawers and the jumble of T-shirts and jeans, shorts and underwear. My hands touch upon the silky material of a football shirt. I pull it out. It's tiny. Harrie's first football shirt. Rob bought it for her on her second birthday. It's all she wanted to wear day after day after day and I had to wash it overnight so it was clean. I didn't know Harrie still has this. The blue material is so tiny now and I hold it in my hands for a long moment remembering Harrie and Elise as toddlers. Pigtails and face paints, dungarees and squealing giggles. It feels like it was a lifetime ago, but also only yesterday. I slide the T-shirt back into place and keep searching.

There's nothing in any of the drawers or the wardrobe, and so I pull off her duvet and the sheet, I lift up the mattress, flick between the pages of books, until an hour has passed and I've found nothing except a half-eaten bag of Haribo that I don't move from its hiding place at the back of a drawer.

I scan the room again. It looks the same as it did before my futile search at least. Despite my certainty that something is wrong with Harrie, I don't like the idea that I'm snooping in their private space.

I'm about to give up when my gaze lands on the storage boxes under the bed that are crammed with toys they no longer play with. Doll outfits and Harrie's Lego City collection and the teeny-tiny Sylvanian Families sets they used to spend hours, days, setting up and would cry about if my foot knocked against a table and sent miniature plates and cutlery flying to the floor.

I slide them out and open them one by one. I run my hands through the Lego. The sound of the plastic bricks knocking together is nostalgic and I find myself longing for the days that a box of toys could make them so happy.

It's as I'm pulling my hand out of the box, ready to give up, that my fingers touch something beneath the Lego. It's a carrier bag, flattened and buried. I pull it out, sending bricks scattering across the carpet.

The bag is squishy. Clothes, I think, and when I open it the smell of dirt and something metallic hits my nostrils, turning my stomach. A noise escapes my throat as I pull out a pair of Harrie's grey school trousers. I hold them up by the waistband and see two large patches of deep rusty brown covering the knees and smeared across the fabric. It's blood. The stain is unmistakable and has soaked through on both sides as though she's knelt in a puddle of it. There is too much of it for a grazed knee, too much for a cut. I think of her pasty white legs on the football pitch yesterday and I know with absolute certainty that this isn't Harrie's blood.

Village Girlies' Group Chat
Monday 26 October, 11.28

Bev Pritchett: That poor man in the car accident last week died in intensive care yesterday. I just saw it in the local paper.

Gina Walker: OMG!! Was that the accident you got stuck in @AnnaJames?

Tracy Campbell: Anthony knew him – it was Dean Stockton's brother. So sad! Just goes to show what reckless driving can do.

Gina Walker: Oh my god! Wasn't that the same night that Dean went missing? Has anyone seen or heard from him?

Sandra Briggs: No. He's still not shown up.

Bev Pritchett: Could Dean have been in the car as well?

Tracy Campbell: Surely not. We'd have heard by now.

Gina Walker: Before I forget, Martin is out on Friday night so drinks at mine? Bring the kids as well. I'll order Domino's for them and put a film on.

Kat Morris: Thanks Gina. Can't wait!

Bev Pritchett: Count me in! I'll bring my nails if anyone needs topping up.

Tracy Campbell: Great.

Kat Morris: @BevPritchett me please! You're a lifesaver.

Sandra Briggs: Yay! Jack gave me a bottle of that pink gin we like. I'll bring it.

Gina Walker: The one from Makro? I LOVE that stuff x

Chapter 28

Anna

I'm late leaving the house and I hurry down the alley in the direction of the new road and the estate. A stuffy Parish Council meeting is the last thing I want to sit through right now. All I can think about is Harrie's trousers.

Stupidly, foolishly, I try calling Dean again. I'm desperate to talk to him. The phone rings but then cuts to voicemail again just like all the other times. He's never made me feel like I was overreacting in the same way Kat and Rob do. I wonder sometimes if they really think telling me not to worry actually helps. Like I can flick a switch. In reality, all their comments do is add a layer of self-loathing to my anxiety.

And there is no amount of 'it'll be fine' that can wash out the blood.

My mouth fills with the taste of metal and for a moment I think I'm going to be sick. I gulp in breath after breath of cold air until the feeling passes. I concentrate on putting one foot in front of the other and quicken my pace as I reach the entrance to Tracy and Anthony's driveway.

Their house is a barn conversion that borders the end of Kat's garden. It's accessible by a long private driveway on the estate, half-hidden with overhanging trees. I eye the canopy above my head, branches bent perfectly into each other in a long arch, and wonder what this driveway will look like in five days' time. The Campbells are the type of family that goes all out for Halloween, decorating the drive with cobwebs and spooky props lit by green fairy lights. Last year, Anthony dressed up as a scarecrow and pretended to be a prop until the very moment a group were walking by when he'd jump out and make them scream. Harrie and Elise loved it but Molly cried.

I gather myself as I reach Tracy and Anthony's huge wooden front door. A deep breath in, hands raking through my hair. This might be the last place I want to be right now, but I promised Kat I'd do this and I need the money.

'Anna, great you're here.' Tracy leans in to kiss my cheek and I catch the coconut scent of her body lotion. 'We were worrying you wouldn't make it.'

I apologize as she leads me down a light hallway, but when I glance at the huge station clock on the wall I realize I'm a minute early.

Tracy is wearing tight jeans and a cream cable-knit jumper. Her braids are loose and there's soft eyeliner etched around her eyes. Sometimes when I look at Tracy, I see a glimpse of the woman she was before I knew her, before her children but after giving up ballet, when she worked for an investment bank in London. It's something in the set of her face, a hard strength I find difficult to read. But then she smiles and she is the Tracy I know again. Mum to Freya and Olivia, member of the Parish Council and the

166

PTA, and married to Anthony Campbell for seventeen years.

Anthony is like Rob – a charmer, always ready with a smile and a wink for whoever is near. He works at Stockton's alongside Dean and I wonder as Tracy leads me into the kitchen if he knows anything more about Dean's whereabouts. Surely Tracy would have said on the message group if he did.

Tracy and Anthony's kitchen is a large perfect square with an entire wall of bi-fold doors that open into a long lawn, scattered with the orange leaves of a huge oak tree that sits at the end of the garden.

The warmth from the heated floors pushes through the wool of my socks and the smell of pastries and coffee fills the kitchen. There's a huge coffee machine in one corner. A silver monster with enough dials and nozzles to rival any coffee shop machinery. On the counter is a plate piled high with croissants and pains au chocolat.

'Here she is,' Tracy announces and the group around the kitchen table fall silent. My gaze lands on Kat. Her hands are wrapped around a tall glass coffee cup. She smiles at me and mouths a hello. Beside her is Bev Pritchett.

> *Broad Bev and Mike the Knight,*
> *Two kids already on their bikes.*

As the rhyme drifts through my head, my eyes fall to Bev's tank top and bare shoulders. They're muscular and round and I remember her telling me once that she used to be a swimmer. I came up with the rhyme long before Mike Pritchett offered to help Elise, but it still fits. He's a knight of sorts for all he does as head teacher.

167

Gina's husband Martin is next around the table. He offers a huge smile and a wave, and I'm quite sure that if he wasn't squashed in between Kat and Bev he'd have stood up and enveloped me in a squishy hug. 'Good to see you, Anna.'

Anthony greets me with a kiss on both cheeks. 'We're so pleased you could join us, Anna. Kat has been raving about your organizational skills.'

'Thanks.' My smile is weak, nervous. 'Although if you saw the state of my washing basket this week you might not think I'm that organized.'

Everyone laughs and I try to relax. This is a local group of volunteers, not a board meeting for a multi-national company, for Christ's sakes.

'Are you all right to sit between me and Tracy?' Anthony asks, resting a hand on the small of my back and guiding me to a chair. 'That way we can keep an eye on what you're writing down and explain things when needed.'

'Oh don't worry,' Tracy says with a reassuring squeeze of my arm. 'It's all very simple. You'll pick it up in a flash. Most of our meetings are about deciding whether we're going to pay for another dog waste bin.'

Another trickle of laughter moves around the table and Tracy fixes me a coffee. When she's sat down beside me, Anthony claps his hands and the meeting starts.

'Thank you all for giving up your lunch hours to be here,' he says. 'We'll keep the meeting to one hour as usual. Let's start with apologies. Barry Glebe and Mary Swanson send theirs as usual.'

'They only come to the AGM,' Tracy whispers in my ear. 'They've been on the council for donkey's years. Barry is ninety-three and Mary isn't far behind him.'

'And Rob James is obviously not joining us this

time,' Anthony continues. 'We're not expecting Dean Stockton either. Jack Briggs sends his apologies. He's on a shift today. First up on the agenda is the dog mess bin.'

Kat shakes her head and groans and the group laugh. I guess Tracy's earlier comment wasn't a joke.

For forty-five minutes I take notes about a request for a conservatory, plans for the next year's summer fete, new toilet facilities needed in the village hall. It's boring. Mind-numbing. I can't believe Rob voluntarily sits through meetings like this when he's back. At least I'm being paid.

'OK. Final point before we can all get on with our days,' Anthony says. 'Jack Briggs has sent a report from the Neighbourhood Watch which I'll read out. Jack is a member of the Parish Council as well as being head of the Neighbourhood Watch,' he adds for my benefit. 'The Neighbourhood Watch committee is just one of several groups, like the school governors and the emergency response volunteers, who we work closely with. Think of it like a big family. We're the mums and dads, and they're the uncles and aunts.'

He unlocks his phone and begins to read. '"There have been no further incidents of vandalism after the school fence was kicked down. While we believe this was a prank that got out of hand, we are still keen to find the culprits. The Neighbourhood Watch have been speaking to residents and requesting any CCTV footage people may have from the day. A few names have cropped up, but further investigation is needed before the matter is taken further."'

When the meeting is officially closed, it's Martin who leans his large hands on the table and asks if there's any word on Dean.

'Not a dicky bird,' Anthony sighs, his lips pursing. 'I'm going to kill him when he gets back.'

'If Sue doesn't kill him first,' Kat quips.

'So sad about his brother, though,' Bev says.

There's murmuring of agreement and for the first time since I scanned the messages on my way here, I realize how devastated Dean will be when he learns of Luke's death. They were so close. Dean didn't talk about his business much, or working with Anthony, or the other men in the village. He didn't talk about Sue much either, but he did talk about Luke, telling me stories about their childhood and the tricks they played on their parents.

My throat aches with emotion and I'm glad when Kat and Bev stay for a subcommittee meeting on the playground resurfacing and Martin drives off, and I'm free to walk home alone with my thoughts.

Images of the crash flash in my head. The speeding car. The sudden change in direction before it launched into the air. Luke was the driver.

My head spins. It feels like another puzzle piece. The bloody trousers. Harrie's fear, Dean missing and now Luke dead, killed the same night. I think of the Neighbourhood Watch and their efforts to track down the vandal. Jack Briggs is going door to door talking to kids, asking for CCTV footage. It's ridiculous, but they've got one thing right – Barton St Martin is a small village. Someone must have seen something that day.

The same is true for the night of the crash. Someone must know something. I just have to find out who.

Chapter 29

Anna

It's gone eight p.m. before I get a chance to speak to Harrie about the trousers. The evening has disappeared in a wash of clubs. I sat beside Harrie for an hour in the gymnastics cafeteria, waiting for Molly and Elise, but I didn't say anything. How could I when I had no idea how she'd react? I couldn't risk her running off.

Every time I looked at her across the table, I saw the trousers and the blood in my mind, and my heart raced with questions and worry. So even though it's late and I need to wrangle a tired Molly into the shower and listen to her read, I go in search of Harrie.

Both twins are in their bedroom. Elise is in bed reading already. Harrie is scrambling to get into her PJs, and when I look at her, I see her eyes flash with something – anger?

'You should have knocked.' Harrie's words are sharp and I feel my own frustration rise.

'You're right,' I say, pushing the feeling down. 'I'm sorry. Can we chat in my bedroom for a minute?'

Harrie's head jerks to Elise and then back to me. 'Both of us?'

'Just you.'

'I'm tired. Can it wait until tomorrow?'

'Now please.'

Harrie sighs, her head dropping, but she follows me anyway, feet dragging on the carpet.

'Come sit down.' I pat a space on the double bed beside me, but Harrie stays by the door, one hand resting on the handle as though ready to escape, to run, at the first opportunity. Our fight yesterday evening swirls in my head. She wouldn't run out of the house again now, would she? It's late, pitch black, bedtime. The truth is, I don't know.

I take a breath. 'I found these trousers in your bedroom.' I slide the carrier bag across the bed and watch Harrie's eyes widen, her mouth open, terror play on her face.

She says nothing and so I carry on pushing. 'They're a pair of your school trousers and they're covered in blood.' My throat pinches with my own fear now. 'Whose blood is it? How did it get on your trousers?'

Silence.

'You have to tell me what's going on. What happened to you last week? Why have you hidden a pair of blood-stained trousers in your bedroom? I'm your mother, Harrie. I am here for you and I want to help you, but you have to talk to me.'

Silence.

'Please.' A single tear rolls down my cheek and I brush it away before Harrie sees it. I have to be strong.

If it's possible for Harrie to shrink closer to the wall, she does, squashing down within herself.

'Harrie.' I force a strength into my voice, an authority

172

that feels false on my lips. 'You *will* tell me why there is blood on your trousers and why I now need to buy a new pair for you because these are ruined.' I slam my hand on the bag in a burst of frustration that makes us both jump. The regret is instant. This isn't about buying new school trousers. This is about the blood, about what happened.

Harrie lifts her gaze and our eyes meet. 'They're not mine,' she says as though it's a dirty cup in the living room that I'm asking her to take out.

The blatant lie hangs between us and if I wasn't so desperate for the truth I'd laugh at the audacity of it. 'Your name is on the label.'

She shrugs. 'I've never seen that bag before. I don't know anything about any blood. Nothing happened the other night. You didn't come home. I went to bed. The end.' Her eyes blaze, daring me to challenge her. The futility of our argument hits me.

The seconds draw out between us. An electric silence. It's Molly's voice that breaks the stand-off. 'Mummmeee?'

And I relent. We're going around in circles and no matter how desperate I am for answers, for the truth, I can't force Harrie to talk to me.

'I'm here for you,' I say softly. 'When you're ready to talk, I'll listen. I'll always be on your side. I love you.' I stand up, my arms open to hug her, but she shrinks away, opening the bedroom door.

'I'm going to bed,' she whispers. 'Goodnight.'

Molly scampers across the hallway as Harrie shuts herself away in her room. A moment later Elise's voice rings out. 'I'm tired, Mum. I'm going to bed too. Night.' And then their light is off and it's just me and Molly.

It hurts – a physical ache – that I can't be the mum Harrie needs me to be right now. I don't know what I'm supposed to do, how I can help her, just that I can't. She won't let me.

Chapter 30

Harrie

The trousers. Her mum found the trousers. Harrie can't believe it. She can't believe she forgot to throw them away.

Stupid, stupid, stupid.

Everything is unravelling. It feels like she's slipped off the side of a cliff and is rolling, tumbling, falling down, down, down. She doesn't know which way is up any more or what the world is going to look like when she eventually lands. The thought makes Harrie's stomach hurt, a burning in the space below her ribs.

At least her mum didn't find the phone. Not that it matters now.

From the bathroom, Harrie hears the rattling hum of the extractor fan and the taps clonking into life as her mum turns on the shower for Molly. It's time to go.

Now or never.

Pulse racing, heart booming like a cannon in her chest, Harrie throws off the covers and moves to the door.

'Don't go,' Elise pleads in the darkness. 'Whatever it is, it can't be worth it.'

'I have to,' Harrie replies.

'Why? You can tell me. I promise I won't tell Mum.' Elise's voice is thick with emotion. The sound of it pulls something deep inside Harrie. She wants to turn around, she really does, but she shakes her head in the dark. She has to keep quiet. It's the only way to protect her family.

'Just cover for me if you can,' Harrie says, hurrying down the stairs and into the kitchen. She strips off her PJs, revealing the dark clothes underneath, the clothes she couldn't let her mum feel the bulk of when she'd tried to hug her a few minutes ago. Wrapping them into a bundle, Harrie stuffs the PJs into the craft cupboard on top of a stack of Molly's old colourings.

Now or never.

Never, never, never. The word circles her thoughts but still she grabs the things she needs and slips silently out the back door, running into the darkness again.

Harrie doesn't stop until she reaches the stable. Every second she's here is another second her mum could find her empty bed. Five minutes in the bathroom helping Molly shower. Ten minutes of reading. That's all Harrie has. As soon as Molly is tucked in bed, their mum will tiptoe across the hall, gently open Elise and Harrie's bedroom door and check they're both settled. Elise is poised to get up and distract her mum on the landing if Harrie isn't back. But that only buys her another few minutes.

'Who's there?' The voice is weaker tonight. A croak followed by a cough.

Harrie swallows hard and steps inside. The smell makes her eyes water, as if a football has hit her in the face. She covers her nose and mouth with her sleeve, but it's pointless.

176

She places the torch upright on the floor. The light bounces off the rafters and casts a shadowy glow across the stable.

'Please, help me,' the man says, wincing as he sits up. His eyes squint as he looks past the torchlight to where Harrie stands. There's a bucket in one corner of the cage and an empty plastic water bottle on the floor.

One of the man's cheeks is swollen and when he says, 'Please,' again it sounds like he's talking with a lump of bread in his mouth.

Harrie's legs buckle at the plea.

'Who are you?' he asks again.

Fear is holding her voice captive just as the cage is doing to the man.

Harrie pulls out the water she's brought with her and twists off the lid. The man picks up the empty plastic bottle and pushes the lip between the metal bars. Drops splash and spill on the floor as she pours from one bottle to another. It would be easier if she moved closer, but even with the locked cage between them, Harrie keeps her distance.

'My name is Dean Stockton.'

Harrie says nothing. She already knows his name, but the ache in her stomach turns from dull to sharp at his words and she bites back a yelp of pain. Does he think telling her his name is going to make this harder for her? It can't get any harder. Surely he must know that. Surely he must see that she doesn't want to do this.

'I live in the village, on the corner of Normandy Road,' the man says. 'Do you know it? The house with the purple wisteria growing across the front.' His voice sounds weird, like he's trying to be normal, like he's chatting away on the street instead of a prisoner in a cage. It's the same voice Harrie's mum uses when she's upset but pretending not to be. All high and cheery.

'I recognize you,' he says with a frown. 'You're one of the twins, aren't you? One of Rob and Anna's kids?'

Harrie can't stop the involuntary step back, the widening of her eyes. The answer she inadvertently gives.

'Are you Harrie or Elise?'

'Harrie.' Her reply is barely audible. She wishes she could stay silent, but she can't keep ignoring his questions, his pleas for help. She can't save this man, but at the very least she can talk to him.

'So you do speak.' He tries to smile and Harrie can see a gap where he's missing a tooth. A memory smacks into her mind. The body. The blood.

Dean's clothes are creased and dirty and Harrie sees a stain on his trousers that makes her look quickly away. He must have wet himself at some point.

'Why do you keep coming here? Why don't you just let me die?' he asks.

Harrie shakes her head but inside she wonders. She wouldn't have to keep coming here if he was dead. But if he was dead, then it would be murder, wouldn't it?

She shakes her head from side to side.

'I didn't have a choice,' she says. It's not an answer, but adults do that all the time. A question with a question, a sweeping statement.

'You can choose to unlock the cage,' he says softly.

She shakes her head.

'I won't hurt you. I promise. Please.' Dean's voice wobbles, a deep rumble in his throat.

'I can't.' Tears threaten behind her eyes. She wants to go now, but her feet won't move.

He sighs, and then catches sight of the bag in her hand. 'What have you got there?'

'A sandwich and some crisps,' Harrie says. She pulls out the food she hid from her mum earlier. Dean shuffles nearer to the bars and Harrie steps closer too, dropping the sandwich into the cage, into Dean's outstretched hands.

'Got any chocolate?'

She shakes her head. 'I'll try and get some next time.' Harrie clamps her mouth shut before she can say any more. Why is she offering to bring him chocolate? It's all so confusing. She shouldn't be helping him, but she can't stop herself.

'And when is that going to be?'

'I don't know.' She shrugs. 'Tomorrow.'

This is the third time Harrie has come here and it isn't getting any easier. If anything, it's getting harder. Harder to get away and harder to be here.

Dean drops his head into his hands. They're covered with dirt, grazes and dried blood.

'Talk to me, please. I've got no one to talk to.'

Harrie opens her mouth to say no, but then she thinks about the cage in her nightmares and how horrible it felt to be trapped, alone.

'I don't know what to talk about.'

'I've got a brother – Luke. He's only a year younger than me. People used to think we were twins. What's it like to have a twin?'

'Really good.' Harrie smiles despite herself. 'We're totally different though. Elise loves pink and girly stuff and gymnastics, but I'm not into any of that. I like sports. She's really smart too. She wants to go to this private school in town, but our mum and dad can't afford it so she's trying to get a scholarship. She's studying all the time. Mum's always helping her.'

'Don't you want to go to that school?' Dean asks.

Harrie shrugs. No one has ever asked her that before. 'I'm not as smart as Elise. She's got a chance at the scholarship, but I haven't.'

'And you have another sister?'

Harrie nods. 'Molly. She's seven. She's a pain sometimes but she's also really funny and totally obsessed with playing Guess Who?'

'It must be hard for you, having one sister studying so much, and another one younger. Your mum can't have much time left for you.'

'I guess.' She's never thought about it like that before. Molly is the youngest and needs their mum more. Elise is the superstar always needing to be taken to gymnastics or helped with her extra work, which leaves Harrie. What does she have?

'I grew up in this village too, you know?' Dean says. 'When Luke and I were younger we decided we wanted an adventure. I think we'd been reading too many *Famous Five* books.'

'My mum's reading *The Famous Five* to us right now.'

'We went across the bridge over the river and into the fields. We thought we could walk all the way to London.'

'What happened?'

'We stopped for a break after ten minutes and ate all our food and then our mum came and got us.'

They sit in silence for a moment before Harrie jumps to her feet with a start. What is she doing? She can't sit here talking to this man.

'I have to go.'

'No, wait.'

'I'll come ba—' Before she can finish Dean moves lightning fast, pushing his fingers through the bars and grabbing her hand in an icy claw.

'Help me. I'll die if you leave me here,' he hisses.

Harrie jumps back, yanking her hand free, stumbling back against the side of the stable.

She's stunned, the wind knocked out of her. All she can do is stare at the man in the cage.

'I'm sorry,' Dean says, breaking the silence. His shoulders shake and he starts to cry. A pitiful whimper sounds from his throat. 'I wasn't trying to hurt you. I didn't mean to scare you. Please let me out. Please, I'll do anything, just let me out of here.'

'No,' she shouts before turning and running, skidding on the straw beneath her feet and almost falling in her desperation to get away.

'Please,' she hears him shout a final time.

Harrie keeps running. She doesn't know if she'll ever come back, even if that makes her a murderer.

Chapter 31

Tuesday, four days until Halloween

Anna

As soon as I'm back from the school run, I throw myself into work. I crave the distraction. Without it, I will think only of Harrie and that grating feeling in the pit of my stomach that I'm missing something.

Bloody trousers.

Dean's name shouted in her sleep.

The bruise.

The mud.

The unlocked back door.

I wish I knew what it all meant. I wish I could open Excel and file what I know in neat little rows and straight columns until answers appear, but I can't. And so I work.

I start with the maintenance jobs from the websites I've designed over the last three years. It's little things. An extra page needed for a new service an accountancy firm is offering, an updated staff member profile for a public-relations company, a contact form for a local children's charity.

When it's done, I move straight on to the Parish Council admin. Organized chaos, Kat called it on Saturday when she showed me how to access the files on Google Drive. She was half right. It's chaos, but there's no semblance of order, no folders, no dates. Just a higgledy-piggledy mishmash of Word documents and PDFs. Meeting minutes from five years ago next to an invoice for plumbing work at the village hall from last month, next to a denied planning application for a house extension. The disorder sucks me in just as I'm sure Kat hoped it would. I spend hours lost in creating dozens of folders and sub-folders. Spending suggestions, fete organization, school, playing field, village hall, invoices. I click on an invoice from Stockton's for a repair on the village hall roof and wince at the cost. There are more invoices. £1,000 on maintenance of the horse field and stable. £5,000 on upkeep of the playing field. It's a mess. Someone has loaded the invoice for the village hall roof twice on different dates, and there's no record of meeting minutes from the last six months.

On and on it goes until my finger aches from clicking with the mouse and my head is pounding. A dull, persistent throb. Like someone is banging two saucepans together inside my brain. A slow and steady *clang, clang, clang*.

Finally, I open the Parish Council email account. It's mostly junk – a new estate agent's in town that wants to put posters on the village noticeboard, a request for clothes to be donated to a jumble sale. There's an enquiry from a Mr and Mrs Randell about

183

renting the empty horse field on the main road for their two ponies.

I trawl through the documents until I find the right form and send it with a reply to the email. It's a little thing, but it feels like I've made progress. It's £200 a month to rent the field and I'm sure the Parish Council will be grateful for the extra income, especially as it's been sat empty for so long.

It's lunchtime by the time I sit back in my chair, bleary-eyed and rubbing at the back of my neck. My mouth is dust dry, my stomach queasy from hunger. I let my gaze drift to the shelf above the table where I keep the cookery books and the little clay pots the children have made me in their art lessons over the years. Sitting beside them is a photo of Rob and the girls cuddled on the sofa at Christmas, wearing upside-down paper hats, Christmas jumpers and big smiles. A lump forms in my throat. Molly's questions on the walk to school this morning prey on my mind.

When is Daddy going to call again?

Will he call this Sunday?

Why didn't he call last week?

Can we give him two riddles to solve because he missed a week?

I smiled brightly and told her what she wanted to hear, jollied her along so she wasn't upset on the way to school. But now the questions return and there is no one to do the same for me. No one to tell me it's going to be OK.

Why did you have to miss the call this week, Rob? The one week when I really need you?

Harrie looked exhausted this morning when she finally appeared for breakfast, like she hadn't slept at all. I don't know which is worse, night terrors or insomnia.

If Rob were here he'd get through to Harrie. He'd take her out to the park or the garden and they'd boot a football back and forth until they were both red-faced and puffing, playing their made-up game, halfway between football and rugby with rules that seem to change every time they play.

Then he'd flop on the ground beside her and would coax and charm the truth right out of her. I realize in that moment that if I can't help Harrie then I must find a way to contact Rob. He will help her.

Chapter 32

Anna

I make a cup of tea and head to my bedroom. Our bedroom. I place the mug on Rob's chest of drawers. He doesn't have many clothes. Ten T-shirts, a few shirts. Two pairs of jeans. One suit that he hasn't worn since the interview with Artax, the contractors who employ him to work on the oil rig. The bottom drawer of the chest is where we keep our paperwork. We used to have an entire study for it in the old house, but now it's crammed into one drawer that's sagging and broken under the weight of the papers.

The drawer snags as I open it, wobbling the unit and slopping tea over the side of my mug. I force the drawer all the way open and lift out the binders one by one. Household bills, bank statements, insurance, the car details, birth and marriage certificates, all the files I've labelled and hole-punched, checked and double-checked. Every time I open one of these folders and add a bill, it blows my mind that I lived the first six years of my marriage without looking at a single bill or paying even a scrap of attention to what was

186

happening under my very nose. What happened to me? I used to look after my finances before Rob. I paid my bills, kept up with the rent, never went overdrawn, but then I fell pregnant so fast and with twins too, and Rob said to leave it all to him and like a fool, I did. Right up until that hot August night.

Sometimes weeks, months even, can go by and I won't give it more than a passing thought. Other times, it's like I'm right there all over again. Stupid really. So stupid. Anyone would think it was a trauma – some kind of attack, a mugging – when it was nothing like that, nothing close. But still it haunts me. Not just that night, but me. Stupid, naive, idiotic me, who thought everything was fine.

'Anna, wake up.' Rob's voice had hammered into my sleep.

My eyes had felt sticky, hard to open. I'd only settled Molly an hour before. 'What's wrong?'

The bedroom lamp switched on.

'We have to go.'

'Go where?' In my sleep-deprived, mummy-fog brain I thought Rob was talking about going to the supermarket for milk. 'There's some coming tomorrow morning. Don't worry.'

'Some what?'

'Milk. Switch off the light.' I turned over, sleep pulling me away, but then Rob's hands were back on my shoulders, shaking me again, this time with more force.

'Anna, you need to get up. We need to pack some things and go.' His voice was choked with emotion and finally I was alert and sitting up in bed.

'What's happened?'

'My business has collapsed. I'm in trouble,' he said, pausing to swallow, and I remember watching his

Adam's apple jut out of his neck and the ashen colour of his face in the orange glow of the lamp.

'What do you mean?'

He covered his face with his hands, a sob shaking his shoulders, and I didn't know whether to comfort him or shout at him to tell me what the hell he was talking about. 'I'm in a lot of debt,' he whispered. 'The company has been struggling for a long time, but I kept expecting things to turn around. There was a big contract I was pitching for, which would have made everything OK, but I didn't get it. I've just found out.'

'There will be other contracts,' I replied, still not grasping what he was telling me.

'No, Anna. There won't be. The company has no money. It's sunk. I'm sunk. I haven't been able to pay any of the staff.'

'But why do we have to leave right now? It doesn't make sense. We can't run away from debt, Rob. If you owe money then we need to pay it back,' I said throwing off the covers, but Rob took my arm, turning me to face him, and finally I saw the panic in his eyes, the severity of the situation.

'Anna, we're in mortgage arrears up to our eyeballs. The bank are repossessing the house tomorrow.'

'Tomorrow? But they can't do that. It's ridiculous. We've got kids. They have to give some warning.'

His silence said it all.

'Oh,' I said. 'They did give you warning, didn't they? How long have you known?'

'A month.'

'A month?' The volume of my voice jumped up and I forced it back to a whisper. The last thing I needed was a crying child in my arms. 'Are you kidding me? You've known for a month that we were going to be

188

homeless and you didn't tell me? Well, I'm not leaving. This is our home and I'm not leaving.'

'It's not our home any more. I'm so sorry, Anna.' Rob's shoulders shook and the tears rolled down his face. 'I know I should've told you, but I really thought I'd get this contract and could get us out of this mess before you found out.'

Before I found out? He'd been lying to me for weeks, months, God knows how long, but I couldn't process the lies. My mind was stuck on our house, our home which was no longer ours.

'The joint account,' I said suddenly. 'There's thousands in there. I saw a statement just the other day.'

'That's all we've got left. The credit cards are maxed out.'

'What credit cards?'

Rob's sadness turned hard before my eyes. 'How did you think we paid for all this shit, Anna? New TVs, a new pushchair because the wheel squeaked on the old one—'

'That wasn't the only reason,' I hissed back. 'And if I'd known we were broke, I wouldn't have bought it, but you didn't tell me, did you?'

'I was trying to protect you.'

'Don't you dare blame me for this.'

He dropped his head into his hands. 'You're right. I'm sorry. This is all me.'

The anger between us dissolved as quickly as it arrived and I slumped on the bed and sighed. Nothing we said to each other was going to change what was happening.

'Where are we going to go?' I asked, wondering how my mum would feel about a call in the middle of the night and all of us cramming into my old bedroom. Not

189

happy, I thought. For a woman who'd never taken any interest in my life or the lives of her grandchildren, she had a lot to say about Rob and my marriage. I didn't think I could face the told-you-so look in her eyes and her sharp belittling words. *I never liked him. I told you from the start. Too much of a charmer, that one.*

'I've found a flat for us on the outskirts of Ipswich,' Rob said. 'It's small but it's only temporary until I find a job.'

'Ipswich? Are you mad? We can't leave London. What about our friends, the girls' school, Molly's nursery?' *My life* is what I meant.

'It's less than two hours away. Ipswich has a couple of good engineering firms nearby. It's my best chance at finding work.'

'But you said you'd never work for anyone but yourself.'

'I don't have a choice. Look, we can still come back and visit, but right now I'm worried about what the lads will do, Anna. They're angry.'

'They're not the only ones.' It hit me then that Rob had found us a place to stay. It wasn't something he'd done in the last hour. Or even the last day. There would have been paperwork and references. A deposit to pay. 'I can't believe this. Why didn't you tell me earlier?'

'Please, Anna. Please, for me and for the kids, can we pack now and get away and talk about this later. I'll tell you everything. No more secrets, I promise.'

I bit back the tears, the hurt, the anger, the questions that pummelled my head, and tried to concentrate on packing everything we needed that would fit into the back of Rob's van. We were halfway to Ipswich when I realized I'd forgotten the new pushchair.

Chapter 33

Anna

The memory leaves my pulse racing, my mouth dry, my face burning crimson. I push it away and reach for the final folder. *Rob's stuff* is written on a sticky label across the top and it occurs to me as I lift it out and sit on the bed how little I know about the company Rob works for.

We should've planned for this. I should know who to call if I can't reach Rob. There should be a number pinned on the fridge and saved in my phone, a name, a contact, anyone who can tell me it's all OK. I must have worried about it. I must have suggested we needed a plan, but it all happened so quickly and Rob was gone in a whirlwind of 'Don't worry,' and 'Everything will be fine,' and it was. He came back every three months and he called every Sunday and so I never asked again.

I sip my tea and flip through the papers in Rob's folder. It's a jumble. No dividers or Post-it notes in sight. There are old letters sent to his company. A dissolution notice from Companies House. An eviction letter from the premises he leased. Reminders of our life before.

There is no contract for Artax here, no paperwork for his current employment. I wonder where else he'd keep it. I make a half-hearted search of the house. I look on the bookshelves and in the drawer in the kitchen where we keep the manuals for the appliances. I climb the loft ladder and search a few dusty boxes, but I find nothing.

In the end I Google the company and find a number for their Human Resources department. A man answers on the second ring.

'This is Frank,' he says by way of hello.

'Oh hi, I'm sorry to trouble you, but my husband works for your company and—'

'Name?' he asks, cutting me off.

'Robert James.'

'Date of birth?' he asks as I hear the *tap tap* of his keyboard.

I reel it off, knowing the digits as well as I know my own.

More tapping, then a pause.

'I'm sorry, there's no one with that name working for us,' he says, his tone signalling the end of the conversation.

'What?' I huff a laugh at his comment. 'But he does. He's worked for you for four years.'

The man sighs, the air rattling in my ear. 'Every employee's name, address, contact details, location and job title is logged on our database the day they start. If your husband worked for us, his name would be on my screen, and it isn't. There's nothing I can do. Is it possible he's working with a different contracting firm? We're not the only ones who do this.'

'I . . . I don't think so. He definitely said Artax,' I reply, my words full of conviction but my tone shrill.

'I'm sorry. There's nothing I can do.'

He ends the call and I stare at my phone for a long time, fighting the desire to phone the number again and speak to someone else. I'm not wrong. I'm not mistaken. Rob showed me the Artax website. The red banner that's open on my laptop right now. He clicked through pages and pages of their security systems, and held my hand in his as he talked me through the lengths they go to to protect their employees. And now it seems Rob isn't one of them. So where the hell is he?

It's safer than working directly for the oil company. Artax will look after me. They'll sort out my airport transfers, they'll make sure I'm safe. Rob's words ring in my mind. Those exact words. I lapped them up, committed them to memory, to trawl out and replay any time the worry mounted too high.

Who else can I contact? What else can I do?

Rob has mentioned a few friends he works with. Sash and Gilbo and Obinna. No surnames. Just a mention here and there. *I played cards with Sash last night again*, or *Gilbo told me the funniest joke the other day*.

They could be fake. Rob could've lied. The thought isn't new. It doesn't leap into my head. More a slow stepping out of the shadows, and for the first time I don't chase it away. Rob wouldn't lie to me, except he's done it before, so maybe he would.

I find myself picking at the last few years of our lives, at everything I know about my husband. I picture Rob's face on the iPad screen. He always sits close to the camera, a bushy black beard taking up most of his face that he won't shave until he's home again. What was in the background? A small room. A plain beige curtain, a desk, an armchair. It could've been anywhere. It could've been on the other side of the world, or the other side of the street.

The black spots disappear and a clarity returns to my thoughts. If I'm going to accept that Rob has lied to me, which really there can be no doubt about, then I also need to face another possibility, one that sends a shooting panic pulsing through my body – Rob could have run away.

If he was dead or kidnapped – tied up, a hood covering his head – wouldn't I have heard? Wouldn't it have been on the news? *British man kidnapped from oil rig in Nigeria.*

Two days have passed since he should have called. Nine days since we last heard from him and I have to face this other possibility.

It wouldn't be the first time he's run away. It wouldn't even be the second. Rob told me about his time in Cardiff on our fifth date. The woman he was living with who thought they'd marry, the job at her father's engineering firm, the life mapped out for him. 'I woke up one day and I knew I had to get away. I was living a life I didn't want, with a woman I didn't love and a job I hated. Every day I stayed it made it harder to leave.' So he packed his bags and left and I was so in love by that point that I didn't spend a single second thinking about the woman he left behind and the devastation he caused.

That was twenty years ago, a voice pipes up in my thoughts. *And he has children now. A family.*

I close my eyes and see a thousand images of Rob with the kids. Molly, his baby girl, tipped upside down in a fireman's carry and squealing with delight as he lifts her up to bed. Charging around the garden with Harrie.

Sat at the table with Elise, patiently explaining long division, going over and over it, late into the evening, heads bent, snacking on popcorn, until the calculations don't feel impossible to her any more. Sitting front row at every show, every competition, every assembly he can make, beaming from ear to ear with joy and love.

He's an amazing dad. Patient and kind, silly and fun. Always making us laugh. That is the Rob I know and those images, those memories, are incongruous with a man who would run away without a goodbye, who would lie to me over and over and over again.

At my laptop, I type *oil companies Nigeria* into Google and watch dozens of names appear. I change the search to *offshore oil company Nigeria*, and find only two names.

The number for the first company is a labyrinth of *press two for this and one for that* and it's forever before I find myself at the end and explaining my search for my husband into a recorded message. It's only when I've hung up that I realize I forgot to give the UK dialling code before my number.

The second company feels just as futile, but eventually I find myself talking to an actual person and try to explain what I want – to find my husband.

'You are press,' the woman on the phone says in heavily accented English.

'No, I'm not. I'm just the wife of a man who works on one of the Nigerian oil rigs.'

'Does he work for us?'

'I . . . I don't know.'

'You're British, yes?'

'Yes.'

'British press?' Her question sounds like an accusation.

'No, I'm not.'

When it becomes apparent that I'm not giving up, the woman reluctantly takes my number and promises to speak to her supervisor and return my call tomorrow. I have zero faith that she will do either of those things.

Reality dawns slow and hard. The only way for me to contact Rob is through his phone and he's not answering. In fact, the last few times I've tried his phone it's been off.

I'm still staring at my phone as a message from Kat arrives.

Fancy a cuppa? Xx

I close my eyes and imagine sitting with Kat right now, whiling the afternoon away. Would I tell her what I've learned about Rob? No. She'd ask me if I think he's lied and I can't bear to hear that question or the hurried 'No,' I'd reply.

After we left London, left our lives behind and squished ourselves into that flat with five-year-old Elise and Harrie, confused and climbing the walls, little Molly too young to understand or remember, but fractious and crying constantly; after the shock had worn away and I was faced with our new reality, I made Rob promise never to lie to me again, never to hide anything. And he did promise. He got down on his knees and begged for my forgiveness and I gave it to him because what choice did I have? Split up our family and take our children to live with my mother and her toxic words? Or find myself a flat I could afford, worse than the one we were already living in? Get a full-time job. Deprive my children of their father and leave them with a mother working too many hours

196

of the day. Despite everything I still loved Rob. I still love him now.

It's the doorbell that saves me from my thoughts. I leap up, grateful for the distraction, but that feeling drops – a glass shattering to the floor – when I see who is standing on my doorstep.

Chapter 34

Anna

Sue Stockton looks older than her forty-eight years. I know she's the same age as Dean, but with her short copper-blonde hair blown by the cold wind, and her lips pursed – her brows too – she looks closer to sixty. But it's the daggers shooting from her gaze that grab me by the throat and leave my mouth gaping. I might as well have a neon flashing GUILTY sign above my head.

Her slight frame is outlined by a bright blue sky streaked with the pale yellow of the autumn sun. From the corner of my eye I see June by the hedge that separates our front gardens. She's holding a pair of gardening loppers, her hands busy, but her gaze is fixed on us. On Dean's wife, standing in a pair of muddied jeans and a long navy parka. She's wearing wellies and holding a lead attached to a scrambling bundle of soft amber fur. The dog yips, breaking the silence. He pulls at the lead, standing on his hind legs as though wondering why my attention is on his owner and not him.

Sue gasps. 'So you're the slapper who's sleeping with my husband.' The words are ice cold and delivered with the impact I'm sure Sue was aiming for.

I stand agog, my head dizzy, playing catch-up with the scene unfolding in front of me.

So you're the slapper.

My heart pounds in my chest as my head moves from side to side. 'No,' I say, finding my voice. 'You're mistaken.' My tone is weak and I'm not even sure I believe me.

'You are Anna James, aren't you?' Sue asks, uncertainty crossing her face.

I nod.

'And you know my husband?'

'Yes, but it's not what you think.' A red heat creeps over my body, my chest, my face, but I realize in that moment that Sue is exactly the person I need to talk to. I don't know what connects Harrie to Dean or why, but there must be a reason Harrie said his name in her sleep and maybe Sue has the answers I need. 'Please, will you come in?' I ask.

Sue's eyes narrow for a moment. She seems as surprised by my offer as I was by her statement. 'I can't leave Timmy outside but he's muddy,' she says, casting her eyes to the dog. 'We've been for a walk.'

I almost laugh then. She's accusing me of having an affair with her husband but is worried about muddy paw prints on my floors.

'Your dog can have a play in our garden, and I really don't care about him being muddy.'

She nods once and I step back, waiting for Sue to slide her feet from her wellies and step into the house in bright-red woolly socks.

As I'm shutting the front door, my gaze draws to

June. She's staring across the fence, her face a mix of surprise and concern, and I feel my cheeks smart and swallow hard.

So you're the slapper.

I lead Sue through to the kitchen and open the back door as she unclips the lead. We stand for a moment and watch Timmy delight in his new freedom, tearing across the lawn to chase an overweight pigeon.

The moment subsides, leaving only awkwardness.

'Would you like a cup of tea?' I ask, already filling the kettle.

She shakes her head. 'No.'

'Water?'

'I've not come here for a damn drink.' The words are hissed, just like her accusation, but this time they're followed by a guttural sob. 'I've come here to find out where my husband is.'

'I don't know where he is,' I reply. 'Why don't you sit down?'

She moves to the table and drops into a chair and I sit too.

'So you don't think he's in Spain playing golf then?' I ask.

'What? Of course he isn't. That's Anthony Campbell's idiot lie he's been telling people so Stockton's doesn't get dragged into the gossip of Dean being missing. We've got a villa in Spain, and yes, Dean often pops over there to play golf, but never without telling me. I usually go with him. We both love it there.'

I nod, remembering how much happier Dean seemed after his last trip to Spain, as though a tension had been lifted from his shoulders. He'd been excited about something, a new plan he wouldn't tell me about. But then the days had slipped by and the excitement died away, leaving only a deep relentless worry I could never get him to talk about.

'Why is Anthony worried about Stockton's?' I ask. 'I thought it was Dean's business.'

'In name yes, but it's grown too much for Dean. He took a step back last year, allowing Anthony to take the reins. Dean is still the majority shareholder and has the final say in everything, but it's Anthony who runs it. He still makes a show of going in every day, but he doesn't do much.'

'So if Dean isn't in Spain, then where do you think he is?'

The hardness slips from Sue's face like a mask falling away and her eyes fill with tears. 'I don't know,' she whispers.

'Do you know what was bothering him?' I blurt out the question, not caring now how guilty it makes me seem.

She lurches slightly at the question. 'Do you?'

I shake my head. 'He wouldn't tell me, but it's felt like there's been something building. He's been so on edge.'

Sue nods. 'He was . . . he was in a dark place last week. I'm so worried about him. I can't shake the feeling that something has happened to him.'

Her words slice through me. It's exactly how I feel about Harrie. Goosebumps pimple my skin as I remember the words Harrie spoke during her night terror.

'When was the last time you spoke to him?' I ask.

Sue raises herself up, lips forming a tight line. 'I think before I answer any more of your questions, you can answer mine.'

A toxic silence stretches between us. I force myself to meet Sue's gaze. 'I'm not having an affair with Dean.'

'But you do spend time together?'

I nod. 'Dean hired me to redevelop Stockton's website and we . . . we became friends.'

'And I'm supposed to believe that he popped round once a week just for a cup of tea?'

'Whether you believe it or not, it's the truth.' Images of last Monday flash into my thoughts but I push them away. 'And I'm worried about Dean too.' I stand up and put the kettle on for tea. I need something to do with my hands whether we drink it or not.

Timmy's paws clatter on the glass of the back door and I let him in. He scampers into the room, nose down, sniffing the new smells, tail wagging furiously. I crouch down to say hello and find Timmy's fur is teddy-bear soft. He licks my hand with a gentle flap of his tongue. He looks just like one of the pictures on Harrie's wall.

When two cups of tea are sitting on the table and I'm back in my chair I ask Sue again when she last spoke to Dean.

She dabs at fresh tears with a ball of tissue she tucks in the sleeve of her jumper. 'He phoned me that Wednesday afternoon to tell me he wouldn't be home for dinner. He sounded agitated, but when I asked him why, he wouldn't say. He just said that he had to see someone and he'd be home late. I didn't think much of it until later when Luke, Dean's brother, called me. I . . . was in the bath and I missed his call.'

Sue pulls out a phone from her pocket and places it on the table. 'This was the voicemail he left.' She presses a button and a moment later the noise of traffic on the road fills the kitchen.

'Sue, it's me,' Luke says, his voice so much like Dean's that I forget to breathe. 'I'm on my way to the village.

Dean's texted me. He says he needs help. If you see him, keep him with you.'

Sue sniffs, wiping away more tears. 'He lives . . . lived in town, you see. So he was driving here that night, but his car crashed and—' Sue covers her face with her hands. Grief fills the kitchen.

'I'm sorry,' I say eventually.

'Dean and Luke were so close. Luke was like a brother to me too. That's how I know something has happened to Dean. If he knew his brother was in hospital, he'd have moved heaven and earth to sit by his bedside. If he knew he was dead, he'd have come home. It will destroy him. I . . . I don't know what to do.'

'Have the police listened to this?'

She laughs then. A single 'ha' devoid of any humour. 'Yes. They've heard it. Dean is filed as a missing person, but they're not interested. Anthony's been telling them and anyone who'll listen that Dean is fine, but Dean hasn't been himself for a few months. He's been . . . very secretive.' Sue stops as if she's expecting me to confess to something, but continues when it's clear I won't. 'We were fighting about things, getting on each other's nerves a bit. He was so down at times. I wanted to move to Spain permanently. We have a nice life out there. Good friends and a climate that suits us, but Dean wasn't sure. I couldn't understand what was keeping him here.

'I suppose in the back of my mind I thought he might have been having an affair.' She looks at me, a flash of accusation, but she must read something in my face as it disappears.

'What about Stockton's? Wouldn't that make Dean want to stay? He built the company from nothing.'

'*We* built it. I spent twenty years working by his

side. It was only when it expanded and Anthony joined the business that I stepped aside. Dean hates it now. He'd gladly sell the whole thing. He loved the building work, the creation of something, but not the business side of things, and the selling.'

'I had no idea. Dean never said.'

Sue's face changes as if she's remembered why she came here.

'So you really haven't been having an affair with my husband? You don't know where he is?'

I shake my head forcefully. 'I promise you. I'm married, and I love my husband very much. I would never do anything to break up my family. Rob works abroad, and Dean . . . for some reason, he understood the loneliness I've been feeling. He used to come over to cheer me up, help with anything that needed fixing around the house . . . He's been a huge support to me. He's a good man.'

She smiles at that. 'He really is.' Timmy paws at Sue's legs and she runs a hand over his back before getting to her feet. 'I think I've taken up enough of your time.'

'I'm sorry about Dean and about Luke.'

'Thank you,' she nods before stepping close, her eyes burning into mine. 'Be careful, Anna.'

'Of what?' The shock of Sue's words causes a bubble of laughter to leave my mouth. I'm not sure if she's warning me or threatening me.

The moment passes and Sue gives a shake of her head. 'Sorry. It's nothing. Just ignore me. I'm not thinking straight,' she says. 'Come on, Timmy. Time we were getting home.'

At the door, Sue turns to me, eyes wide and tearful. 'If you hear anything, please will you tell me?'

I nod. 'Of course.'

'I'm sorry for what I said on the doorstep. That'll teach me to listen to gossip.'

She slips her feet into her wellies and is striding away before her final word sinks in. Gossip. People have been gossiping about me.

Chapter 35

Anna

I've barely had time to sit down, to process what Sue has told me, when the doorbell rings again and I find June on my doorstep. My face grows hot thinking of the accusation I'm sure she heard.

'Oh, Anna,' she says with her usual smile. 'Could I ask a favour?'

'Of course.'

'I've got some cookie cutters in a tin in the top cupboard and I can't reach it. I've been trying for twenty minutes with my little steps and a broom, but they're right at the back and so I'm admitting defeat and asking for help. I don't suppose you'd mind having a try, would you, please? They're Halloween-shaped, you see. I like to bake biscuits for the trick-or-treaters.'

'No problem at all. Lead the way.'

I follow June around the hedge and into her house. It's the same layout as mine, but feels bigger. There's less clutter I suppose. No overloaded shoe racks, no toys scattered around the floor, no stacks of school letters, homework sheets or colourings on the sides. The walls are painted a soft peach and the carpet beneath my feet looks new, although I'm sure it's not. There are beautiful landscape oil paintings covering the walls and I can't help but step closer.

'Is this the river in the village?' I ask.

June steps up beside me and taps the glass frame. 'Yes. I caught it about this time of year actually, just before it flooded.'

'You painted this?' My voice rings with surprise and I turn to face June.

'Well yes, although admittedly it was some years ago. My eyesight isn't as good as it was so I don't paint as much.'

'It's amazing. You're very talented.'

'Thank you. Now, these cutters,' she says, leading me through to a white kitchen with marble-effect work-tops. It's dated but spotlessly clean. A top cupboard is open in the corner and there's a small stepladder resting beside it.

'Here?' I point.

'Yes please, Anna.'

A moment later the tin is in my hands and I pass it to a thankful June. 'Oh you're so kind. Can I tempt you to stay for a slice of Bakewell tart? Made this morning,' she adds, and even though I want to be alone with my thoughts, to process Sue's visit, I say yes.

She makes a pot of tea and we sit at the oval kitchen table.

'Now tell me,' she says, sliding the plate of cake towards me. 'Are you OK, Anna? Really OK? I can't help but notice you've been looking rather strained this week, and then Sue Stockton appearing like that . . . If I'm honest, I'm worried about you.'

'You are?'

'Yes dear, of course I am.' She encloses my hand in hers. It's cool, her skin soft. The gesture tightens my throat with emotion.

I hang my head and let the wisps of my hair droop forwards. A single tear traces a line down my face. 'I guess you heard what Sue said to me?'

June nods.

'It's not true,' I say as she pours two cups of steaming hot tea from a floral patterned pot. 'At least, I don't think it's true.'

'I don't claim to have any experience with infidelity,' June says, adding milk to our cups. 'I married Derek when I was twenty-three and as far as I know we were both faithful to each other until the day he died. But I don't imagine there is much grey area with affairs. You're either having one or you're not.'

I shrug and dab a finger to my eye where a second tear is forming. 'I've not slept with Dean and I've not kissed him.' I swallow hard and think of his touch on Monday, the comfort in it.

'So what would make you think you are having an affair?'

'It's not physical, but maybe on an emotional level I am. I don't think Dean sees it that way. He's just been a friend. We've both been struggling – me with Rob being away and Dean with his own issues – but over the last few months I've come to rely on him. I've felt so lonely and down at times. Rob being away feels like a punishment for me and the girls, and I know that's not what he's trying to do, but I resent it. I'm so angry with Rob sometimes. And when I've felt lonely, it's Dean who I've turned to, and he's cheered me up and made me feel more alive. I've looked forward to his visits. I've confided in him. I don't think I'd have done that if Rob was here, and I've not told a soul about my friendship with him. If it was innocent, why wouldn't I have told my best friend about it?'

June wraps her hands around the teacup and takes a sip, her face thoughtful for a moment. 'Two things,' she says. 'First of all, the answer to why you've not told anyone is obvious – this village is a toxic sewer of gossip. And word would get around within ten minutes that you and Dean were friends and I guarantee there would be speculation as to the nature of that friendship.'

'I think there already is.'

'My point exactly.'

'And the second thing?'

'The second thing is this – if you'd developed a friendship with a woman, if you'd phoned me when you were down and we'd chatted, if I'd been your confidante instead of a man, would you have thought for a single moment that there was anything wrong with that? Would you have questioned whether we were having an affair?'

I laugh and shake my head.

'There you are then. If you're friends, you're friends. And a good friend is hard to come by. The rest, excuse my French, is a load of bollocks.'

'Thank you.' I take a bite of the cake. It's warm and chewy, and an explosion of sugary jam takes over my senses. 'This is delicious.'

'It is rather, isn't it? Now tell me, what else is going on with you?'

My instinct is to shake my head and sugar-coat my woes, to steer the conversation around to easier topics, but there is something in June's warmth, her kindness, that makes me feel safe. My secret – what happened on Monday last week – shoots forwards, dancing on the tip of my tongue, but I can't face it. Not yet. Not now. Instead I tell June about Harrie and the night of the crash. I tell her about the sudden change in her behaviour, the unexplained bruise, the night terrors and shouting Dean's name. I speak fast, the words tumbling out, leaving me breathless and panicky all over again. I stop before I reach Harrie's bloody clothes. I'm not sure why. Only that an instinctive part of me wants to protect Harrie from whatever trouble she's in and until I know how she got herself covered in blood, I want to keep the trousers to myself.

It's only when I'm finished that I realize how alone I've felt this past week.

'My oh my,' June says, her face now pale. 'I don't know what to say. It does sound like something happened that night.'

I nod, surprised, relieved at June's agreement. I'm so used to Kat and Rob brushing away my worries, it feels strange to have someone agree. 'What do I do?'

'I don't think there is anything you can do. As you say, you can't force Harrie to tell you what happened—'

'Although I've tried. I've begged her to talk to me.'

'She knows you're concerned and she knows you're there for her when she's ready. Until then, I guess all you can do is wait and watch her like a hawk.'

It's much later, when the pot of tea is drunk and I've eaten two slices of Bakewell tart and have three slices in a cake tin for the girls, when I'm home again among the mess and the clutter, that June's words sink in.

I don't think there is anything you can do.

Is that really true? I want to believe it's not, and yet I can't find a single solution to help Harrie or find Rob. But the thought of waiting makes my stomach knot. I can't stop the worry and the what-ifs from consuming me.

Chapter 36

Harrie

Terror seizes Harrie's body, pinning her to the ground. She closes her eyes but the blood is still there, streaking through her mind. The scream stops. It wasn't her. She wasn't the one making the noise. A silence settles over the kitchen and Harrie realizes that someone else is with the two men. Someone standing in the doorway that Harrie can't see.

Run. Run. Run. The one word plays over and over in her head and she forces herself to open her eyes and focus on the back door. It's not far. She could reach it in seconds. But the door opens inwards and it'll take time to stop to open it, precious seconds she doesn't have. The man, the murderer, is standing right there. There's no way she can make it.

Harrie can hear her breath coming in short bursts. It sounds so loud, but she can't stop it.

He's going to hear her.

Her eyes pull back to the body on the floor and the

thick red blood, a growing puddle. She whimpers, like an injured dog. She clamps her mouth shut. But it's too late. The man is turning in the direction of the table.

'What the hell?' The voice is an angry panting growl and for a split second he's staring right at Harrie. 'Hey.' He turns to talk to the person out of Harrie's eyeline. 'Come here.'

Run.

And this time Harrie does move. She's slow and clumsy, her legs weak as though she's run for miles. She stumbles as she throws herself towards the back door, reaching the handle, pulling back, slipping through.

Cold air hits her face and she's out, running back to the gate.

She's going to make it. She's going to get home and then she can forget about the blood and the dead man on the floor. She will. She has to.

The gate is in darkness. Harrie's hands fly out, rubbing the wood. A sharp splinter digs into her skin but she doesn't care. She finds the handle just as footsteps tap on the concrete behind her. She throws open the gate and in the second it takes for it to open, for her body to move, Harrie realizes her mistake.

She's running home, retracing her steps. But the back door and then the gate – it's too much stop–start. She should have run straight down the garden, hidden in the shadows, found a fence to climb over. Done a hundred other things that weren't this.

She makes it one step on to the driveway when a weight hits her shoulder. A firm hand squeezing tight, pulling her back. She cries out in pain and thrashes, trying to duck out of the grasp, but he's got two hands on her now and is picking her up, wrapping her in a bear hug like her dad has done a hundred times, but that was playing and this is not.

'No,' she cries out, wriggling and kicking, moving everything she can move inside the tightness of his arms as he carries her back inside. Her heel connects with his shin and he groans, his grip slipping so her head is covered with his arm.

They're in the kitchen now. The warmth and the smell of metal encircling her again. She has to get away. Harrie bites down on his arm as hard as she can, harder than she's ever bitten anything. Warm liquid – blood – fills her mouth.

'Argh,' he yells and then she's no longer in his arms but flying to the ground, too fast to steady herself, too fast to change her course. She can see exactly where she's going to land and there's nothing she can do to stop the splatting sound of her body skidding into the puddle of the dead man's blood.

Village Girlies' Group Chat,
Tuesday 27 October, 18.40

Bev Pritchett: BREAKING NEWS KLAXON

Sandra Briggs: ???

Bev Pritchett: That new boy Kai in Year 5 who Tracy thought was the vandal is leaving the school!!

Gina Walker: Really? Do you know why?

Tracy Campbell: I was only speculating. It could've been anyone. @SandraBriggs has Jack found anything else?

Sandra Briggs: Not yet.

Bev Pritchett: Kai's mum told Mike that Kai hasn't settled well and she's moving him to a new school AGAIN!

Kat Morris: I thought he'd made quite a few friends.

Bev Pritchett: Just between us, Mike says that the mum felt like nobody wanted him there, which obviously Mike said was crazy.

Gina Walker: That's a shame she felt like that. She didn't exactly make any effort to come and talk to us though. We're a friendly bunch.

Tracy Campbell: Well I for one am relieved. He was a bad influence!!

Bev Pritchett: Mike thinks it was definitely Kai who vandalized the school.

Kat Morris: That's that then. What on earth are we all going to talk about from now on?

Village Girlies' Secret Group Chat
Tuesday 27 October, 18.46

Bev Pritchett: @KatMorris still plenty more things to talk about!! Like the fact I bumped into Sue Stockton yesterday and she was a total mess.

Tracy Campbell: She's always a mess!

Bev Pritchett: She is convinced Dean isn't in Spain.

Sandra Briggs: What did you say to that?

Bev Pritchett: I told her she should speak to Anna as she and Dean were 'friends'.

Tracy Campbell: YOU DIDN'T!! LOL

Bev Pritchett: I did :-)

Kat Morris: OMG you guys are the worst!

Sandra Briggs: @KatMorris like you're not LOLs.

Chapter 37

Harrie

Harrie's hands wrap around the bobbled sides of the rugby ball at the exact moment that Rufus reaches for it. They tussle for a second before falling to the ground in a heap. A peal of laughter escapes from Rufus's mouth. The sound makes Harrie laugh too. She feels almost normal in that moment. Almost.

The wet grass seeps through her trousers but Harrie doesn't care.

'I got it first,' Rufus says with another boyish giggle.

'No you didn't,' she grins, releasing a hand to tickle Rufus under the arm.

Then the moment changes. 'Harriet James.' Her name is said with a deep authority that makes Harrie release the ball and leap up with the speed of an electric shock. 'What do you think you're doing?'

Mr Pritchett is standing a metre away, arms crossed, face scowling with displeasure. Harrie looks from him to Rufus, still lying on the grass but no longer laughing.

217

A hush falls over the school playing field. From the corner of her eye, Harrie sees Ben and Tyler stop dead, watching. The football they were kicking rolls towards Harrie's feet but she doesn't kick it back.

'Well?' Mr Pritchett barks.

'We were just playing. Sorry,' she adds, although she doesn't know why. They're not really supposed to wrestle on the ground when it's wet, but they all do it. Yesterday, Ben and Tyler were mud-wrestling under the big oak tree and were so mucky after lunch break that they had to change into their PE kits, and no one told them off.

'Go sit on the chair outside my office.' His eyes are piercing and never leave Harrie's face. 'Fighting of any kind is not tolerated.'

She almost laughs then, shaking her head with relief. Mr Pritchett must have got the wrong end of the stick. She shoots a look at Rufus. 'We were just—'

'There'll be time for an explanation later. Go now, please.'

'Mr Pritchett,' Rufus starts, his voice small. 'We weren't—'

'Thank you, Rufus, but there is no need to defend Harriet. I know exactly what I saw. The bell will be going soon. Brush some of that mud off.'

Harrie's head drops as she walks quickly off the playing field and into the school. She hears Elise call out to her. Harrie looks up, about to answer, but Mr Pritchett is right behind her, his hand reaching for Harrie's shoulder to guide her in. Panic shoots through her body. She can't let him touch her. What if she freaks out like when Tyler bumped into her? She quickens her pace, eyes fixing on the floor as she walks through the school to Mr Pritchett's office.

'Wait here,' he says, pointing to the old plastic naughty chair. His voice has yet to soften like it normally does when he's told someone off. 'This is very serious, Harrie. Very serious indeed. You cannot go around punching people and expecting to get away with it.'

Harrie looks up, her mouth opening, the denial on her lips, but the look on Mr Pritchett's face tells her not to bother. Instead she bites down on her lip, her hands moving to rub at her knees.

The minutes pass. The school bustles around her. A kid from Year Two comes in to get a plaster for a grazed hand. A phone rings unanswered in the main office. Teachers trail out of the staff room one by one, folders and mugs in their hands. Miss Holloway stops at the sight of Harrie and frowns. Harrie can't tell if she's worried or disappointed to see her. Both probably.

The bell rings. Harrie waits, expecting Mr Pritchett to reappear and tell her to go back to class. Except the door remains shut. Has he forgotten she's out here? More time passes. Her class will be in their seats by now. She can imagine Elise asking Miss Holloway twenty questions. *Where is Harrie? What did she do? Why isn't she back?*

It's only as the classes file noisily into the school hall for assembly that Mr Pritchett appears, his expression still stony. 'Go join your class, Harrie,' he says. 'And if I were you, I would listen very carefully this afternoon. Is that understood?'

Harrie nods. Tears of humiliation threaten behind her eyes, but she keeps them in as she walks into the hall. The smell of boiled carrot cubes still hangs in the air from lunch. A hundred pairs of eyes watch her as she passes the little Reception kids, fidgeting on their bottoms, then the other classes, until she reaches the benches at the back. Elise waves her over, scooting along the smooth wood to make space for Harrie.

Harrie keeps her head down, not bothering to listen at first. Her mind is still turning over what happened at lunch. She replays the moment she and Rufus fell to the ground, both grabbing at the ball. Mr Pritchett must have thought they were fighting, not playing. But why didn't he ask Rufus what happened?

Mr Pritchett's voice rises a notch, penetrating Harrie's thoughts. 'Stealing is at the very heart of a corrupt society,' he says.

Her skin tingles. Her eyes pull up and she finds Mr Pritchett's gaze on her. He carries on. A whole twenty-five minutes of booming words that seem directed straight at Harrie.

She swallows hard. Is this about the phone she slipped into her pocket that night?

Harrie gives a small shake of her head. She's being paranoid. He can't know what happened. He can't know about the phone she took. He just can't.

Chapter 38

Anna

The routine of my life – the work, washing, tidying, cleaning – takes over today. I let it take over. Yesterday, all I could think about was Harrie and Rob. Rob and Harrie. I flipped from one to the other, feeling helpless and lost. Dean was mixed among it all, like sticky weed in my thoughts. I woke up this morning with nothing left but autopilot, my emotions coated with an immovable treacle of worry.

By the time I reach the school playground to collect the girls, my head is pounding with a headache and the thought of another night of gymnastics fills me with loathing. A light rain drizzles slowly from the sky, more mist than droplets, frizzing my hair and echoing my mood.

I spot Kat across the playground, standing in a huddle with Gina, Sandra and Tracy. Their backs are to me and I'm glad they've not spotted me. Sue's comment about gossip plays through my mind and I don't have the energy to talk to them today. I pull my hood up and stand in the corner.

The younger classes pile out first and despite everything a sweeping joy floods my body as Molly comes skipping towards me.

'Hey baby,' I say, opening my arms for a hug. She throws herself into me and we squeeze each other tight.

'Mummy.' Molly pulls away, glancing across the playground before hopping from foot to foot. 'Can I go to Olivia's house to play?'

Before I have a chance to answer, Tracy is by my side with Olivia, and both girls are grinning from ear to ear.

'Looks like you've just been ambushed too,' Tracy smiles.

I laugh. 'Yes.'

'We'd love to have Molly to play this afternoon, if she'd like to come over? She can stay for tea too.'

'Yessssss,' Molly says, the single word a long hiss.

'OK, thanks. If you're sure you don't mind?'

'Not at all. Saves me having to play dressing up.' Tracy laughs again. 'Do you want to pick her up about five thirty?'

'Perfect. Thank you.' I drop to a crouch and hug Molly. 'Be a good girl,' I tell her, before she hands me her book bag and skips off hand in hand with Olivia.

'Mum.' I look up to see Elise and Harrie side by side. 'Mr Pritchett wants to talk to you,' Elise says.

'Right,' I nod, looking past them to where the head teacher is standing. He's holding a large navy golf umbrella and is talking to a Year One parent with a toddler in her arms. 'It's probably about your extra tuition,' I say. 'Wait here. It won't take long.'

'Can we go back?' Harrie asks. There is something desperate in her eyes but with it a flash of defiance as

222

though she's going to walk away whether I say yes or not.

I shake my head and keep my voice firm. 'No. Just wait, please.'

Harrie sighs and drops her school bag on the floor. There's a thud from where her water bottle hits the concrete and I bite back a remark about looking after her things and console myself with the fact that she hasn't walked off.

Rain starts to patter on my coat. A gust of wind blows drops of it into my face.

The playground empties around us and I linger behind the other parent still talking to Mr Pritchett. From the tone of their voices it sounds like a chat, a bit of fun, and I will them to hurry up. I have to make dinner early tonight so Elise can eat before gymnastics. Something inside me sinks at the battle I'll face with Harrie. She'll want to be left alone. Of course she will. But there's no way I will let her, not after last week.

Mr Pritchett looks my way and raises one dark-grey eyebrow in a silent 'I won't be a moment' gesture. A gust of wind whips around the school building, lifting a few strands of his comb-over. He pats them back into place and turns slightly away from the direction of the wind.

Mike Pritchett has one of those down-turned mouths so he seems sad even when he's smiling, but he's a good head teacher and clearly committed to the school and each of its pupils. He's gone out of his way to help Elise with her extra studying, something that would have cost us a fortune in private tuition.

But five minutes later my patience is running thin. I glance back at the girls. I can't hear what they're saying, but I can tell from their stances and the looks on their faces that they're bickering, something they rarely do. It's usually Molly and Elise who fall out, squabbling over something Molly has borrowed without asking or whose turn it is to watch something, and Harrie is stuck in the middle trying to placate them both.

Surely whatever Mr Pritchett wants to discuss can wait until tomorrow, but as I take a step towards the girls, toes like ice blocks, Mr Pritchett ends his conversation with the other parent and she leaves the playground, offering me an apologetic smile as she hurries past.

'Anna, I'm sorry about that,' he says, giving a final wave to the other parent. 'I didn't mean to keep you but I need to discuss an incident that happened at school today. Harriet was fighting with a boy during lunch break.'

'Harrie? Are you sure?' I glance back at my daughter. Her face is bright red and she's glaring back at me, her expression a deep scowl.

'Yes. I'm afraid there is no doubt. I was on duty at lunchtime and it was me that stepped in to stop the fight. Harriet was sitting on top of the boy and punching him.'

'I can't believe it. Which boy?'

'Does that matter?' he asks and I feel my own cheeks redden, as though it is me who is being scolded.

'No, I guess not. I just—'

'I'm afraid we're not allowed to give out that information. We've had instances in the past of parents taking matters into their own hands, talking to other children or shouting at parents. It's better to let the school deal with it. Obviously, we put Harriet on a red warning, which means she will miss play at break and lunch tomorrow. It isn't the kind of behaviour we expect from our Year Six students and, as you know, we pride ourselves on being a small community school, a family really.'

'Of course.' I shake my head. 'I'm very sorry. I'll speak to her tonight.'

'I believe you're aware that this isn't an isolated incident. Miss Holloway informed me that Harrie has been pushing other pupils.'

'I ... I only know about the one time last Thursday.'

'There have been other times. Harrie's behaviour has been very out of character this week. We're all concerned about her. Have there been any changes at home?' he asks.

I sigh and feel the weight of the last seven days pull me down. Where do I start? 'Their dad didn't call on Sunday. He normally does and Harrie is worried about him.' I'm not sure if that's true. The night terrors and the moods started before Rob's missed call, but it's all I have to offer Mr Pritchett. 'It's no excuse,' I add quickly.

'I see,' the head teacher nods. He makes an effort to rearrange his features into what I think is sympathy and yet the judgement is still wafting off him. I can't blame him. Fighting is not OK. Not ever, and yet I'm struggling to match what he's saying with my loving, sweet daughter. Harrie is competitive. Loves sports. Hates cheaters, but she's never hit anyone before.

'Please speak to Harrie and make sure she understands that violence cannot be condoned in any school, but especially not a village one like ours. Trust is a big part of our ethos. If it happens again it will be a more serious matter.'

'I will. There won't be a next time, I promise.' My heart is thumping in my chest. The disbelief is contorting into anger. How could Harrie do this? Blood thumps in my ears as I stride back to the girls. They see the look on my face and even Harrie ducks her head. The defiance gone.

'What on earth were you thinking?' I hiss at Harrie as we leave the playground.

'As if you care.' Harrie's words are sharp.

'Of course I care. And you can forget about even asking if you can stay home tonight. I'm not letting you out of my sight.'

'Mum,' Elise says from beside me. 'It wasn't—'

'Not now, Elise,' I mutter. I need a moment to collect my thoughts, to scoop up my anger and make it manageable.

Harrie walks ahead and I let her. Too angry, too stunned, to know what the hell I'm supposed to do.

The desperation to understand what is going on inside my daughter's head burns through me. Why won't she tell me? When did I become someone she can't talk to? I close my eyes for a moment and wish I could unzip her head and pull out her thoughts, her worries, and take them from her.

One thing is for sure – doing nothing is not an option. I can't sit back and wait for her to come to me. There must be someone else in this village who knows what the hell has happened to my daughter and I'm going to find out. I'll ask the village mums on the group chat. Someone must have seen something.

Village Girlies' Group Chat
Wednesday 28 October, 15.47

Me: Strange question, but does anyone remember seeing anything odd going on last Wednesday evening? @BevPritchett you said you saw Dean's car driving into the village. What time was that? @TracyCampbell did you notice anything while you were walking the dog?

Kat Morris: Everything OK Anna? Is this about Harrie?

Gina Walker: Have I missed something? What's up?

Me: I think something happened to Harrie the night I was stuck on the road, but she won't tell me anything.

Gina Walker: Clarissa did mention that Harrie and Elise have been acting weird this week. What do you think happened?

Tracy Campbell: I didn't see anything. Sorry!

Bev Pritchett: Sorry @AnnaJames I don't think it was Dean's car I saw. I was only looking out the window for a minute. It could've been any blue car. Do you want Mike to have a chat with Harrie tomorrow?

Me: @BevPritchett thanks but I don't think it will do any good. So no one saw anything at all that night?

Village Girlies' Secret Group Chat
Wednesday 28 October, 15.59

Sandra Briggs: What are those messages about? Anyone else find them a bit accusing?

Bev Pritchett: No idea!! Weird, right?!

Kat Morris: Think Anna is just worried about Harrie!

Tracy Campbell: I get that @KatMorris, but not sure what she thinks we might know. If any of us saw anything strange that night, especially something involving Harrie, then we'd have mentioned it.

Kat Morris: I know, but you can't blame Anna for trying. She's worried.

Tracy Campbell: She's always worried about something! @SandraBriggs remember when it snowed that time and Anna was having a fit on the message group about getting out of the house? Jack ended up clearing her path.

Sandra Briggs: YEP! As if there is anything to worry about living here!

Chapter 39

The night of the crash, *8.19–8.31 p.m.*

Harrie

'Don't hurt me.' The words fly from Harrie's mouth as she pushes herself across the floor, away from the murderer who grabbed her, away from the blood and away from the body lying motionless. When she's by the table once more, she stands, instinctively holding her forearms up to protect her face.

'Calm down,' the man says, rubbing at the bite Harrie gave him. 'I'm not going to hurt you.' There's a strange humour in his tone as though Harrie's assumption is ridiculous. It's the same tone her mum uses when Molly is crying over something silly. Calming but also amused.

Harrie drops her arms and lifts her eyes to the man as he steps back to the door. He turns the key before slipping it into his pocket. She's trapped.

Silence rings in her ears.

'Elise? Is that you?'

Harrie turns to the voice and for the first time she

230

sees the other person in the room and the source of the scream.

It's Kat.

Relief sweeps through Harrie so fast that she feels dizzy. Kat won't let anything happen to her.

'He killed him,' Harrie says, too scared to correct Kat's mistake. Harrie means it as a warning, she means to shout it, to tell Kat to run away and get help, but the voice that comes out is little and scared. Suddenly she's aware of the blood soaking through her trousers. Her eyes fill with tears. She wants to be home with her mum, Elise and Molly.

The man laughs. A deep bellow of a noise. 'He's not dead. He's drunk. He'll be fine in an hour or so. It's only a nosebleed.'

Harrie's eyes fall back to the body on the kitchen floor. He's not moving, and there is still a lot of blood, but the other man is right. It's coming from his nose. Harrie has had plenty of nosebleeds and none of them have killed her.

The man turns to Kat and points a thumb at Harrie. 'You know this girl?'

'Yes, of course. It's Elise – Ben's friend. One of Anna and Rob's twins,' Kat answers, her gaze never leaving Harrie's. Kat's eyes are wide. Harrie can see the whites surrounding the pupils. Her mascara is smudged, so is her lipstick. She looks as scared as Harrie feels. 'What are you doing here so late? Does your mum know you're out?'

She shakes her head. 'No.' The single word is a croak. Her throat hurts. Her vision blurs. 'She's gone to collect Elise from gymnastics,' Harrie blurts. A tremor takes hold. She's shaking all over like she's cold, freezing, when she's not. What's going to happen now? Can Kat protect her from this man?

'To collect Elise?' Kat's eyes narrow as she stares at Harrie with a why-did-you-lie? frown. 'Harrie?'

She nods and then the man steps closer and Harrie feels herself shrink down. 'Why don't you take a seat.' He pulls out a chair and, taking her by the shoulder, he pushes her down.

The relief at seeing Kat morphs back into fear. Kat should've called the police by now, but she hasn't.

Interview with Anthony Campbell, head
of Barton St Martin Parish Council,
Chief Financial Officer for Stockton's
Builders and Contractors
Interview conducted by Melissa Hart,
The Daily Gazette, 3 November

MH: Mr Campbell, Melissa Hart from *The
Daily Gazette*. Have you got time for a
few questions, please?

Anthony: I do, yes, although you should
know that some people in my village have
mentioned that you're harassing them. I've
told them that's not the case. You're just
trying to get answers, which is what we
all want, isn't it?

MH: Yes it is. Thank you. Is it your
village?

Anthony: I suppose my answer to that is that it's perhaps more my village than it is yours, but what I meant is that as head of the Parish Council, people bring their complaints to me, but I'm on your side. If you need anything, anything at all, please let me know. We all want the same thing.

MH: And what is that?

Anthony: To understand what happened on Halloween night and the following morning. And let me tell you something – there is no one more surprised about what happened than me. I'm sure we're all taking a long hard look at ourselves right now. This happened right under our noses. Someone must have seen this coming. Someone must have been able to prevent this tragedy. I guess what I'm trying to say is that maybe we're not the close-knit community I thought we were.

MH: And you knew the victims?

Anthony: Of course I did. We all did.

MH: Where was Dean Stockton last week?

Anthony: What does that have to do with anything?

MH: I'm trying to get a clear picture of the events that happened before two people were killed.

Anthony: Murdered.

MH: I'm sorry?

Anthony: Two people weren't killed. It wasn't an accident. It was murder - plain and simple. I really must get going now. And in answer to your question, I don't know. I'm as much in the dark about all this as everyone.

MH: I find that hard to believe, Mr Campbell. A man of your stature in the community. Working alongside Dean Stockton in his business and on the Parish Council, and you knew nothing?

Anthony: Believe what you want, it's the truth.

Chapter 40

Anna

'Come on, Harrie, time to get up.' My tone is light, almost sing-song cheery. I'm trying to start the day on a fresh note, trying to forget her outburst yesterday, the 'as if you care' comment flung at me. She didn't say a word on the drive to and from gymnastics, preferring to sit in the back with Molly than up front with me.

I draw back the curtains, allowing the grey morning light to fill the bedroom. Elise's bed is already empty. I can hear her in the bathroom brushing her teeth.

'You need to get ready for school,' I say when Harrie still doesn't move. I feel the frustration prickle inside me. So much for a fresh note, a new day. It's not even eight a.m. and I'm frayed, nerves jittery.

'I'm not going,' she replies, her voice muffled under the covers.

'What do you mean? Of course you're going.' I laugh because even after the week we've had, it's still so un-Harrie-like.

'I'm not. And you can't make me.'

'Of course I can make you.' No laughter now. Sparks of yesterday's anger ignite inside me. I step towards the bed and yank off the covers. 'You live under this roof and you will obey the rules.' I hate the tone of my voice, the words I'm using. I sound like a mother I don't want to be – my own – and yet I'm so angry too. Angry at Harrie for changing and not telling me why, and angry at myself that no matter what I do, I can't get through to her.

Harrie sighs and says something I don't catch.

'Sorry?'

'I SAID,' she shouts, leaping up and stepping towards me so she's only inches away from my face. Our eyes meet and I see a wildness I don't recognize. 'FUCK OFF!'

I gasp, too stunned to reply as the swear word hangs between us. Harrie has never sworn before. I don't even let the girls say 'damn it' like their friends do. Then the shock of her words slips away and all that's left is the hate in her voice. I back away from her bed and stand in the doorway. Lost. Infuriated.

The silence drags out between us. Heat burns through my body. But there's worry there too, water and oil, neither mixing but both present.

'I hate you,' she says, throwing the words at me like she really means it. They hit like a punch and suddenly the rage is no longer a spark but a lit flare – burning and intense.

'Don't you dare speak to me like that.' I spin around, pulling open the wardrobe door before grabbing her uniform and throwing it at her feet. I step closer, jabbing my finger at the clothes. 'Get dressed now,' I say, teeth gritted.

We stand like that for a second, neither of us sure where this fight will go next.

Then I see the tears welling in Harrie's eyes, the tremor in her bottom lip, and just like that the anger is gone, dropping to the floor with Harrie's uniform. What the hell am I doing?

Suddenly I feel like the worst mother alive, the worst person. What kind of mother leaves their child home alone like I did? What kind of mother shouts at their child when they're upset like this? Harrie might not be telling me everything, but her actions are shouting loud and clear and all I can do is throw her clothes, pull off her covers.

My chest, my heart, aches with emotion. I don't know what to do. I don't know how to make this right.

I reach out a hand – a gesture. 'Harrie—'

She yelps, shrinking away from me as though I've hit her.

'I'm sorry,' I say, forcing myself to step back, to give her space, when all I want to do is pick her up and cradle her in my arms like she's a baby again. 'I've got this all wrong, haven't I? If you want to stay home with me today, that's OK. I think you should.'

Harrie's eyes drop, her shoulders too, and she sits back on the bed, hands rubbing at her knees like she did during the night terrors. I picture the trousers – the coppery-brown blood stains on her knees – and now I get it. She's trying to rub it away, rub herself clean.

'Harrie?' I sink to the carpet, kneeling before her. 'Please tell me what happened that night. Please. Whatever it is, I'm here for you. I'm on your side. There's nothing you can say, nothing that you could've done that will change the way I feel about you, but please tell me so I can help you.'

I wait. The silence loaded with anticipation. Harrie takes a shuddering breath, her eyes meeting mine. Her lips part and I hold my breath, waiting for her to speak.

There's the creak of floorboards on the landing and I realize too late that the sounds of Elise in the bathroom have stopped. A second later I sense her in the doorway, but my gaze remains fixed, pleading with Harrie to talk, but already she's retreating into her shell.

'Nothing happened,' she whispers. 'I'm just ... I keep getting in trouble at school and I don't know why.'

'You must be doing something—'

'She's not, Mum,' Elise jumps in. 'It wasn't Harrie's fault. She wasn't fighting with Rufus. They were just playing with a rugby ball like they normally do and Mr Pritchett went out and told them to stop and that Harrie needed to go to his office. Rufus wasn't hurt or anything.'

'Did you see it?'

She pauses. 'No, but Georgia did. She told me.'

This is the same Georgia who told the entire school that she'd got a pony over the summer holidays. The story went on for weeks until Georgia's mum heard about it and put everyone straight. No pony. Not even a hamster. 'Maybe Mr Pritchett saw Harrie from another angle or misunderstood.'

'Ask Kat if you don't believe me. She can ask Ben. He was standing right there.'

'So why didn't he ask Harrie and Rufus about it then?'

'After lunch, Rufus wanted to go and tell Mr Pritchett that they were only playing, but Miss Holloway wouldn't let him.'

My insides curl. I wish I'd questioned Mr Pritchett more. I wish I'd stuck up for Harrie.

'Why didn't you tell me this yesterday?' I ask Elise.

'You weren't exactly in the listening mood.' Elise frowns and it feels like another slap.

'Elise, it doesn't matter what mood I'm in, I will always listen to you and help you. I promise.' The words fall flat. Elise's expression doesn't change. I think of my behaviour last night. I was distracted by Harrie and the trousers, Dean, Rob. I need to do better.

'I will speak to Mr Pritchett today. If what you say is true—'

Elise makes a noise in her throat – a 'huh' – as though I'm accusing her of lying.

'I believe you. I know Harrie wouldn't punch anyone. We'll get this cleared up today and Mr Pritchett can apologize to Harrie. I'll speak to him this morning at drop-off.'

'No,' Harrie says, picking up her uniform from where I'd thrown it. The navy of her school jumper matches perfectly with the dark circles around her eyes. 'Don't, Mum. Leave it. Talking to Mr Pritchett is only going to make it worse.'

'But if you've done nothing wrong—'

'Please,' she begs, hands clasping together, tears forming in her eyes. 'Please leave it.'

I nod, sad and scared for my daughter. What has made her this upset? 'OK. If that's what you want.'

'I'll go to school,' Harrie says.

'Don't.' I shake my head, adamant now that I want Harrie home with me. She was so close to telling me something before Elise walked in.

Harrie looks at me uncertainly for a moment and I push the point. 'Stay in bed for a bit. I'll get June to pop in while I take the girls to school and then you can camp out on the sofa and have a TV day.'

She nods and I see the relief in her face and feel it too.

'Is Harrie staying home?' Molly asks, appearing in the twins' bedroom, hairbrush in hand.

I nod. 'She's not feeling well.'

Molly gives a little cough. 'I think I've got it too.' The corners of her mouth turn down and at the same time she lifts her big brown eyes up to look at me.

'You're fine. Come on. Harrie needs some rest and Elise needs to get dressed.'

I shoo Molly out and close the door.

We stand on the landing to brush her hair and as I strain to hear the quiet mumbles of Harrie and Elise my phone rings from my back pocket. I snatch it up, my heart soaring as I see Rob's name on the display.

Chapter 41

Anna

'Rob?' I say, urgent and loud.

'Daddy?' Molly squeals, jumping up and down, hands already reaching towards the phone now pressed to my ear.

Harrie and Elise's bedroom door flies open and they rush to my side.

There's static on the line. A low hum. A crackle. 'Rob? Rob?'

'Can I speak to him?' Molly asks.

'Me first,' Elise replies.

I press a finger to my lips and urge them to be quiet.

'Anna?' Rob's voice is distant. He sounds miles away. Thousands of miles.

'Rob?'

He says something but the signal is so bad that his words are lost in a stuttering of broken silence. The only thing I catch is a muffled, 'Don't worry.'

'I can't hear you.' Static is scratching in my eardrums. I know he'll be gone in a second and so I say the only thing I can. 'Come home.'

The line cuts dead. He's gone and I've no idea if he heard me. No idea what he was trying to say, but tears of relief roll down my cheeks because he's not dead. He's not left me either. Something has happened out there but he's told me not to worry. I take a long breath and turn to the girls.

'Daddy's OK,' I say, reading the fearful expressions on their faces. 'His phone isn't working, but he's going to call again as soon as he can.' It's another lie but this time it feels like the truth.

I finish Molly's hair in a rush and slip into the kitchen to collect my thoughts, to calm my racing heart. Rob called. He's alive. Did he hear me tell him to come home? Hearing his voice has made me realize how much I need him. Right now. Today. This very second.

Ten minutes later, I'm still rattled and jittery, but June is on my doorstep and I push Elise and Molly out of the house, leaving Harrie in bed.

Elise is by my side and Molly a few paces ahead, skipping as she sings to herself.

'Was Dad really OK?' Elise asks.

I take a long breath in and out before I speak. 'I heard his voice and he told me not to worry. If he wasn't OK, he wouldn't have been able to call.' I hope it's true. 'Try not to worry. How's your homework this week? Are you meeting Mr Pritchett at lunch today?'

'Yes. He's got a practice paper for me.'

We're at the alley now, five minutes until we're at school. Elise sticks to my side and it feels like she wants to tell me something.

'Are you OK?' I ask.

She shakes her head. 'I'm worried about Harrie.'

'Me too. If you know anything, Elise. Anything at all. Will you tell me?'

Silence.

I turn to look at Elise. Her head is dipped, her gaze fixed on the concrete.

'Elise?'

'I've tried talking to her, but she won't tell me anything.'

I keep staring, wanting to believe her, but I'm not sure I do. We walk through the estate in silence.

'Anna,' Kat shouts from across the road as she pushes Ben out of the front door. She jogs towards me, Ben by her side.

'Hi Ben, how are you?' I ask.

'Good.' He throws a look at Elise and I wait for her to fall back and walk with him but she's two steps ahead, talking with Molly, and doesn't turn around. I'm surprised but pleased. It's nice to see her making more effort with Molly.

'I've been meaning to call you.' Kat takes my arm and gives it a squeeze. 'You didn't reply to my text about a cuppa the other day?'

'Sorry, I forgot. It's been a strange week.'

'Are you OK? Your message on the group chat sounded a little stressed.'

'I'm just worried about Harrie. She's at home today. She's really not herself, Kat.'

'Has she told you anything about that night?'

I shake my head. 'She's still saying she didn't go out.'

'Maybe—'

'There's something going on here,' I say, cutting Kat off and ignoring the look of doubt, of pity, on her face.

'Do you want to come back to mine after drop-off and talk about it?' she asks.

'I can't. June's watching Harrie, so I need to get back. Do you want to come to mine?'

'I'd love to, but I've got a delivery coming this morning.' She checks her watch. 'In fact, I'd better get back. I'll speak to you later.'

Kat spins around, saying a hurried goodbye to Ben. She's already jogging back to the house when she shouts back to me. 'Oh my God, Anna. I forgot to tell you. Dean got in contact with Anthony. He's fine. He's in Scotland. He had a bit of a breakdown by the sounds of it, but at least he's OK.'

She gives a thumbs-up and is gone before I can form the words to reply.

Dean has had a breakdown and run off to Scotland. I frown as the news sinks in. It makes sense. Almost. Dean was struggling with something. It wasn't just me who thought so. Sue mentioned his dark mood too. And yet there's something about Dean being in Scotland that doesn't fit. If Dean is in Scotland then does it mean he wasn't even in the village the night Harrie was alone, or does it mean he was, and whatever happened is the reason he's run?

Chapter 42

Harrie

Harrie flies out the gate at the side of the house, the bag in her hand knocking against her legs as she sprints ahead.

She hates this village. She hates the field and the stable. She hates Dean and the cage he's in, but most of all she hates herself for what she's done and what she's still doing.

Each night she lies awake, her head filled with images of Dean, and she promises herself she won't go back. She'll fall asleep and when she wakes up, she'll pretend it never happened. None of it. But then the dreams come and it's Harrie locked in the cage, Harrie who is a prisoner, alone and dying with no one to save her, and she wakes up crying, and she knows she has to return.

'Who's there?' Dean shouts as she reaches the doorway, steadying herself for what awaits her – a dying man and a smell worse than death. It must be what hell smells like, Harrie thinks.

'I know someone is there. Please help me. I'm

trapped.' It's the crack in Dean's voice that makes Harrie step forward. His desperation pulling her in so he can see it's her and not his rescuer.

She watches his face fall, the disappointment hitting hard.

'What day is it?' he asks, the question half lost in a coughing fit that makes his whole body shudder.

'Thursday,' she says.

'Shit.' His shoulders sag and he starts to cry again.

Shut up! Shut up! Shut up! Harrie bites the inside of her mouth. He sounds like Molly does when she's tired. He takes a long breath and looks up at her. 'I've been here for more than a week. My wife and my brother will be going out of their minds. Please, help me. Just write a note or something. No one has to know it came from you. I'll never tell anyone you were here.'

Harrie shakes her head and closes her eyes, then opens them quickly. The smell is worse when her eyes are closed. 'I can't.'

She reaches in the bag for a blanket she found in the back of the coat cupboard. The wool is rough with age but she thinks it will still be warm.

'How long is this going to go on for?' he asks, not bothering to take the blanket she pushes through the bars.

'I don't know.'

'Harrie. Please. You're a good girl. Your mum and dad are always saying what good kids you are.'

Harrie's eyes narrow a fraction as she looks at Dean. 'You know my mum and dad?'

'Yes, we're friends. Your mum designed the website for my building firm and I was the one helping your dad with the lights for the band at the summer fete.

Do you remember? Martin Walker was there too. You know Martin. He's got a daughter your age.'

She nods, thinking of Clarissa.

'When will your dad be back?'

'In a couple of months.' Harrie sucks in her bottom lip to stop it trembling. She doesn't want to talk about her mum and dad. Her mum is pretending everything is fine, that nothing is wrong, but Harrie heard her crying in the living room last week when she thought they were all asleep. She knows it's about her dad.

Harrie reaches for the food next. She needs to hurry. It's risky being here now. June could walk upstairs and check on her any minute. But she had to come now. She couldn't bear another trip in the dark later. And besides, as soon as her mum is back she'll be watching Harrie so closely there'll be no way she can sneak out again, even if Elise agreed to help.

Elise is worrying, threatening to tell their mum everything if Harrie doesn't stop sneaking out. Elise only knows a fraction – why Harrie left the house that night – but it's enough. Harrie can't let her do that. The fear rises so fast it chokes her.

You tell anyone about this and I promise you I will know. The threat is a constant whisper in her head. She shivers and grabs at the food.

A pack of crisps pops as Harrie squeezes it through the bars of the cage, making her jump. She doesn't like being this close. Dean didn't want to hurt her last time, he just wanted to make her listen, but his touch still scared her. Sometimes she'll be sat at her desk at school, or in the car, or drifting off to sleep, and she'll feel his icy fingers touching her skin and she'll shudder, a scream lodged in her throat.

Dean is still talking about her dad. On and on. Stuff Harrie doesn't understand. She wants to tell him to stop.

'I can't do this any more,' she whispers.

'What was that?' Dean asks.

'I can't do this any more,' she says, forcing herself to speak up.

'But you have to.' His eyes grow wide and Harrie looks away. His face is so thin. It reminds her of a skeleton. 'I need you,' he says. 'Please. Your visits are the only thing I have.'

'I'm sorry.'

'I was leaving, you know? Selling up and moving away from here, and now look at me. I didn't mean to get you involved. You know that, don't you? I'm not a bad man, Harrie.'

Dean's shoulders shake and he starts to cry again. Horrible loud sobs.

Without another word, Harrie covers her ears and runs away. She can't listen any more. She wishes Dean would die so she could be free.

Harrie runs across the field, climbs the gate and keeps going into the road, only seeing the silver car when she's already in motion, when it's too late to stop or hide or run. It brakes suddenly, stopping a metre away from her, the engine loud beside her.

The driver's window buzzes down. He leans out. She wants to run again, but her legs are wobbling beneath her. She didn't look before she crossed the road and she was almost hit by a car. His car.

'What are you doing here, Harrie?' The sound of his voice makes her heart stutter in her chest.

Then his door opens. The sound is enough to send a rocket of terror blasting through her, and she sprints away before he can grab her, only stopping to draw breath when she reaches the back gate.

Hot tears stream down her face. Her hands shake violently as she pushes the bolts across and creeps back into the house. The sound of the news on the TV drifts from the living room as Harrie hurries back to her bedroom before her mum gets home.

Chapter 43

Anna

The post is waiting for me on the doormat when I arrive home. I scoop it up and dump it on the side as I flick the kettle on to boil.

'Cup of tea, June?' I call from the kitchen.

'No thanks, love. I'm catching the bus into town this morning. Don't want to miss it.'

June shuffles into the kitchen, laying a hand on my back. 'How are you, dear?'

'OK, I think,' I say. 'Worried about Harrie. Has she said anything to you?'

'No, not a peep. I think she's gone back to sleep. It's the best thing for her. Anything else I can do, you just give me a call.'

'I will, thank you.'

June leaves and the kettle finishes boiling. I pour the water over the teabag and thumb through the post. It's junk, sort of. An advert for a local business networking event that I really should go to, and I will one day. Once I have a few more websites in my portfolio, once I feel less like a phoney – a mum trying to make ends meet – and more like the professional I want to be.

The second letter is addressed to Mr and Mrs James and I rip through the envelope without hesitation. The header at the top leaps out at me in bold navy lettering – *DCC Collection Services* – and I feel the world, the house, the kitchen fall away as I read on.

Dear Mr & Mrs James,

We are writing to inform you that we have acquired your outstanding mortgage debt of £150,000 from Willow Mortgage Providers. The above-mentioned amount is now due in full by the end of November.

If you are unable to make full payment, please call us immediately to arrange a repayment schedule that will show your commitment to clearing this debt. 23.43% p.a. interest will be charged on any outstanding debt. If you are unable to make payments, we will send bailiffs to the above-mentioned address to reclaim lost monies.

If the payment has already been made, please accept our thanks and ignore this letter.

Regards,
P. Robinson
Debt Collection Officer
DCC Collection Services

By the time I finish reading, the letter is shaking in my hands. The paper rustling and flapping. It doesn't make sense. We never had a second mortgage on the London house. Rob showed me everything. The half dozen credit cards, the loans for the business, the interest rates, the mortgage arrears. It was a steaming pile of shit I thought would drown us, but there was no second mortgage.

The only sound in the kitchen is my ragged breathing as I read the letter again, peering at each word. It's on this second time round that I really see my name at the top of the page. Mrs James. Me. All the credit cards Rob took out, the loans, the failed repayments – everything was in Rob's name alone. It was his mess and I would sit right down in it and take it as my own, but it has always been his.

This – this £150,000 – isn't just Rob's though. It's mine too. It's both our names on the letter. The realization makes my head spin. Black spots float across my eyes. We owe this company £150,000.

I can't think straight. Can't breathe.

Why did Rob hide this debt from me? Something else he's lied about.

My phone is silent in my pocket but I snatch it up as though it's ringing and stare at the blank screen. I'm desperate to call someone.

I try Rob first. It doesn't even ring. It just hums – a dead tone.

Out of desperation I call Dean. I try to picture him in Scotland, holed up in a hotel. The picture doesn't fit. Dean likes warmth and sunshine and he hates the rain. Scotland at this time of year would be his worst nightmare. The voicemail clicks on, but I don't leave a message.

Part of me wants to throw open the front door and chase after June. I know she'll be a shoulder to cry on for me, the supportive friend I need right now, but I've already asked so much of her.

I think of Kat next. She'd ditch the delivery she's waiting in for and be round in a flash if I called her, but something makes me hold back. I picture Sue Stockton on my doorstep, the hissed accusation, and later her own admonishment. *That'll teach me to listen to gossip.*

I'm almost certain the gossip is nothing to do with Kat, and yet I don't call her. This is my problem and mine alone.

There is no one else. Literally no one. Out of obligation, I speak to my mother once a month. The life I tell her about isn't so much Instagram-filtered as CGI-edited. I long ago stopped trying to win her approval. She has always been a hard woman to love and if she's not someone I can turn to at midnight when there is nowhere else to go, then she's not someone I can call for help now.

My father is long gone. I have no cousins, no other family to speak of.

Rob is equally alone. His mother died the year before we met and his father is in a care home in Brighton. We visited last time Rob was home, taking the girls to the beach and making a day of it. Graham was having a good day and although he couldn't remember the girls' names, he seemed to know who we were.

My thoughts flip from Rob back to the letter still in my hand. The edges are damp from my clammy grasp. I fold the letter in half and half again and slide it into my pocket before climbing the stairs to check on Harrie.

The curtains are drawn, the room in gloom. Harrie is curled up under her covers, breathing softly, and I leave her to sleep.

I have never felt so alone.

Second interview with Bev Pritchett,
member of Barton St Martin Parish
Council
Interview conducted by Melissa Hart,
The Daily Gazette, 3 November

Bev: I'm so sorry about yesterday.

MH: It's completely understandable, Mrs Pritchett. It's becoming quite clear to me that this is a very close community. The events that have taken place here must have come as a huge shock.

Bev: Yes, that's very true. We are all close.

MH: Will Mr Pritchett be joining us today?

Bev: Oh . . . no, he's gone in to the school. Even when the kids aren't there, there is always paperwork that needs to be completed. He's very dedicated. Some schools don't go as far as they should to teach the kids. It's not all about maths and English, you know? Mike feels he has a duty to give each and every child the best opportunity in life. The Year Fives are learning to manage a budget this term. And he likes the school to be involved with the village events, get the community behind it.

MH: Mrs Pritchett, what was your husband's interest in Elise James? I understand they spent a lot of time together?

Bev: Well yes, they did. Elise wanted to go to a private school which has an entrance exam. Mike was helping her study for it. He knew Anna didn't have the money for a tutor and entry to the school is very competitive. It's all for nothing now, sadly. I just wish I knew what Harrie had been up to last week. I'm sure Mike's already told you this, but she wasn't herself. Something was wrong. Anna messaged us a couple of times asking if we knew something. God knows what she thought we knew. Anyway, Mike did what he could for Elise.

MH: It sounds like you're a very dedicated couple, Mrs Pritchett. You've been on the Parish Council for how long now?

Bev: Oh, ten years at least. Dean and I joined around the same time.

MH: What can you tell me about Dean Stockton?

Bev: Nothing I'm sure you don't already know.

MH: Do you know his wife?

Bev: Sue? Yes. She used to come with Dean to the parties, but she stopped. I don't know why.

MH: What parties are these?

Bev: The normal kind. Anthony and Tracy Campbell normally host. They've got the biggest garden, you see. But we all take it in turns. Mike and I do a Burns Night celebration. Gina and Martin do the summer solstice.

MH: And who came to the parties? I'm assuming not all of the village.

Bev: Oh no. Just the usual group. Kat and Steve, obviously. Gina and Martin. Tracy and Anthony. Jack and Sandra. Dean. Anna and Rob were always invited but they only tended to join us when Rob was home. I wish I could be more help. Have you spoken to Tracy?

Chapter 44

Anna

Harrie sleeps until lunchtime then drags her duvet downstairs and watches a film. I try to talk to her, to find that moment again when she was prepared to open up to me, but it's gone – a locked room I can't get into.

Instead I clean the inside of the kitchen cupboards, pulling everything out first, scrubbing and then packing it all away. It's a job that doesn't need doing but I find comfort in it.

The day disappears and I'm just rallying Harrie to come with me for the school pick-up in the rain when June arrives on my doorstep, proffering a baking tin.

'I thought Harrie might prefer to stay here. I've baked some Halloween biscuits I need some help decorating. That is if you're game, Harrie?'

Harrie smiles for the first time in what feels like forever, and the hardness, the worry inside me, softens.

'We'll save some for Molly and Elise to do too, of course.'

'Thanks, June. You're the best.'

She hands me a biscuit as I'm leaving. 'Eat this,' she says. 'You look like you need it.'

I smile and do as I'm told before walking out into the rain. It's been drizzling since lunchtime and the pavements are slick with it. Puddles dot the road and I walk fast, head down against the cold droplets.

'Anna,' a voice calls from behind me as I reach the alley. I turn to find Tracy jogging towards me, her chocolate Labrador running alongside her, pink tongue flopping out of its mouth. She's wearing her usual activewear beneath a yellow Joules rain mac and looks lithe and radiant. My eyes travel to my black jeans, faded and baggy in the wrong places, and my cheap coat that's already damp on the inside. I feel frumpy and haggard under her gaze.

'Hi, how are you, Tracy?' I say out of politeness. I'm too tired, too everything, to chat. 'All set for Halloween on Saturday?'

'Almost,' she laughs. 'Every year Olivia and Freya egg us on and we end up going crazy. I've had Amazon boxes arriving every day this week. Even Buster here has a devil costume this year.'

I smile and ignore the stab of jealousy that cuts far deeper than it should. The mortgage debt weighs heavy on my mind, but it's not Tracy's fault she has expendable income. I used to be exactly like her, buying whatever took my fancy. It's hard to think of a time when I'll have enough money, let alone anything spare, but if that day comes I will never be frivolous again.

'I was just coming to knock for you,' Tracy says and we pause as Buster cocks his leg and splashes urine up an overgrown thorn bush.

'Oh?'

'It's about the Parish Council clerk role.'

'Actually, that's great because I have a question,' I reply.

'Fire away.'

'I've been reading through the rules of the Parish Council and it states that three quotes are needed for any job undertaken over £500, but I'm sorting everything into folders and I can only find the one quote from Stockton's for the village hall roof. Am I looking in the wrong place for the other quotes? I need to add them to the files in case the Parish Council is ever audited.'

'Oh I'm sure they're somewhere. Can I ask who gave you access to the Google drive?'

'Kat did,' I reply. 'Why? Is there a problem?'

'It's just that we've historically never given a clerk access to all of our files. There is some very confidential information in them and we can't have it getting into the wrong hands.'

'Am I the wrong hands?' I raise my eyebrows and muster a laugh, understanding now why the files are such a mess. They've never had anyone to organize them before.

'I don't know. Are you? You're not exactly the first person to offer to help.' Tracy laughs and nudges me. 'I'm joking, obviously.'

I force myself to smile but the malice in her question stings more than I care to admit.

'I'm sure the other quotes for the village hall roof are somewhere around. I'll dig them out for you.'

'Thank you.'

'Kat wasn't wrong about your organizational skills.' There's something in Tracy's tone that makes it sound far from a compliment and I glance at the side profile of her face and wonder if I'm misreading something.

This whole conversation feels strange, like I'm being told off and I don't know why.

'What did you want to talk about?' I ask as we leave the alley and walk towards the school.

'It's about the emails you've sent to the PC members.'

'Is there a problem?'

'No, of course not. We're so grateful to have you on board and helping out.' She smiles, flashing beautiful white teeth. 'It's just that some of these issues don't need to be sent to all members. As I'm sure you can imagine, some of us are more invested in the work we do than others. As I said at the meeting, Barry Glebe and Mary Swanson are elderly and only attend the AGM. We don't like to bother them with the little things.'

'I see.' I really don't. 'So who shouldn't I be sending emails to?'

'And the horse field rental query that came in,' she continues without answering my question. 'Obviously, it's great that you took the initiative to send out the forms to Mr and Mrs Randell, but we can't rent the field at the moment. It's not in a good state. If we're going to allow live animals in the field then we have a duty of care to ensure it's safe. There's a fence at the back that's fallen down and I'm told the stable roof is leaking. They're relatively easy fixes and we'll get round to them at some point but right now we can't rent the field. If you'd checked with me or Anthony first it would've saved disappointing the Randells.'

'I'm sorry, I didn't realize. I assumed you'd be glad of the income. I'll let Mr Randell know. I'm sure he'll be fine. There's another field in the next village he was looking at too.'

'It's fine. How about for now, you send all the emails

and questions you have to me and I will share them with the relevant people.'

'No problem,' I say as we approach the school, glad of the rain and my hood hiding the worst of my flaming face. Something niggles in the back of my mind but I'm flustered from the conversation and can't pin it down.

Cars are parked in a long snaking line down the road and I'm about to change the subject when Sandra jogs up beside us. She glances between us quickly and from the questioning look on her face I wonder if she can sense the tension too.

'Hey ladies,' Sandra says. 'You'll never guess what.'

'What?' Tracy raises an eyebrow and smiles at me and then Sandra. It's as though the last few minutes didn't happen and I wonder again if I've misinterpreted Tracy's tone.

'Jack just told me that he knows who vandalized the school.'

'Really?' Tracy's voice jumps with excitement. 'Was it that boy Kai?'

'He wouldn't tell me. Apparently he thinks I'm a gossip.' She places a hand on her chest as though the very notion hurts and then she laughs. 'He did say that it wasn't Kai, but that it was someone at the school and that the parents are going to be invited in to a special meeting on Monday.'

'Wow,' Tracy says. 'I wonder who it was. There are some feisty characters in Year Five, don't you think?'

As we enter the playground to collect the children, Sandra and Tracy step away and I stand alone. They bend their heads together and I wonder who they're gossiping about now. Sandra flicks a glance at me before dropping her eyes and my cheeks smart as I realize the answer.

Village Girlies' Secret Group Chat
Thursday 29 October, 16.04

Tracy Campbell: OMG I still can't believe it!

Sandra Briggs: I was pretty surprised too.

Bev Pritchett: What? TELL ME NOW! I hate that you all get to meet without me during the school run.

Sandra Briggs: LOL! You can pick my kids up for me any time, Bev.

Tracy Campbell: Is Jack sure?

Sandra Briggs: 100%.

Kat Morris: What's this about?

Sandra Briggs: Jack knows who vandalized the fence and threw the toilet roll everywhere.

Bev Pritchett: OMG! Just spoke to Mike. Is it bad that I'm not surprised???

**Village Girlies' Secret Group Chat
Friday 30 October, 08.55**

Bev Pritchett: Can't stop thinking about
it! Is anyone going to tell Anna?

Chapter 45

Anna

I step into the school playground, wincing at the noise of the children. My head is pounding from a night of broken sleep and what-ifs. My thoughts flit from one thing to another. Harrie, Rob, debt, Dean, Harrie again and again. In the space of nine days Harrie has faded, morphed – whatever the word – into a child I barely recognize, one I don't know how to read or talk to, and my desperation for answers is eating me alive.

The rain has stopped but the clouds are still looming, threatening to start again at any moment. It feels more like dusk than morning.

'Hey you,' Kat says, nudging her shoulder against mine like she always does. 'How's it going? Are you feeling any better today?'

'Me? I'm fine. It's Harrie I've been worried about.'

'I know. That's what I meant,' she says, but I don't think it was, and I realize with a flash of anger how belittling it is to be constantly told I worry too much, that the problem is me and not the world. I know I'm anxious sometimes, but that doesn't mean I'm wrong or stupid or less than anyone else.

'Can I ask you something?' I say, turning to Kat. Her smile falters but she nods. 'Do you know about this rumour that I'm having an affair with Dean Stockton?'

The answer is there in her silence. No wide-eyed surprise, no 'OMG, what?' She gives a short nod. 'I didn't believe it.'

'Who started it? Where did it come from?'

Kat shrugs. 'Where do any of these stupid rumours come from? Every time I've heard it, I've said it's rubbish.'

'It is.'

'Exactly. Don't worry. It's just village gossip at its worst. I dread to think what people say about me. By the way, did you see that letter from the school about the Christmas Fair? I wondered if you wanted to run a stall together selling hot chocolates and cookies or something.'

'Who did you hear the rumour from?' I ask, ignoring Kat's attempt to change the subject.

'God, I can't even remember. Anna – it doesn't matter. No one believes it. People haven't got anything better to do with their time.'

My heart is thundering in my chest. Heat is pulsing through my body and I want to keep pressing Kat for answers but I know she won't tell me anything more.

'I meant to say,' Kat continues, her voice light and bubbly again, like we're having any other conversation. 'Anthony was asking me if I thought you might be interested in a job working at Stockton's.'

The question throws me. 'What kind of job? I've already done their website.'

'Admin, I think, and also some kind of internet advertising thing. He said a special name ...' She frowns, waving her hand in front of me like a terrible game of charades. 'It's called search something. Anyway, I think you've impressed him with your organizational skills. Just like I knew you would. So what do you think? I think Anthony wants me to sound you out about it first, so he's not putting you on the spot by asking.'

My immediate answer is no. My website business is growing slowly, but it is growing. I need to put myself out there more. Go to one of these local networking events. That's where my focus should be, but the letter from the debt collectors rushes through my mind and I know we need all the money we can get right now. 'I ... guess, maybe. It would depend on the hours.'

'Great,' Kat beams. 'I'll let him know.'

'Thanks.'

'Has there been any word from Rob?' Kat asks then.

Hurt rises up and I think again how Rob has chosen the worst week to disappear. His lies are stacking up. I'm starting to believe that his disappearance is connected to them. Did he know the debt collectors would be getting in touch this week? Is that the real reason he's not called us?

My eyes roam the playground, watching Molly play hopscotch with Olivia. Harrie and Elise are in the corner of the playground talking to Ben. Their heads are bent close. Whatever they're talking about, it looks serious. It looks like they're arguing, in fact.

Mr Pritchett arrives in the playground, checking his watch and nodding to one of the teachers before turning to face me. Our eyes meet for a moment and I smile, lifting my hand in a wave. He stares back for a beat before turning away as though he didn't see my greeting.

'Anna?' Kat says.

'Sorry. Yes, Rob called yesterday. The line was terrible. I don't know what's going on.' My voice cracks. 'I'm hoping he'll call on Sunday or I don't know what I'm going to do. Go to the police, maybe.'

'Oh Anna. Why didn't you call me yesterday? You know I'm here for you. I'm sure Rob is fine. I bet the Wi-Fi is down or something. How's Harrie?'

The bell rings before I can answer and I make a fuss of saying goodbye to the girls. Molly first and then the twins.

'Mum, can I skip gymnastics tonight?' Elise asks as I kiss the top of her head.

'Um . . . I don't know. I guess so. Why? Are you feeling OK?'

She gives a slow nod, her eyes looking from Harrie to the rest of her class, now trudging into school. 'Just tired.'

'All right. Let's see how you are later. Are you sure you're OK to be here today?' I ask Harrie before she can walk away.

She hesitates for a moment. Her face has a gaunt paleness that churns my stomach. 'Think so. Last day before half-term,' she adds with a shrug.

'I'm not going to leave her side today,' Elise says. 'So she can't get in trouble for something she doesn't do.'

I watch Harrie and Elise walk in together, a metre behind the rest of their class, as though separate from them somehow. When I turn around Tracy is standing by Kat's side and they're waiting for me at the gate.

'I just told Tracy about Rob,' Kat says as I approach. 'Is there anything we can do?' Tracy's smile is sympathetic and I find myself searching her face for the tension I felt yesterday, but all I see is concern.

I shake my head. 'I'm sure it's fine. You know what a worrier I am,' I say, hiding behind the very thing I know they all think about me.

We start to move, Tracy one side of me, Kat the other.

'Here.' Tracy pulls out her phone. 'This will cheer you up.' She opens a video and hands me the phone so Kat and I can both watch Buster chasing around the garden like a loon in a red devil costume. Kat laughs and says something to Tracy, but I'm not listening any more. I'm too busy reading my name in the message from Bev that has dropped down from the top of the screen.

I take an extra step forwards and click on the message. The app opens and a stream of messages appear before my eyes. Village Girlies' Secret Group. *What the hell?*

I keep scrolling and take a sharp intake of breath at seeing Kat's name.

'You OK?' Kat asks.

I say nothing as Tracy steps closer, her hand stretched out to take back her phone, but I carry on reading, scrolling up and up. My face feels hot, my skin clammy despite the cold.

'What's this about the vandal?' I ask. 'Why is Bev asking if someone should tell me?'

Kat and Tracy exchange a look. They have the decency to look sheepish.

'I'm not sure how,' Kat says, 'but Jack found out that Harrie was responsible for vandalizing the school.'

My gaze shifts from Tracy to Kat and back again.

'No.' I shake my head. 'Harrie and Elise were with you that day. They came over to play with Ben.'

Kat shrugs. 'I let them go to the park for a bit. She must have done it then.'

I shake my head again.

Harrie is the vandal.

It's not true. It can't be.

Chapter 46

Anna

'We're sorry,' Tracy says, reaching towards me, and I realize I'm still holding her phone.

I jerk my hand, keeping it out of reach. 'Sorry because Harrie is responsible for damaging a fence, or sorry for having a secret message group to gossip about me? What are we, teenagers again?'

'It's an old group,' Tracy tries to explain. 'From before you moved here. It only says "secret" as a joke about not telling the husbands. It's not about—'

'If you've got something to say to me about my children, at least have the decency to say it to my face.' I shove the phone back at Tracy and stride away.

'Anna, wait,' Kat calls after me.

I spin around. 'Don't.' Our eyes meet and I'm ambushed by a sudden wave of hurt. This is my best friend and I don't recognize her at all.

The rain starts as I storm away. Big fat drops of it that soak through my trainers in seconds, but I don't care.

Harrie is the vandal.

I don't believe it.

Harrie wouldn't kick down a fence. I don't care how much she's changed these last few days; I will not believe spiteful gossip without speaking to Harrie and hearing her side of things. I made the mistake of believing Mike Pritchett when he told me Harrie had punched a boy. I won't do the same again.

I have a sudden urge to turn on my heels, march back to the school and get Harrie. I want to scream and shout and beg her to tell me everything, but what good will it do me right now? I need to pull myself together before I speak to Harrie. So I squash it down, and when I reach my front door, I keep walking.

I'm wound up, coiled like a spring, and there is nothing in my house that can relieve this feeling.

I walk to the end of the road, past the empty horse field. The rain stops, the day brightens. I'm hot and frazzled, inside and out. It's only when I reach the edge of the village that I realize where I'm going.

Dean and Sue's house is an old Tudor property, on the corner of the main road. The walls are dark pink, the window frames white. It looks like the wooden doll's house Molly wants for Christmas. A huge wisteria stretches its gnarly branches across the house. I bet it's beautiful in bloom.

The front door is blocked by flowerpots and hanging baskets filled with winter pansies. A brass *Beware of the dog* sign is screwed to a black gate at the side of the house and I hear the first yap as I lift the handle.

Sue looks even older today as she opens a door at the side. Dark circles ring her eyes and there's a tremor in her hand as she scoops Timmy into her arms.

'I'm sorry to bother you,' I stammer, suddenly unsure why I'm here.

Sue doesn't reply and so I carry on. 'I don't really know why I've come, except to ask if Dean is OK. I heard he's in Scotland.'

Sue's eyes widen then narrow. 'Who told you that?'

I open my mouth to reply and realize as I stare into Sue's eyes that they are not the eyes of a woman who knows where her husband is. They are the eyes of worry and fear. The expression is one I recognize. 'So it's not true?'

She shifts Timmy to her other arm and pulls out a ragged tissue from her sleeve. 'Of course it isn't.' Timmy wriggles again and she sighs. 'You might as well come in.'

I slip out of my trainers on the doormat, aware of how rain-soaked I must look, and follow Sue through an old-fashioned kitchen with a huge Aga that takes up an entire wall. Timmy skitters around my feet, jumping at my hand as I bend down to stroke him.

The house is smaller than I expected from the grand pink walls and huge black beams that stretch across the outside. It's long but narrow, the rooms poky. Sue leads me into a fussy living room with floral sofas positioned around a fireplace. There's a large framed photo on the wall of a younger Dean and Sue on their wedding day, and tiny dog ornaments on the mantelpiece.

Sue points at one of the sofas and I sit. 'Do you . . . can I make you a cup of tea?' I ask, feeling stupid because this is her house not mine, and yet Sue looks like a woman who needs a strong cup of tea and a hug.

She shakes her head and sits on the opposite chair. Timmy bounds on to her lap and curls into a ball, tail wagging softly as she pats his head.

'Dean would never go to Scotland. He hates the

weather up there this time of year,' Sue says, reinforcing what I'd already suspected.

'Do you have any idea where he is?'

She shakes her head, freeing a stream of tears. 'You said it yourself, something was bothering Dean. He's been secretive with me in the last few months. But it's more than that. Dean has always struggled with dark moods now and again. Bouts of depression, I suppose, although he never went to the doctor. He'd get them two or three times a year for a few weeks. They'd lift on their own eventually, but this time it kept on and on. He was worried about something happening to him and kept talking about what I should do if he wasn't here any more. It was stupid stuff like where he keeps the deeds for the land and the wills. I thought he was just in a bad place but now I wonder if . . . I wonder if he was so depressed he thought about killing himself, and he called Luke that night because he felt like he might do it and when Luke didn't turn up . . .'

Sue reaches to a glass coffee table and plucks a fresh tissue from a box, dabbing at her eyes. When she looks at me again I see raw pain etched across her face. 'I should've done more to help him, but I thought it would pass like all the rest. I kept telling myself that if I could get him away from this place and to Spain then he'd be happier. He's a different person when he's out there, like the weight of all this is left behind.'

'Why haven't you moved before?'

'Dean kept saying it wasn't the right time. He would come home from the office stressed and drained. He suddenly stopped talking about work, but I got the impression from a few things he said that Anthony was pressuring him to sell more of the business. Whatever was going on it made Dean secretive and unhappy.'

'Unhappy enough to kill himself?'

'Maybe,' she shrugs. 'His car hasn't turned up. Did you know that?' Sue asks. 'The police checked local traffic cameras and they've got Dean driving home from work in the direction of the village and that's it. Nothing more.'

We fall silent for a moment and I can feel my time here winding up. Any minute now Sue will stand and show me to the door and I'll be no closer to understanding what happened that night.

'Sue,' I ask. 'Why did you tell me to be careful the other day? What do I need to be careful about?'

'Not what, but who,' Sue says.

Frustration rears up inside me. I feel myself being dragged into a cryptic conversation I don't understand.

'Sue, please, tell me what you know. Something happened to my daughter the same night Dean went missing. She was home alone, but she may have left the house and whatever happened, I think it's connected to Dean somehow. She's eleven years old and I'm trying to help her. Please.'

Sue swallows, her gaze moving from me to the tissue in her hand. She's tearing it into tiny pieces – a pile of white on her lap.

'Sue—'

'We couldn't have children,' she says, cuddling Timmy closer. 'We tried many times, but it just wouldn't happen. We thought about adopting, obviously,' she says, reading my mind. 'But the last time I was pregnant we made it to twenty-eight weeks before Elizabeth was born. She lived for two hours, but her body wasn't developed enough to survive and so we lost her. It destroyed us in a way I can't begin to explain and I think neither of us wanted to get hurt like that again.'

My hand moves involuntarily towards my stomach as I think of my beautiful children and how lucky I am to have them. My desperation to help Harrie feels suddenly sharp, heightened. 'I'm so sorry.'

'The reason I'm telling you this is so you understand the next bit. Life goes on, sometimes cruelly so, and we began to socialize again. We saw our group of friends in the village. People I'm sure you know well. It took some years but the grief changed me. I no longer felt as though I fitted in. I became more of an observer and that's when I realized there was a sort of subset of people within the friendship group – a group within the group – who stayed later than everyone else at the parties.

'I'm not much of a night person so I was often one of the first to leave. And Dean was one of the last. Sometimes he wouldn't come home until three or four in the morning. As time went on I began to think there was something else going on. I withdrew from the village crowd, but I knew without children to cement our marriage that I had to – or perhaps I chose to – turn a blind eye to whatever Dean was doing, or risk him leaving me.'

'What do you mean a subgroup? Who are you talking about?'

She shrugs. 'Your friend Kat for one. Bev and Mike Pritchett. There are others, I'm sure of it.'

'What kind of things do you think—'

'Sex.' Sue hisses the word like a naughty whisper. 'Or drugs, although I've never seen Dean anything other than a bit tipsy. Whatever it was, something changed in the last few months. Dean went from seeing his friends every week to not seeing them at all. Like I said, I thought he was having a spell of depression.'

'And you think whatever was happening has something to do with Dean going missing?'

'I don't know,' she cries. 'I don't have the answers, Anna. I wish I did. All I know is that he left the office last Wednesday and was seen driving towards the village. He told me he had a stop to make, but never made it home. He texted Luke and said he was in some kind of trouble. I keep turning it over in my mind. But if he killed himself, if he jumped in the river or however he did it, where is his car?'

Sue's voice chokes, her body trembles and I move to sit beside her, rubbing her back as she cries.

'Will you call me if you find out anything about Dean?'

'Of course. I'll do everything I can to find out what happened that night.' We stand and for a moment neither of us knows whether to hug.

Sue shows me out and it's as I'm leaving the garden that she rushes after me. 'I've just remembered something.'

'What?'

'There was a man here a couple of months ago. I was upstairs cleaning, but the windows were open and I heard Dean arguing with someone on the driveway. I looked out and saw this man shouting at Dean, and then out of nowhere the man punches Dean in the face.'

'Was it someone you knew?' I think of Anthony. Always in control. Was he angry that Dean wouldn't sell more of the business to him?

Sue shakes her head. 'I don't think so. He was average-looking but I didn't think I'd seen him before. I wanted to call the police but Dean said not to. He told me it was a carpenter who used to work with Stockton's and was angry at Dean for letting him go. The man said

278

something, some phrase that I thought was odd. Oh, what was it?' A pained expression crosses her face before she shakes her head again. 'I can't remember. At the time, I accepted Dean's explanation, but now I think about it, his dark mood started straight after that.'

On my walk home I turn over in my mind what Sue told me about the parties. A group within a group. What is it? Sex? Drugs? Something else?

Anthony and Tracy.

Kat and Steve.

Gina and Martin.

Bev and Mike.

Jack and Sandra.

Anna and Rob.

I add our names in my head and cast my mind back to the few occasions I've socialized with these people, but I can't remember anything out of the ordinary. I only went when Rob was home, and only to the odd child-friendly BBQ at Tracy's house.

What-ifs float around my thoughts like lost helium balloons, but I still can't see how Harrie fits into this.

What am I missing?

Chapter 47

The night of the crash, 8.31–9.10 p.m.

Harrie

The desire to run throbs through Harrie's body but there's nowhere to go. No escape. Why hasn't Kat called the police? The answer sends a sickening wave of fear crashing into her thoughts. Kat is helping the man, not Harrie.

'It's all right. You're all right.' Kat's voice is far away, floating above Harrie's head. Harrie wants to push Kat away, to shout at her to help, but her body isn't listening to her head any more.

There's blood on Harrie's hands and her clothes. It's drying cold and sticky. She can't stop looking at it. She can't breathe properly.

'Calm down.' Kat's arms wrap around Harrie. 'Breathe slowly, in through the nose and out through the mouth. In, two, three. Out, two, three.'

Harrie does as she's told, counting in her head, and she blinks, her focus returning to the room.

Kat fetches something from the sink and returns

with a dishcloth. She takes one of Harrie's hands in hers and wipes away the blood as though Harrie is a little toddler with ice cream all over her. Kat's touch is gentle, mothering. Tears roll down Harrie's cheeks. Her nose runs too, teeth chattering.

'I want to go home now,' Harrie says in a voice that sounds more like Molly's than her own.

'You will,' Kat says, giving Harrie's hand a squeeze. 'We just need to sort this out. I'd better call your mum. She'll be worried.'

Kat pulls a phone from the pocket of the grey cardigan she always wears and frowns. 'Anna's texted,' she says, looking to the man. 'There's been an accident on the road. She's stuck in traffic. It's going to be a few hours by the looks of it. She's asked me to go round and check on Harrie. What should I reply?'

The man looks at something on his own phone – checking the time, Harrie thinks, because a second later he nods. 'Don't say anything. Pretend you didn't see the message. Let's sort this mess out, shall we?' he says before turning to Harrie. 'Why are you here?'

Harrie takes a gulp of the water Kat has placed on the table beside her. The cold liquid slides too fast down her throat and she chokes.

The man laughs. 'What have you given her? Vodka?'

'Don't be an idiot,' Kat hisses back. 'Can't you see she's terrified?'

Harrie flinches, waiting for the man to retaliate. Kat has called him an idiot. He'll be mad. He'll hit them both, but instead he laughs again. Harrie forces her eyes up from the blood on her knees to Kat's face. She thought Kat was scared, she thought they were both trapped here, but now she isn't so sure. Kat doesn't seem scared any more, she seems angry.

'Harrie,' Kat prompts, her eyes searching Harrie's face in a way that makes her feel exposed. 'Why did you come here tonight?'

'I wanted . . .' Harrie touches the hard plastic of the phone still hidden in her pocket. 'I wanted to ask Ben a question about the homework.' Harrie picks up the glass and takes another sip, this time slower, hoping Kat won't ask what homework.

'Ben's not here. He's gone to watch West Ham play with Steve. And this homework question, it couldn't wait until tomorrow?'

'I didn't know Ben wasn't here. I thought it would be fun to come at night while Mum was out,' Harrie lies. Nothing about this has been fun, but at least she's got Ben's phone. It doesn't seem important any more, but she knows it still is.

Harrie thinks about Elise and how badly she wishes her sister was here. How will she tell Elise about the mess she's in? About the man bleeding on the floor and the other one, standing over her.

That stupid video. She hates Ben. This is all his fault.

Chapter 48

Anna

I watch Harrie scoop up a football from the floor of her bedroom, hugging it like a teddy. Molly is downstairs in front of the TV. Elise is at the kitchen table doing homework and Harrie is here, not talking.

I sit beside her, trying so hard to be patient, to be two parents in one – good cop, bad cop – supportive but firm. I push at a discarded T-shirt with my foot and feel like I'm failing at both.

'I don't care about the fence or the toilet roll. I'm on your side. I just want you to tell me what happened.'

'It wasn't me. Why don't you believe me?'

'I do believe you.' My words lack conviction and Harrie knows it. 'But let's not pretend that something hasn't been going on with you since that night I left you. You can deny it all you want, you can lie to my face, but I know something happened that night. So I think you can understand why I have to ask about the vandalism.'

'I'm telling the truth. It wasn't me.'

There's a noise from outside the door.

Harrie leaps up, slamming her hand on the wood. 'Go away, Elise. This is nothing to do with you.' I jump at the sharpness to Harrie's tone. It's Elise who snaps at Molly, not Harrie at Elise. They've never spoken to each other like that before.

'Harrie?' I cry out.

'What?' She spins back to me. 'She was eavesdropping.' Tears roll down Harrie's cheeks. Her face is blotchy red. She kicks the football in the air with her foot. Tap, tap, tap.

'Do you know who did cause the damage at the school?'

Tap. Tap. Tap.

'Harrie? Answer me, or there is no trick-or-treating for you tomorrow.'

Harrie sighs, letting the ball drop and roll across the carpet. 'It was Ben, OK? Ben did it. But everyone is blaming me for everything. It's not my fault.' Harrie throws herself face down on to the bed.

'I believe you,' I tell her, meaning it this time.

I find Elise slumped on the stairs, tears streaming down her face. 'Hey,' I say. 'It's OK. Harrie didn't mean to shout.'

'I know,' Elise sniffs. 'Can you help with my maths now?'

'Sure.'

'Mummy.' Molly appears at the bottom of the stairs. 'Since we're not going to gymnastics tonight, can we play hide and seek?'

I nod. 'But I just need to help Elise first, OK baby? Can we play in twenty minutes?'

'I'll play with you,' Harrie says from her bedroom doorway. Harrie looks at Elise and something passes between them – a silent apology, I think.

'Yaaay! I'll hide first,' Molly shouts.

'Let's play in the garden,' Harrie says.

We troop downstairs. Me to the table with Elise, and Harrie and Molly to play in the garden.

'Just until it gets dark,' I say as they rush outside into the dusky late afternoon.

'Mum?' Elise says. 'Is Harrie OK?'

'I don't know, sweetheart.'

I explain dividing fractions to Elise and as she bends her head over her books I replay Harrie's words over and over in my mind.

It was Ben.

So why does the whole village think it was Harrie? I'll speak to the school and Jack Briggs and find out what they know.

'Mummy.' Molly's voice drags me back to the kitchen. 'I can't find Harrie,' she says from the back door.

I'm about to stand and help Molly when Elise pushes her book towards me. 'Mum, I don't think this one is right. Was I supposed to make the bottom numbers the same? It's so hard. I'm never going to do well enough for the scholarship, am I?' Fresh tears brim in Elise's eyes and I take her hand and squeeze it in mine.

'You can do this,' I tell Elise. 'You've been working so hard.'

'Mummy?' Molly calls again.

'Keep looking, Molly,' I call out. 'It'll be cheating if I help you. Try the shed.'

Molly spins around and races down the garden and I try to help Elise with the maths I barely understand myself.

Chapter 49

Harrie

Harrie sobs as she stares at the cage. Why isn't he moving?

'Dean?' She sniffs and the putrid smell makes her gag. 'Wake up.'

There's something wrong with the way Dean is sitting, Harrie thinks. He's upright against the back of the cage like he always is, but the top half of his body is slumped to one side and his head is drooping so far down to his chest it's like it's not even connected to his neck any more.

'Dean?' Her voice trembles. Her mouth is dry and she wants to run away and never come back to this place, but her feet are rooted to the spot.

The only reply is the slow lazy hum of a fly hovering nearby.

She wished he was dead but she didn't mean it.

It's all her fault.

She should never have taken the phone. The wrong phone, it turns out.

It was supposed to be Ben's. It looked exactly the

same as Ben's one. Black cover. White face. But when Ben came into school that Thursday he still had his phone. He still had the video. And the stupid thing – the unbelievable thing – is that when he told them again that he was going to share it and Harrie said, 'Go on then,' instead of pressing send, Ben shrugged and told them he'd only been messing around.

Everything she'd done was for nothing. And now a man is dead and she could've saved him. Tears blur her eyes and she turns away, walking on legs that don't feel like her own.

It's over.

She never has to come back here again.

Except it's not over, Harrie realizes. She still has Dean's phone. She's still in a heap of trouble. Her mum and Elise and Molly are still in danger.

What does she do now? She can't go to the police and she can't tell Elise or her mum.

You tell anyone about this and I promise you I will know, and then I'll kill your mum and your sisters, and I'll make you watch and then I'll kill you.

An idea starts to form in Harrie's thoughts. She could speak to Kat. She could give Kat Dean's phone, and then Kat will sort it all out. Harrie will go to Kat's tomorrow. It will be easy to slip away during trick-or-treating.

Harrie runs across the field as fast as her legs will carry her, wishing it was Dean's voice chasing her away and not his silence.

Chapter 50

Saturday, Halloween

Anna

I'm jittery. Distracted. Going through the motions of normal life. Clubs and lunch and playing with Molly. Checking on the twins. Washing and cleaning like everything is fine, and I keep catching myself doing it and thinking *what the hell?* I can't carry on as normal any more. Too much is happening. Rob, Dean, Harrie. A village group up to something. Bloody trousers. My head spins with it all – an out-of-control carousel.

And yet it's Halloween and Molly is bouncing with excitement and I have to focus. She's been staring out of the window every ten minutes and declaring it almost dark since three p.m., and now it really is almost time to go and I'm on my tiptoes, digging through the top shelf of the wardrobe in the twins' room, searching for the black silk gloves to go with Molly's witch's costume, which I know are in here but can't for the life of me find. I stretch a little further, arm muscles crying out in pain, and the edge of my hand brushes against something hard. I tease it towards me with the tips of my fingers until the weight of it is clasped in my hand and I know before I see it that it's a phone.

I pull it from the shelf and then it's lying in the palm of my hand. An iPhone.

This isn't Harrie's or Elise's. Neither of them has a phone and there's no way they could have bought one without me knowing. Even second-hand it would cost hundreds of pounds and neither of them has that kind of money.

I press a button and the screen lights up. It's locked, password-protected, but I can see an ominous red empty-battery symbol in the top right corner and a list of missed calls and text messages. There are dozens. Some are withheld but others I recognize. Anthony Campbell is one. Sue is another. And one name that stands out above all the rest. My own.

Anna James: 3 missed calls.

My pulse is racing as I look past the call list to the photo in the background, the sky-blue Stockton's logo I know so well from working on the website.

I rush downstairs, phone in hand, and find my own sitting on the side. Dean's name is in my recent contacts and I know before I press it that when I do, my name will appear on the other phone's screen.

I connect the dots from what I know to what I don't. Dean was last seen in the village ten days ago. The same evening that I got stuck on the road and left Harrie alone for hours. The same evening Dean's brother was speeding towards the village and died in a car crash.

There was mud on the floor in the kitchen that night. The back door was unlocked. There was blood on Harrie's clothes. She said Dean's name in her sleep and she has his phone. I don't know what happened yet or what connects them, but I'm going to find out.

'Did you find the gloves, Mummy?' Molly says from beside me, her little voice making me jump. I slip Dean's phone into my pocket and turn to face her.

'No, I didn't, but you can wear my woolly ones if you promise not to drop them?'

'I promise,' she grins, oblivious to the shake in my voice. 'Can we get dressed now?'

Outside the last of the light is slipping from the day.

'Good idea. Elise, Harrie,' I call out. 'Time to get dressed in your costumes.'

'I want to be Cruella De Vil from *101 Dalmatians*,' Molly announces.

I'm too distracted by the weight of the phone in my pocket, the weight of questions lying heavy on my mind, to listen. Elise and Harrie appear from the living room and run upstairs without a word. I want to call Harrie back and ask her about the phone, but what is the point? It will just end with another tearful argument and we're already running late. I promised Molly she could trick-or-treat with Olivia and the rest of her class. The phone, the questions – it will have to wait an hour until we're back and Molly is watching TV with a bucket of chocolate and sweets.

'Mummy? I said I want to be Cruella De Vil.'

'But you said you wanted to be a witch,' I reply, my gaze moving to the kitchen table, now strewn with Halloween paraphernalia. Face paints and cotton pads, vampire teeth and devil's horns. No Cruella De Vil outfit, nothing I can cobble together to look even remotely like the evil character with one half of her hair white and the other black.

'But I don't want to be a witch,' Molly says, her face a deep frown.

'Sweetheart,' I start, injecting as much calm, as much understanding, into my voice as I can. 'Last month when I asked you, you said you wanted to be a witch and so I've made you a witch's costume.' I don't mention staying up until midnight cutting up an old black cocktail dress and sewing it into a cape because last year's one came from Poundland and ripped after two minutes. 'I've even put spooky green thread on your hat so it looks like you have green hair.'

The frown remains but she doesn't argue as she reaches out to caress the hat. 'Will you paint my face green too, so I look really spooky like that witch in that show that Olivia went to see?'

I stare down at the face paints on the table. The green is almost empty from Elise's Frankenstein face last year. I can see the bottom of the pot and the edges are dried and cracked. Surely some water will revive it. There might be just enough to cover Molly's face. 'Absolutely.' I paste on a smile as the twins appear in the kitchen.

Harrie is wearing last year's werewolf costume. It's too small around the legs and I can see skinny ankles sticking out the bottom of the brown baggy trousers. It has gloves with matted grey fur and a full head mask.

Elise stands beside her, wearing her favourite pink PJs. The ones with the black stars and the swirly writing. *Dream Big*.

'Where's your costume?' I ask Elise. 'You're not going out in PJs, are you?'

'I don't want to go,' she says.

'Why not? Are you feeling all right?'

Molly dances at my feet and I grab the face paint and dab it with a damp ball of cotton wool. It remains like a rock. Only when I slop some water into the dish and rub it against the paint does the cotton wool turn a hopeful green.

'Not really,' Elise replies. 'Can I stay here?'

I hesitate, feeling torn in two, right down the middle. I don't want to drag Elise out in the cold if she's unwell. But Molly's lip is already wobbling and I can't let her down. I've been so focused on Harrie this last week I've neglected Molly. She's always been my go-with-the-flow baby – not that she's ever had much choice in the matter, being born the younger sister to twins. But Molly is just as aware as her sisters that she hasn't spoken to her daddy this week and the brief moment he called on Thursday has done nothing to settle any of our worries.

I'll go to the police on Monday, I decide suddenly. I should've done it earlier. What I'll say dances tauntingly in my head and I wonder if Rob will be nothing more than a case number like Dean. *My husband has been lying to me for years about where he's been and about a mortgage debt I knew nothing about, and now he's not come back at all.* Hardly a priority case.

I'll have to tell the children something soon. The weight of my own secret lies like a stone in my belly. I'll have to tell them a lot of things soon.

'Are we still going?' Molly's voice is soft and whiny.

'Of course,' I smile. 'Now stay still and let me pop this face paint on.' I run the cotton-wool ball over Molly's skin until her whole face is a pale green. It's a washed-out version of a witch but Molly grins when she looks in the mirror and that's enough for me.

I grab the house phone from its holder and June answers on the second ring.

'Say no more,' June says when I explain about Elise. 'I'll be around in five.' Her voice is so full of joy, it's as though I've just invited her on an all-inclusive holiday to the Caribbean. June has been a rock to me this past week. I think about what she said about my closeness to Dean. *If you'd developed a friendship with a woman . . . would you have questioned whether we were having an affair?* Now I wish it had been June I'd been close to.

She hangs up and I turn back to Elise who is pulling an 'I don't need a babysitter' face, but she says nothing. The battle is already won and I smile gratefully and kiss the top of her head.

'We'll only be an hour. We're just going to do the estate.'

'And Olivia's house,' Molly says. 'We have to do Olivia's house.'

'Of course.' I cringe inwardly. Tracy is the last person I want to see. I wonder briefly if it's too late to hide behind a costume.

'Mum, it's five. Can I go? I can see Sandra on the corner with the others,' Harrie says, her voice muffled by the mask.

'I thought you were meeting at five thirty? I was going to walk with you.' I glance around for my phone to check the messages but it's hiding somewhere in the mess. I'm trying not to think about the secret group, their gossip about Harrie and Elise. Kat and Tracy have texted a few times, but I've ignored them. They've simultaneously managed to apologize and tell me it's no big deal and not what I think. *Silly Anna worrying*

293

again. I can't ignore them forever, but it's something else that can wait until Monday.

'Mum?' Harrie says. 'It's definitely five. I can see them.'

'We just need a few minutes,' I say, grabbing Molly's witch dress from the kitchen table.

'Mum,' Harrie whines now, sounding just as upset as Molly did a minute ago. 'Please. I said I'd meet them and you said I could go. Sandra is taking us. It's not like we're on our own.'

Harrie inches towards the front door and I must hesitate a moment too long because it swings open and before I can protest she is leaving, just as June is walking in.

'I'll meet you on the way round,' I call after her. 'Sandra said you're going clockwise around the estate, so we'll go the other way and we'll bump into you at some point. Elise and June will be here to let you in if we miss each other. And make sure Sandra drops you back.'

'Yes, Mum,' Harrie shouts, already running down the dark street. I watch her jog towards a group of trick-or-treaters. She slows as she reaches them and I close the door and turn to June.

'Thanks so much for doing this.'

She bats my thanks away. A pesky fly. 'Any instructions?' June asks.

I think of the debris from the Halloween costumes scattered across the table. 'I . . . I'm sorry about the mess.' For a moment I'm floundering, half of me still with Harrie running down the road, another part anchored here, wanting to wait for her to return. 'No, no instructions.'

'Mummy, can we go?' Molly asks. She's pulled the

294

dress over her leggings and T-shirt and is clutching an empty plastic cauldron, ready to be filled with sweets.

June waves us off with a don't-worry smile that radiates such kindness it almost breaks me, and then I'm pulled away into the cold night.

Chapter 51

Anna

It's well over an hour before I'm home from trick-or-treating with Molly. Longer than I thought. Longer than I wanted. I searched for Harrie in every group of children but I didn't see her. I didn't see Sandra or any of Harrie's friends either. They must have gone a different route.

My body is bone tired, running on empty. All I want to do is snuggle with the girls in our PJs.

'We're back,' I call out as I unpeel my layers – my coat, my scarf, my hat, the extra jumper. I tried to smile for Molly, to laugh and enjoy this for her. There won't be many more years that Molly will want my company. Soon, she'll be like Harrie and want to go with her friends, or like Elise and decide not to bother at all. But I couldn't keep the worry from chasing me.

I find June knitting on the sofa in the living room. Elise is sat beside her holding a ball of baby-blue wool.

'Did you have a nice time?' June asks.

'Yessss,' Molly answers. 'Look how many sweets I got.' She holds up the bucket. It's overflowing with

Haribo packets and lollies and eyeball-shaped chocolates. 'You can share some with me,' Molly says, smiling at Elise.

'Thanks,' she replies.

'Is Harrie upstairs?'

A look of surprise crosses June's face at the exact moment Elise says, 'No, she's not back yet.'

'Oh.' I check my watch. It's been an hour and a half. 'I'm sure she'll be back any minute.'

'I'll leave you to it.' June scoops up her wool and pats Elise's shoulder. 'Nice to talk to you.' She turns to me as she leaves. 'You know where I am, Anna, if you need me.'

'Thank you. You're a lifesaver.'

'Can I watch TV?' Molly asks the second it's just the three of us in the house. She's jiggling from foot to foot. Already she's had too much sugar. There's a rim of chocolate around her lips and her cheeks are rosy from the cold night.

'Yes, but just while I cook the pizzas.'

'Pizza? Yessssss. Is it a takeaway? Olivia is getting Domino's tonight.'

I shake my head. 'Homemade, but with extra cheese. No more treats until after dinner.'

Molly sticks out her bottom lip for a moment before skipping away to the living room.

Elise shuffles towards me. Her movements are slow, like how she drags her feet when it's time to get in the car for Molly's swimming lesson and she doesn't want to go.

'Are you hungry?' I ask, switching on the oven. My eyes pull to the clock on the wall. Where is Harrie? 'Pizza will be ready in ten minutes.'

She shakes her head and instead of walking upstairs, she slides into a chair at the table.

'You have to eat something.'

'I'll wait until Harrie gets back.'

'I'm sure she'll be back any minute.' I pick up my phone and check the messages. Nothing from Sandra on the village group.

It's only when the pizza is on the table and Harrie isn't back that I allow the worry to take over.

'Where's Harrie?' Molly asks, the words muffled by the crust she's eating.

'I don't know,' I say, too distracted to tell her not to talk with her mouth full. I reach for my phone and message the village girlies' chat group.

Me: Has anyone got Harrie with them? She hasn't come back from trick-or-treating yet. @SandraBriggs she said she was meeting you at 5 p.m. Have you seen her?

Tracy Campbell: Sorry, no.

Gina Walker: She's not here. Clarissa says Harrie wasn't with them.

The panic circles closer and closer as the messages ping on to my phone.

Me: Really? Are you sure?

Sandra Briggs: I kept an eye on all of them and Harrie definitely wasn't there. What costume was she wearing?

Me: A werewolf. Same as last year. If anyone sees her, please call me!

Gina Walker: Will do. Let us know when she's home safe x

'Mum?' Elise's voice drifts in the background. 'Mum?'

My focus is on my phone and the messages I read two then three times. It doesn't make sense. Blood rushes through my body. My head feels light. My eyes move to the clock. It's nearly seven p.m. Harrie left the house two hours ago to meet her friends. Except she didn't. So where is she?

'Mum?' The urgency in Elise's voice startles me from my thoughts and I look up. Elise's face has drained of all its colour. She's pale, her eyes wide – scared – and she's biting her bottom lip. 'I have to tell you something.' There's a breathlessness about the way she says it and I wonder if I hold my own breath, stay completely still, will I be able to hear her heart beating as fast as my own?

'Molly, sweetheart,' I say, my eyes still fixed on Elise. 'As a special treat, why don't you take your pizza and eat it in front of the TV?'

'Really? Thank you. Thank you.' She jumps up and is gone in a flash, her pizza slices sliding around the plate. A moment later the sound of cartoons fills the silence.

I place my phone on the table and look at Elise. 'Do you know where Harrie is?'

She nods.

Chapter 52

Anna

Tears swim in Elise's eyes. 'I'm the one who broke the fence and threw the toilet roll over the school field.'

'What?'

'I'm sorry.'

'But Harrie said it was Ben.'

'She just said that to protect me. I wanted to tell you yesterday but Harrie wouldn't let me. That's why she shouted at me. She said it didn't matter that everyone thinks it's her, but it does. It matters to me.'

'If you're trying to protect Harrie—'

'No.' Elise shakes her head. 'It wasn't Harrie, Mum. It was just me. I'm sorry.' The tears leak from her eyes and for a moment she can't speak from the emotion gripping her.

'It's OK,' I say. 'You should've come to me earlier and told me, but it's OK. It's only toilet roll.'

She nods and takes a shuddering breath. 'I didn't mean for the fence to break. It fell over as I was climbing back over it. I didn't kick it down like they said.'

'Tell me what happened.'

'We . . . we were at Ben's house and Kat doesn't mind us going out to the park by ourselves.' She looks up, her face sheepish. 'You wouldn't have let us go on our own. Kat said she wouldn't say anything.'

I bite down on the inside of my lip, hiding my frustration. Kat had no right to let them play out alone. They're too young to always make the right choices, but 'I told you so' are my mother's words, not mine. 'Go on,' I say encouragingly.

'We were playing truth and dare. Ben dared me to throw the toilet roll over the tree in the school field, and I know it was stupid, but he was saying I was boring because all I did was my schoolwork. So I did it and then the fence broke and everyone started saying it was vandalism and the person who did it was in big trouble.' She gasps and takes a breath but I don't tell her to slow down.

'And then . . .' She swallows, fighting back the tears. 'I hadn't known at the time but Ben filmed it on his phone and was threatening to share it round the class. But if he did that then I knew Mr Pritchett would find out and he wouldn't help me with my tutoring any more and he wouldn't write me a recommendation for the scholarship and I wouldn't be able to go to St Benedict's.' Elise sobs, and the weight of what she's carried with her for the past couple of weeks leaks on to the table, my own guilt with it. I've been so focused on Harrie – did I miss something with Elise?

I want to take her in my arms and tell her everything will be all right, but she's not done yet and I know by the look on her face that the worst is still to come.

'How did Harrie get involved?'

'At first Harrie said she'd tell everyone it was her

301

that did it and take the blame, but it wouldn't have worked because I'm wearing my gymnastics hoody with my name on and you can hear Harrie calling to me to stop. So then we begged Ben to delete the video and he just laughed and said he would if I kissed him.' Red spots appear on Elise's face. An anger bubbles inside me. 'I thought if he'd delete the video then it would be OK.'

'And he didn't?'

'No,' she cries out. 'So Harrie came up with this plan to sneak into his house when he wasn't expecting us and take his phone. Kat always keeps her back door open and makes Ben leave his phone in their spare room on charge in the evenings. We thought it would be easy to get in and out. It was just to delete the video. We would've given it back to him afterwards,' she says quickly, as if I care one iota about Ben's phone right now. If I had the thing in front of me I'd smash it to pieces myself.

Then it all starts to click into place.

'That Wednesday we got stuck, that's when Harrie went out?'

She nods, dropping her head. 'I'm sorry.'

'What happened?'

'I don't know, but it was bad, Mum. Harrie went into Kat's kitchen and saw a phone and took it and then something happened but she wouldn't tell me what, but it wasn't Ben's phone. I've been begging her to tell me, but she just keeps saying she can't. And then today just before she left she said the phone belonged to that man.'

My mouth drops open. I can't believe it.

Elise makes a face.

'Harrie didn't go trick-or-treating with the others, did she?' I ask, the panic gripping me tighter.

Elise shakes her head. 'She went to speak to Kat to ask her to help and give Dean's phone back, but we can't find it. We've lost it, Mum.'

'Kat?'

'I think she was there that night. She knows what happened to Harrie.'

Something inside me breaks – a hairline fracture tracing its way right down my middle. I think of my friendship with Kat. All those cups of tea, the laughter, the support we've given each other. The play dates, the wine, the gossip. I trusted her with my girls and she let them play out behind my back. She told them to lie to me.

Kat's voice rings in my head. *Harrie is fine . . . it's probably hormones.*

I told her the day after the crash that I thought something was wrong. She tried to convince me I was worrying over nothing, while the whole time she knew what had happened to my daughter.

'I think Mr Pritchett knows Harrie took the phone as well,' Elise says, filling the silence.

'What?'

'He did this whole assembly on stealing and was looking at Harrie the whole time. Plus he totally made up that stuff about Harrie being in a fight. Why else would he do that, Mum? Harrie thinks Kat can help us, and . . .' Elise drops her head. 'She's been sneaking out and won't tell me where she's going.'

I close my eyes, thinking of the argument with Harrie last Sunday. She stormed off, returning with mud covering her shoes.

'She was supposed to go to Kat's and then come back and I'd stay here and let her in and we'd pretend she finished trick-or-treating early. But she hasn't come back and I think it's because we couldn't find the phone.' Elise crumbles into a heap of sobbing and I reach over and wrap her tight in my arms.

'I have the phone,' I tell Elise. 'I found it earlier when I was looking for the Halloween costumes.'

'You have to give it to Kat,' Elise half shouts. 'Harrie was only trying to help me. This is all my fault.'

'None of this is your fault, Elise. You should have come to me straight away, but it's not your fault.'

There is so much of what Elise has told me that I can't wrap my head around. I've always thought of myself as an observant mother. I'm here in the morning and after school. I talk to them. I'm watchful, but I've been clueless. Truly and utterly clueless.

'Are you going to go to Kat's?'

I nod, already standing up.

'I'll look after Molly,' Elise says and I don't know whether to laugh or cry at her offer. Instead I say nothing. After another pleading call, June is back at my door in less than a minute.

'Thank you,' I say as she steps inside, still in her slippers, with a shawl over her shoulders.

I say a hurried goodbye to Molly and tell Elise to call me if Harrie comes home, and then I run from the house, my mind sticking on Kat's involvement. I might not have known Kat as well as I thought I did, but she'd never hurt Harrie, would she?

Chapter 53

Harrie

The dark streets are alive with children and noise. Little kids in bright costumes sticking out from winter coats. Parents and pushchairs and dogs dressed up too. There are older kids as well. Groups of teenagers who Harrie probably knows but the paint and the masks hide their faces just as Harrie is hiding hers. Fake cobwebs and skeletons decorate people's driveways. Huge orange pumpkins glow from doorsteps.

Nobody notices the lone werewolf walking down the road. Nobody stops to ask her why she is alone, why she hasn't got a bucket for sweets. Harrie feels invisible as she makes her way to Kat's house. Ben will be leaving to join their friends for trick-or-treating soon and Harrie will be ready when he does.

She feels a pang then, a deep unsettling longing. It's not for the trick-or-treating or the sweets and chocolates they'll collect, it's not the jokes her friends will share without her and the laughter she'll miss out on, it's something else she can't explain. She wants to undo everything that has happened and be like her friends

305

again, be able to trust adults, and most of all she wishes she didn't know that there's a man lying dead in a cage.

Harrie has lied to her mum again. It feels as bad this time as it did the first time and she wishes it would all stop. But without the phone, Harrie doesn't know if it will ever stop.

How could she have lost the phone? It was there yesterday. Harrie checked. But when she went to get it just now, it was gone. She wonders for a moment if Molly could have taken it. She's always sneaking into their room to borrow books or hairbands. But the phone was on the top shelf of the wardrobe. There's no way Molly could have reached it.

Harrie has played that night in Kat's kitchen over and over in her head and she's sure now that Kat didn't know what was going to happen to Dean. Kat is nice. She's a normal mum. Maybe if Harrie had gone to Kat earlier, Dean would still be alive.

An image of Dean's body flashes in Harrie's thoughts. Pain slices through her stomach. She has to make this OK, if not for her then for Elise. Elise will be OK. She can get the scholarship to the fancy school. She can be happy enough for both of them. Harrie isn't sure she'll ever be happy again.

Harrie slips through the gate and into Kat's garden. She sticks close to the wall, retracing her steps from ten days ago. She hears Kat's voice from the driveway calling out to Ben. 'Have a good time.' Then the front door closes and a moment later the kitchen light flicks on. Harrie steps through the back door and into the kitchen.

'Hello?' Kat says, her face frowning with confusion.

Harrie pulls off her mask and stuffs it into her pocket. Her face is already wet with tears.

'Harrie?'

She nods.

'You all right, love? Ben's just left. You'll catch him if you run.'

'No.' Harrie shakes her head and hair falls out of its ponytail, dropping over her face. 'I need your help. Please. Dean is locked in a cage.' The words tumble out and Harrie is crying and struggling to breathe and talk at the same time, but she can't stop. 'He left Dean there to die and I've been taking him food and water but I couldn't unlock the cage and now he's . . .' A sob shudders through Harrie's body. 'He's dead.'

'Oh my God.' Kat reaches out and hugs Harrie tight. 'You poor thing. Why didn't you say something sooner?'

'I didn't want to get put in the cage too. He said . . . he said he'd hurt my mum and Elise and Molly if I told anyone.'

'Hey, come on now. No one is going to hurt anyone and no one is locking you in the stable. We can sort this out.' Kat rubs Harrie's back. 'You're freezing. Let me get you one of Ben's jumpers to put on. Stay here. You'll be all right now. I'll help you, I promise.'

Harrie stands frozen to the spot, her body trembling with cold and fear and relief all jumbled together. Kat is going to help her. Harrie covers her face with her hands, allowing the silent tears to stream down her face. But something is nagging in the back of her mind. Harrie didn't mention the stable, so how does Kat know where the cage is?

In three steps she's by the kitchen door, peering through the gap into the hall. Kat is by the front door, her back to the kitchen, and she's whispering into her phone.

'Just shut up a minute. We need to be careful. Anna

has been poking her nose in . . . I know, I know. I was wrong. We have to stop her. Just get here now . . . Fine. I will.'

For a second it feels like the floor is giving way to empty space and Harrie is going to fall right through it.

Kat isn't going to help her.

Harrie bites down on her lip as angry tears pool in her eyes. She needs to get away before it's too late again. She needs to escape this house, this horrible village that she hates more than anything else in the world. The promise tears at her chest. If she stays, they'll hurt her mum and sisters and it will be Harrie's fault. She has to leave or they'll never be safe.

Harrie runs out the back door, out the gate. She pulls on her mask and threads through the groups of trick-or-treaters. Every step she expects to feel a hand on her shoulder.

Chapter 54

Anna

I head straight through the gate and fly through the back door into Kat's kitchen. She's standing by the sink with a glass of wine in one hand and her phone in the other. The house is warm, the kitchen tidy and bathed in the soft glow of the lights beneath the cabinets. If it wasn't for my desperation to find Harrie, I'd find it inviting.

'I was just texting you,' she smiles as though it's nothing that I've burst straight through her door. Like the secret group is all forgotten, like she hasn't lied and lied and lied to me.

'Where's Harrie? HARRIE?' I shout her name, moving straight to the hall and shouting again.

'She's not here, Anna. What's going on?' Kat's face is the picture of concern and for a moment all I see is my best friend, the person who is kind and loving and makes me laugh. The moment passes and I round on Kat.

'Let's stop pretending. I know all about your secret group.'

She sighs and picks up a hand cream from the side.

It's one from the beauty range she sells and smells of coconuts and long-ago holidays by glistening pools. 'I've explained that, Anna. Don't make more of it than it is. You can join it right now if you want.'

'Not that group.'

'What then?'

I stare at Kat's face and think I see an unease lurking beneath her cooler-than-cool facade.

'You, Dean, Mike and the others.' I sound vague, but I don't know who else is involved. It could be more. 'What is it? Sex parties? Drugs?'

Kat laughs and something in her posture relaxes. 'You've got an active imagination, Anna. Jealous, are you? Well, there's no need to be. Can you really see us all swapping partners on a Friday night? Steve and Bev? Me and Mike? Please. I'm afraid you've got this all wrong. We're a close friendship group, a close community – surely you've figured that out by now. There's nothing else going on here. Listen to yourself, Anna. You're always worrying—'

'No, don't you dare do that,' I snap. 'I know there's something dodgy going on. Is this about Dean's business? Anthony wanted him to sell it to him and you're helping Anthony.'

Kat stiffens. It's a game of find the missing object. Colder or hotter, and I've just got hot. Kat and Anthony. Anthony and Kat. For a moment I wonder if they're having an affair. Is she helping Anthony for love? It doesn't fit somehow. I might not know Kat as well as I thought I did, but she and Steve are rock solid. An affair isn't Kat's style.

Anthony, Kat, Dean. Mike.

How are they connected?

They're all on the Parish Council except Mike. He

isn't, but Bev is. Is that the link I'm missing? Frustration courses through my veins but I keep coming back to one thing – Harrie. She is all that matters in this.

'Where is Harrie? I know she came here.'

Something in Kat's face changes. I see a fear I've never seen before. 'I don't know. I thought she went home.'

I sigh through gritted teeth and fight back the surge of rage. I want to ask what happened that night, but I'm sick of the questions. Everyone is lying. I must find Harrie.

My phone buzzes in my hand and I pray it's Elise calling to tell me Harrie is home, but it's not. It's a message from Gina.

```
Hi Anna, have you found Harrie? I think
I just saw her running up towards the
river. Tried to call to her but she dis-
appeared. Let me know if she's OK! xx
```

'What is it?' Kat asks, leaning closer and trying to look at my phone. 'Let me see.'

I lock the screen and slip it into my pocket as Kat reaches out, grabbing my arm.

'Let her go, Kat,' a voice says from behind me as I yank myself free from Kat's grasp. I spin around, my jaw dropping. And I see it. The silver car pulled up outside my house. I thought it looked familiar because I'd seen it before. It's Sandra's car.

It's not Anthony Kat is helping. It's Jack Briggs.

He's a policeman, a father. He's supposed to help people, but he's involved in this.

More questions pummel my thoughts, but I ignore them and run.

Chapter 55

The night of the crash, 9.10–10.30 p.m.

Harrie

Kat reaches for a bottle of wine. She twists off the lid and pours a glass before taking three long gulps.

Harrie wishes she could change her trousers. The blood on them is stiff and sticky. It's making her feel sick.

The man moves closer then and Harrie shrinks down in the chair.

'Do you know who I am?' he asks.

She shakes her head.

'I'm Jack Briggs.'

'Tyler's dad?' Harrie asks, thinking of the blond-haired boy in her class. Harrie gets on well with most of the boys at school, but she doesn't like Tyler very much. He's always bragging about the holidays he goes on and the stuff his parents buy him, like he's trying to make Harrie jealous. Sometimes it works. Plus, Tyler was mean to Elise last year when she forgot her lines in the school play, and Harrie hasn't forgotten that nasty snigger, even if Elise has.

Harrie looks at the man again. It's always Tyler's mum at the drop-off with Tyler and his little sister, but there is something familiar about the man now that Harrie looks at him again.

Then it hits her.

Of course she knows him. Her mind is all jumbled and she didn't recognize him without his uniform. He came into the school once to talk to them about internet safety. He was at the summer fete too, talking for ages with her mum and dad.

Tyler is always bragging about his dad, another thing he does just to annoy Harrie. *My dad can run a marathon. My dad is building me a tree house. My dad is taking us to Barbados next year. My dad is a police officer. He can arrest you.*

But police officers are supposed to help people, not beat them up. Harrie's eyes flick to the body on the floor as though she's expecting it to have disappeared, as though she might have imagined the whole thing. The man is still there. He's moved a little. His hand is resting on the top of his head.

'You're a police officer,' she whispers.

'That's right, Harrie, I am.' Jack nods and smiles at Harrie. His tone is different now. More official than it was a minute ago. 'So you don't need to worry about any of this, do you?'

Harrie wants to shake her head and agree with Jack but she can't. The man on the floor groans. The blood on Harrie's trousers is sticking to the hair on her legs. She rubs at it and wishes she was at home, wishes she'd never left the house.

Jack leans against the counter and folds his arms. 'Look, you're not a little kid any more. I'm going to tell you what happened so you understand why I hit him. I think you're old enough to understand that sometimes grown-ups do stupid things.' Jack pauses, waiting for Harrie to agree and so she nods.

'Well, that man there is called Dean and he had too much to drink. I'm sure you've seen your mum and dad have a few too many beers now and again.'

Harrie's head bobs up and down.

'Dean came to see Kat,' Jack continues. 'And he tried to kiss Kat, which he shouldn't have done. I happened to be popping in to borrow something and I saw. I stopped Dean from hurting Kat. I lost my temper more than I should have done, I'll admit that, but now I'm going to get Dean home to his wife. I'm sure he'll have a sore head in the morning and feel pretty stupid. But that's all there is to it.'

Harrie stares between the two men and feels an uncertainty churn in her stomach. Five minutes ago, the man on the floor was dead and the one who grabbed Harrie was a murderer. But now the man isn't dead and Jack was only trying to protect Kat from him.

'Shouldn't you call the police?' Harrie asks.

'What Dean did is very wrong, but he's been punished and now the best thing to do is to move on.'

Harrie glances at Kat and she smiles tightly. 'Jack's right, Harrie. We should all just go to bed and forget about it.'

'What about me?' Harrie asks. 'Can I go home now?' Harrie's heart isn't beating as fast as it was but there's a horrible sick feeling in her tummy and she's still shaking.

'Of course you can,' Jack says. 'It sounds to me like you've had a lucky escape with your mum being stuck in traffic tonight. I'm sure you'd be in a lot of trouble if she found out you'd left the house at night without permission. Am I right?'

Harrie nods again.

'That's what I thought. But I don't see why she needs to know about this though, do you?'

Harrie stares at Jack and then Kat. 'You won't tell my mum?'

'No,' Jack says.

Kat shakes her head. 'Promise.'

'It'll be our secret,' Jack continues. 'We won't tell your mum that you've left the house when you shouldn't have and sneaked into someone else's home without them knowing, and in return you won't mention anything about this to her or anyone else, will you?'

Harrie bites down on her lip and stares at the man on the floor. 'No.'

Jack's face breaks into a smile. It's the same closed-mouthed smug smile that Tyler uses. He steps towards the back door and fishes out the key. A moment later it's open. Cold air blasts the kitchen. 'What are you waiting for? Go on.'

Harrie stands, her legs wobbling beneath her. She takes a hesitant step, half expecting Jack to change his mind, but he's smiling, one hand on the open door, the other waving her through. She's one step away from leaving, one step from escape, when Jack's hand comes down, his grasp landing hard on her shoulder. Pain shoots through her body and she tries to wriggle free but his fingers are pressing into her skin so tight.

He leans down, his mouth close to her face, his breath hot in her ear as he whispers, low and fast. 'I know everything that goes on in this village. You tell anyone about this and I promise you I will know, and

315

then I'll kill your mum and your sisters, and I'll make you watch and then I'll kill you. Understand?'

A sob shakes her body but her head bobs up and down until his grip loosens and she's free.

Outside, the chill of the night hits her face. She moves away and leans against the wall, gasping for breath. She should run home now before anything else can happen, but her head is spinning so fast.

She draws in a breath and pushes herself away from the wall. The light from the kitchen is spilling on to the paving stones and Harrie can see the back door is ajar. Jack's voice carries through the gap.

'What are we going to do about Harrie?' Kat asks.

'I don't think she'll be telling anyone in a hurry. I'll keep an eye on her. Who did you say her parents were?'

'Anna and Rob.'

'Keep an eye on Anna. See if you can find a way to bring her into the fold. Now come on, let's sort this mess out and get Dean out of here. Where's his phone?'

'I'm not sure.'

Harrie swallows hard and closes her eyes. Jack's words fly around in her head. *You tell anyone about this and I promise you I will know, and then I'll kill your mum and your sisters.*

And she believes him. The man half-dead on the floor is proof of what Jack can do. She can't tell anyone about this. Not Elise, not her mum, no one.

A cold shiver runs through Harrie's body. Her legs are aching from where she's squatting beside the back door. She's tired and thirsty and wants to go home.

'Are you sure about this?' There's a wobble to Kat's voice. 'It feels—'

'Stop it. You know this is what needs to be done. You know better than anyone what this idiot tried to do. A few days, a week max, and everything will be back to normal. Dean just needs to remember which side his bread is buttered.'

'You're right, I'm sorry.'

A second later Harrie feels a presence by the back door, inches from where she's hiding. Every muscle in her body tenses and she closes her eyes, waiting to be seen again, to be grabbed. But then the door closes and Harrie is alone in the darkness.

She waits a few seconds before hurrying to the gate. She opens it quietly, staying in the shadows as she steps on to the driveway. There's a silver car parked on the drive and another blue car on the street. She must have missed them when she ran up to the house.

The front door opens and she hears Jack's voice. 'Make sure you clean properly.' He appears on the drive with Dean propped against him like they're about to do a three-legged race. Dean's head is drooped forward but he's walking. 'Use bleach. I'll come back for Dean's car and park it in my garage later.'

The silver car pulls away and a moment later the front door closes.

Harrie darts across the road and cuts down the alley. Her hands are shaking. She's running on aching legs back to her home at last. It feels darker than when she ran to Kat's house, but the darkness doesn't scare her any more.

Her mum's car isn't outside the house when Harrie approaches it. Harrie doesn't know if she's relieved or not.

Her hand is on the gate into her garden when she sees the headlights of a car on the main road through the village. It's Jack's car. He's come to threaten Harrie again or, worse, hurt her. Harrie stands frozen, unable to breathe, as she watches Jack pull over by the gate to the horse field. He unlocks the long silver gate before going to the passenger door and helping Dean out.

Harrie knows the field. It's the one her dad took them camping in last summer. The only thing in there is an old stable at the back.

She watches Jack hoist Dean out of the car and with a final glance down the road, he leads Dean into the field. But why? He told Harrie he was taking Dean home.

Go inside, a voice tells her. *Forget it happened.* But she can't. Before she can question what she's doing, she's racing across the road and into the horse field.

Away from the streetlights, the pitch black of the night is absolute. Harrie can't even see her hand in front of her face, but she can see torchlight halfway across the field, bouncing up and down with each step and moving in the direction of the stable.

Harrie follows, her shoes sinking into thick clumpy mud. The light disappears inside the stable just as she stumbles on the uneven ground. She finds the entrance and keeps moving, hiding at the side.

Her heart is racing so fast it's making her stomach gurgle and she feels sick. Her legs give way from under her and she sinks to the ground and waits. The light returns a few minutes later and Harrie covers her mouth, silencing the scream fighting to get out as Jack walks back across the field.

When she's sure Jack is gone, Harrie pulls herself up and digs out her torch, banging it against the palm of her hand, almost laughing with relief when a dim flickering light appears. She swallows a final time and walks into the stable.

There's nothing to see at first. It's just empty horse stalls and a dusty floor and clutter. Then Harrie's gaze finds the cage.

Chapter 56

Anna

The night is completely still as I race through the village.

Please be OK. Please be OK. I chant the words as I run, flat out, as fast as my legs can carry me.

The clouds have drifted away, leaving a perfect crescent moon in the sky and stars stretching out into the darkness like a spilt glitter pot. The temperature has dropped. My breath puffs out in a trail of smoke and I shiver inside my coat. It'll be even colder by the river.

I need to call the police. I should've done it as soon as Elise told me everything. But I thought Harrie would be with Kat. I thought she'd be safe. The face of Jack Briggs flashes in my mind. Will the police even help me if Jack is involved?

The air burns in my lungs and my boots rub against my heels but I don't stop until I reach the river. There are fewer streetlights on this stretch of the village and it takes a moment for my eyes to adjust to the darkness. I reach into my pocket for my phone and open the torch app, increasing the brightness to max.

The white beam of light illuminates the squelching grass of the riverbank by my feet and I lift it up and walk towards the bridge. Fear is shuddering through my body and I fight back a sob.

'Harrie?' I shout her name.

The bridge is a narrow wooden walkway that leads into the open countryside. I can't see the river below but I can hear it. The noise is monstrous. A beast that could leap up and swallow the bridge, swallow me in a heartbeat.

'Harrie?' I call her name again but the sound is lost, stolen by the wind and the current racing below me.

Why would Harrie come here?

I picture Harrie on the bridge, her feet slipping on the wood, falling, tumbling into the river, her scream lost to the noise of the water. I see her body swept away as easily as a twig snapped from a tree. The image causes a nausea, a raw unwavering fear, to rise up inside me and I swallow hard and push the thought away.

The wind drops suddenly and I hear something. A whimper, a footstep. I lift the torch up and peer into the middle of the bridge. There's a shadow, a figure huddled against the railing. I hold up the light of my phone and cry out as I see Harrie.

'Harrie.' I rush towards her, my feet skidding on the wood.

The Halloween costume is gone and she's shivering in a pair of black leggings and a black jumper. Her face is deathly white and puffy from crying. I reach a hand to her and she leaps at me, sobbing in my arms.

'It's OK. You're safe now. I'm here. I'm here.'

'I'm not safe, Mum.' Her voice is a whisper and barely audible over the noise of the water. 'I have to run away. I can't stay here.'

'You're not going anywhere. I know it was Elise who threw the toilet roll and Ben filmed it. I know you were at Kat's house that night to get Ben's phone.'

'You do?'

I nod.

'I was trying to help Elise. She really wants to go to that school. I'm sorry I snuck out. I was trying to help her.'

'I know, baby. It's OK. Let's go home and get you warm and then you can tell me everything and we'll fix it together. I'm on your side, Harrie, and I will fix this.'

She shakes her head. 'I can't go home. He'll find me there.'

'Who?' I ask. 'Jack?'

She nods, the movement furtive, panicked. 'When I . . . when I went to get Ben's phone, he was there and he was fighting with Dean. I thought Jack had killed him.' Tears stream down her face and I unzip my coat and wrap it around her body. 'Then Jack said that Dean had tried to hurt Kat and he was helping. I knew he was a policeman so I thought he was good and Dean was bad. But then Jack said he'd kill you and Elise and Molly if I told anyone what I'd seen. They sent me home and I saw Jack take Dean to the stable.'

'Which stable?'

'The one in the field opposite our road. I waited until Jack had left and then I . . . I went inside the stable. He'd put him in a cage, Mum.'

An icy chill spreads through me, like I'm plunging into the river. 'What do you mean?'

'Like a dog kennel that had a big padlock on it. I couldn't open the cage. And . . .' She gasps another sob. 'I couldn't call the police or speak to anyone because Jack is the police. He said he knows everything that goes on in the village and he'd kill us if I told anyone. But he ... doesn't know that I saw him at the stable. I couldn't just leave Dean there and so I took him food and water every day and talked to him.'

'Oh Harrie.' The words, the comfort I want to offer, lodge in my throat. I think back to the day Jack came to the house. I told the girls they could trust Jack. This is all on me.

I can't comprehend what Harrie has been through, the burden she has carried. Dean has been locked in a cage this whole time.

'Then Jack must have found out that I had Dean's phone and he drove by one day to threaten me, but he got me and Elise mixed up because I was wearing her coat that night. He tried to grab her. He said if I didn't give the phone back he'd make sure I got in loads of trouble and it would only be the start. And then he came to the house and you were acting like he was this really great guy, and he said he's got eyes everywhere and we weren't safe.'

Tears race down my cheeks. Hurt and anger vie for space in my body. 'Harrie—'

'Then I ... I went to the stable yesterday, but Dean wouldn't wake up. I think he was dead, Mummy. I couldn't save him. I'm sorry. I'm so sorry.' Big heaving sobs shudder through Harrie's body and my heart breaks for her. 'It's my fault Dean was locked in there. I took his phone and Jack wanted it.'

'Harrie, Harriet, this is not your fault. None of this is your fault.' I pull out my phone and tap the screen.

'Who are you calling?' Harrie's question is laced with panic.

'The police,' I say.

'No,' she cries out, slapping the phone out of my

hand. It hits the wooden bridge slats before bouncing into the darkness. 'Jack will come. He'll kill us.'

I shake my head and hold her tighter. 'Jack is only one man, Harrie. He's not the whole police. Let's get you home. I'll call them then.'

'Do you think Dean was dead?' she asks, pulling back and wiping her hands across her face.

'I don't know.'

'Can we . . . can we go and check?'

'I'll go. I need you to be safe. I'll take you home first. June is there with Molly and Elise. You can tell her as much as you like but ask her to call the police.' My voice shakes and I move us to our feet.

As we stand up, I zip my coat around Harrie's body just like when she was too little to do the zip herself.

I turn away, but before I can take a single step I feel the gap between us, sense the distance that shouldn't be there, and when I spin back, Harrie has moved further to the middle of the bridge and is clinging to the railing.

'I can't go back,' she cries. 'I'm sorry. I can't. I can't.' Her eyes drop from mine to the river gushing below us. The noise seems to rise up then, a crashing roar of water, a rapids that freezes my heart. Sprinkles of water splash my jeans.

'Harrie, walk towards me.'

'I can't,' she says again, her eyes still focused on the river.

I take a step but she jumps back. Her foot slips on the slick wood and she skids, one leg flying out towards the river. But she's got the railing tight in her grip and rights herself. 'I can't.'

'Harrie, look at me.'

'I have to run away. I need to keep you and Elise

and Molly safe.' She's shouting now, her eyes wild like an animal caught in a trap. I swallow, fighting back my own fear. I have to concentrate. I have to be strong for Harrie.

'I need you with me,' I say.

'You've got Elise and Molly.'

Tears form in my eyes. 'I need you too, Harriet. You're my daughter and I love you. There is nothing I love more in this world than my children and right now I need you more than ever because ...' Memories of that Monday in my kitchen with Dean flash into my thoughts. His kindness, the warmth of his arms around me when I told him what I'd just found out.

'I'm pregnant,' I say, shouting the words to be heard over the river. 'I'm pregnant and I need you, Harrie. I can't do this without you. You're everything to me. We're a family and we're going to stick together, no matter what. If you ...' I look down to the water and can't bring myself to finish the sentence. 'If you go, we follow ... We stick together. You, me, Elise, Molly and Dad.'

Harrie's shoulders slump, her grip loosens on the railing. She moves towards me and then we're wrapped tight in each other's arms. I walk us away from the bridge.

Only when there is pavement beneath our feet do I glance back at the dark icy river, my stomach flipping and tumbling at what could've been.

What if Gina hadn't texted me?

What if I'd not made it in time?

Chapter 57

Anna

We start to run, hand in hand. My heart pounds with fear and rage. So much rage. It's burning through my veins. Rage at Jack and Kat. My best friend. The person I trusted more than anyone else. A mother too. How could she do this to Harrie, to me?

'Mum,' Harrie says as we reach the house. 'Promise you'll be careful.' She shrugs off my coat and hands it back to me.

It's such a motherly thing to say that in spite of everything, I smile. 'I promise. Now go inside, tell June everything and ask her to call the police.'

I open the front door for Harrie and make sure she's in before turning on my heel and hurrying towards the horse field. I'm at the end of the road when I see a figure running towards me from the opposite direction.

Fear coils itself around me, that vulnerable 'woman on her own' fear plus something else. I've no idea what I'm walking into. If Jack can beat a man half to death and keep him locked in a cage for over a week, if he can torment an eleven-year-old, what will he do to me? I stop dead. My feet refuse to move and the desire to run back to the house and wait for the police is fierce.

Then a voice carries through the night and everything changes. 'Anna?'

The man approaches and suddenly I'm bursting with a hundred emotions. 'Rob?'

He rushes forward, throws his rucksack to the ground and takes me in his arms, holding me so close, so tight, and I squeeze him back, burying my face in the scent of him.

Rob is here.

The relief rushes through me and I realize in that second that I've been holding it together – for the kids, for myself, for the baby inside me – with sticky-tape patches and dried Blu-Tack, forever one step away from breaking down, and not just this week, this month, but for years.

'Where have you been?' The words leave my mouth in a rush as I pull away and take him in. Even under the glow of the streetlight he looks done in, exhausted, like he hasn't slept for days.

'The oil rig was attacked. We were under siege with no electricity or internet. The army came and I was smuggled off and taken to the British Embassy. Then they flew me home and there were a million transfers. It's taken days. The first time I had a moment to call was Thursday, but the signal was terrible. I'm so sorry for worrying you. I've just got back. Then the bloody taxi broke down at the edge of the village and I've literally been running to get back to you.'

'Why wasn't the attack in the news?' I step back, desperately wanting to believe Rob, but there's a barrier. The mortgage arrears. The debt. Another lie.

'The oil companies pay to keep it quiet when they

can. Bad PR to have their rigs and their employees attacked.'

'I know about the mortgage debt from the house.' It's not the time or the place to have this conversation, but I blurt it out anyway, unable to keep it in any more. There is so much to tell him.

'What debt?' He frowns and rubs his beard. I've never seen it in real life before. It's thicker than it looks on the videos.

'The second mortgage from the house. £150,000.'

'Anna . . .' He places his hands on my arms and I let him pull me closer. 'I promise you, there is no second mortgage. I know nothing about this. It's probably a scam letter.'

I search Rob's eyes, but find only honesty and love. A giddy fluttering swoops through me so fast it makes me lightheaded. There's no debt. Rob was in Nigeria on an oil rig all along. He hasn't lied to me.

'What's going on, Anna? Why are you out here?'

Rob holds me tight and God, I've missed him. I've missed his warmth and his love, and even though it winds me up sometimes, I miss his don't-worry words and the little eye-rolls that make me laugh and feel silly. I've missed it all.

I tell Rob what's been happening. A condensed version, anyway. I tell him about the night Harrie was alone. Jack, Kat and Dean, and my suspicions that this is about Anthony pressuring Dean to sell Stockton's. I tell him about the cage, the stable and Harrie's visits to take Dean food, blaming herself. There's so much more I want to say but there's no time.

It sounds absurd and I brace myself for Rob's laughter, but it doesn't come.

'Bloody hell, Anna. I can't believe it. Where's Harrie

now?' The fact that he believes me, this crazy story, that he hasn't questioned it, makes me feel weak with relief.

'At home with June. I told her to call the police. I was on my way to see if Dean is still alive.'

'I'll go,' Rob says. 'You get back to Harrie.'

I almost nod. It would be so easy to let Rob take over. I can go home and hug all three of my girls and tell them Daddy is back, but I don't. I'm the one who has been here, I'm the one who looked Sue in the eyes and told her I'd try my best to find her husband. I have to see it through. 'I'm coming with you.'

Chapter 58

Anna

The padlock on the gate is unlocked and Rob pushes it open and takes my hand as we walk across the field together. Away from the streetlights, the darkness surrounds us. The clouds have covered the sky and there is no moon to guide us now. I realize too late that I should've brought a torch, but I can see an orange glow of light coming from the stable and we hurry towards it, tripping on the uneven earth.

The field is bigger than I thought and surrounded by trees. It might be right in the middle of the village but it's private too. There's no way anyone on the road would hear shouts or screams from the stable. It's too far back. The thought sends a shudder down my body.

Every rustle of my coat, every footfall sounds like it's being broadcast through speakers as I draw nearer.

What if we're walking into danger?

The murmur of voices carries through the night. It sounds like they're arguing. How many people are involved? Jack and Kat, I know. Mike? Anthony?

A cry sounds from inside the stable. A yell of pain. Rob looks at me, his face full of concern.

'Go home. Please, Anna,' he pleads quietly. 'We don't know what we're walking into.' It's the first time I've heard Rob echo my own what-ifs but I shake my head, the decision made, and we take the final steps into the stable together.

The stench smacks right into me – urine and faeces, sweat and blood. It coats the inside of my nose all the way to the back of my throat and makes me gag. My knees buckle for a moment as I fight the urge to retch. Rob coughs beside me, his reaction the same as mine.

There's a chunky black torch sat upright in the middle of the floor casting a shadowy orange glow. In the corner is a metal crate like a kennel for a large dog. It's exactly as Harrie described but worse somehow too. The door is open and it's empty. Are we too late? Is Dean dead? Even in the dim light I can see the blood where it has soaked into the straw on the ground. There's a bucket in one corner and a balled-up blanket that I recognize in the other.

I lift my eyes to the faces now staring at me.

Kat looks startled by our entrance. Jack rolls his eyes. Neither of them I'm surprised to see. Standing beside Jack is his wife, Sandra, and Mike Pritchett and Anthony Campbell are also here.

Jack steps aside and then I see him – Dean. He's sitting on a wooden crate, head in his hands.

'Dean?' I cover my mouth, unable to comprehend what I'm seeing.

He looks up, his face sallow, body gaunt. He's aged twenty years since I last saw him.

'I'm fine.' He coughs as he speaks – a deep wheezing croak – sounding anything but.

331

My eyes scan the group again. Sandra's face is hard and unreadable. Mike is staring at the floor. Anthony is shaking his head. Kat looks horrified, her eyes puffy, and she's wiping her nose on the sleeves of her cardigan.

'What the hell is going on here?' Rob says from beside me. 'Anthony?'

Anthony steps forward. Always the leader. Even now. He holds up his hands, a peace offering. 'Clearly things have got out of hand,' he says.

I scoff. 'You call locking a man up for ten days "out of hand"?'

'Jack acted on his own.' Mike is quick to jump in. 'We didn't know anything about this until tonight.'

'Shut up,' Jack growls. 'You don't want to get your hands dirty because you don't have the balls, but you still want me to do the dirty work and protect us.'

'How is locking a man up protecting anyone?' I cry out. 'What the hell is going on here?'

A stony silence falls over the group. The start of a scream builds in my throat.

'They're on the take,' Dean says, looking from the group to me. 'I'm in it up to my eyeballs too, so don't go feeling sorry for me, Anna.'

'Don't say another word.' Jack steps towards him, warning in his voice.

'Give it a rest, Jack. You really think Anna's going to walk away from this without knowing the truth? What else can you do to me?'

Jack raises his eyebrows. His answer silent, but there anyway. *A lot.*

'The take from what? Your business?' I ask.

'In a way. The Parish Council have been paying Stockton's for bogus work for years, then Stockton's pays me and Anthony and we give it out to these guys, and they funnel it through their little side businesses. We also take hefty chunks from the money raised from the summer fete, creating bogus projects with the school or the Neighbourhood Watch.' Dean leans forward, his body convulsing in another coughing fit.

I try to wrap my head around what he's telling me as I look from one person to another. And finally it starts to make sense.

My eyes fall on Kat and for the first time it occurs to me that I've never seen her lift a finger to sell her beauty products to anyone outside of her friendship group, and now the reason is obvious – it's a front. A way to pretend to make money. No doubt it's the same for Bev's nail business, Tracy's jewellery and Sandra's candles. I've been so blind.

'Steve doesn't know,' Kat whispers, tears falling down her face. 'It was only supposed to be a little bit, you know? Because we all do so much for the village. But they got greedy,' she says, her tone full of spite as she nods at Anthony. 'I was just trying to do my bit to protect the village.'

'Protect it?' I scoff.

'Don't be so naive, Anna.' Sandra snaps the words so fast I take an involuntary step back.

'You're stealing from the council funds, from money the people in this village raise, so you can have nice holidays and fancy cars. I'm not being naive.'

'It's hardly stealing,' she replies. 'We take a contribution for our efforts. This village would be unrecognizable if it wasn't for us. If you only knew how many times we've had people trying to build on the land here, put up housing estates all over the place like they've done in the other villages, you'd be thanking us right now.'

'You lying bitch,' Dean hisses, trying to laugh but

333

coughing instead. 'None of you give a shit about this village. If you did, I wouldn't be here, would I?' Dean slugs back a mouthful of water before looking at me with hollow eyes. 'I was selling the land I own,' he says. 'The meadow by the playing field and two fields on the edge of the village. That's why I'm here, but don't believe a word of what Sandra is telling you. They don't care about new houses going up. All they care about is me selling my land to Stockton's so they get their cut. Anthony's been trying to get me to agree to make this lot directors so they can split the profits that way.

'Then they found out I was selling it to someone else.' He holds his hands up and shrugs in a 'now look where I am' gesture.

The final penny drops – a stone plopping into the depths of the sea. This wasn't about Dean selling his business; it was about his land and the money to be made on building houses. A lot of money.

'And that's what Harrie walked in on that night, was it?' I ask, my voice thick with emotion. 'You' – I nod at Jack – 'found out about this and wanted to beat some sense into Dean. But he wouldn't agree, so you locked him in a cage for days on end.' I shake my head. 'You're all monsters.'

Sandra has the decency to look uncomfortable as her eyes travel to Jack, but it's Kat who answers. 'She shouldn't have been there. I'm sorry, Anna. I'm so sorry. This has all gone too far. I never wanted this.'

'But you wanted the extra money, didn't you?' Jack hisses.

'Hey, hey, hey,' Anthony steps in. 'Let's all take a breath, Rob, Anna, this is all going to be smoothed out, I promise you. I'm terribly sorry for everything that happened to Harrie.' He shoots Jack and Mike a look. 'But I didn't know. I never would've let it happen. We can all move on from this.'

'You're right,' I nod. 'We can, when the police arrive.'

A shocked silence falls across the stable. Jack spins to face me, his hand reaching for something in his back pocket.

Chapter 59

Anna

Jack pulls the object free and for the smallest of seconds I think it's a gun. My heart stops. I don't breathe as I inch closer to Rob. My head fills with thoughts of the baby and I wish then that I'd listened to Rob and was home right now.

Where the hell are the police?

And then I realize, even as Jack is tapping on the screen of the mobile in his hands, a triumphant smile playing on his lips. I realize no one is coming. Harrie hasn't told June and June hasn't called the police. Harrie said it on the bridge. She thinks Jack is the police. I told her it wasn't true but she's spent days terrified he's coming to get her, that she'll be next to be beaten and locked in a cage or worse. A single reassurance from me isn't going to have changed her mind.

'The thing is, Anna,' Jack says. 'If the police are called to Barton St Martin, I get an alert.' He holds up his phone. 'No alert.'

'You better hope they're not,' Sandra hisses. 'Because if one of us goes down, we all go down. You're involved in this too.' She throws a look my way and I pale as her meaning hits me. I'm the Parish Council clerk. I've built Stockton's website. According to Kat, Anthony was about to offer me a job. They've been sucking me in, trying to make me complicit.

They knew my weakness. Money. The letter from the debt collectors flashes in my mind. A debt neither Rob nor I know anything about. 'Who sent the letter?' I ask, my eyes flitting between them.

'What letter?' Mike asks, checking his watch like he's got some place more important to be.

'DCC Debt Collectors. £150,000 mortgage arrears ring any bells?'

My gaze lands on Kat and I see the look on her face of someone who has just been caught.

'I'm sorry about that,' she whispers. 'Truly I am. But I did it for you. I was trying to help.'

'How is sending me a letter threatening bailiffs coming to my home helping me?' My voice is a screech.

'I knew money was tight for you and I knew about the debt you'd had. Everyone did,' she says, and despite everything my face smarts. 'But I knew you'd be reluctant to take a job because of your business and the girls, so I faked that letter' – she shrugs – 'to help you make the right decision. I was doing it for you. Anna, come on,' she says, looking at me with pleading eyes. 'We're best friends. I know you better than anyone, and you know me.'

'I never would've agreed to the work if I'd known it was . . . blood money.'

'Blood money?' Sandra laughs. 'You didn't just say that.'

Jack clears his throat. 'I think everyone is missing the point.'

'And that is?' Anthony asks.

'Even if the police were on their way, Dean isn't going to tell them diddly squat. Are you, Dean?'

I'm silent. Stunned. Dean looks around the faces before landing on Rob then me. There is such pain in his eyes that I feel the emotion clogging my throat.

'I'm sorry, Anna. Jack's right.' Dean stops for a moment, leaning over himself and coughing so hard I swear I can hear the rattle in his lungs. 'Being stuck here has given me time to think and I've realized I want to sell the land to Stockton's. I thought I could teach them a lesson by selling the land to a competitor. There'd be no more fiddling the books then, but I'm just as bad as everyone else in this room.' His voice has a robotic quality to it, like he's going through the motions. A broken man.

I want to protest, to tell him he's not, but Jack jumps in again. 'So it's Harrie's story against Dean's. An eleven-year-old kid, a known troublemaker around the village and at school—'

'She's not,' I snap.

Jack shrugs. 'She is if we say she is. Harrie versus a respected businessman who denies everything. Who would you believe?'

For the whole time we've been standing here, Rob has kept by my side, a silent rock of support, listening, catching up on what he's just walked into, but his body stiffens with the mention of Harrie.

'Just wait a minute,' Rob says, lunging at Jack. 'You leave my daughter out of this.'

In two steps the pair have become a brawling force of fists and legs.

It lasts five seconds before Anthony and Mike are stepping in, pulling the men apart, and Rob and Jack are glaring at each other like a couple of boys fighting in the playground.

'This is over,' Anthony says, bending down to pick up the torch. 'I promise you, Anna, I will get this smoothed out and the Parish Council back on track. But Dean and Jack are right. One of us goes down, we all go down. Mutual assured destruction.'

My eyes flit back to Dean, ready to plead with him again to say something, do something. How can anyone just walk away from this? But then I see it – the only way he can walk away is if he says nothing at all.

The atmosphere around us changes. It's like the end of a meeting, when everyone knows it's time to leave. Sandra and Jack go first, hand in hand, and I wonder with a fresh wave of red-hot anger if this is what counts as a date night in their messed-up world.

I want to scream for them to come back. This isn't over. It can't be. Where is the justice?

Anthony hands Rob the torch before he and Mike step either side of Dean. They help him to his feet and out of the stable, the prison he has been kept in for ten days. I think of the food Harrie brought here, the trips she made without me knowing, the fear she must have felt with every step across the field, and the burden weighing on her that she and only she could keep him alive. But they didn't put Dean here to die, that much is obvious. They want Dean alive so they all get rich building houses on his land. They must have been bringing him food and water too. They must have unlocked the cage and emptied the bucket every day.

'Dean,' I try one more time. 'You're not this person. I know you're not.'

'I am,' is all he says, before dropping his head.

Then it's only Kat. She hesitates, her eyes conveying

something that yesterday I would have understood, but she seems closer to a stranger to me now.

'Anna,' Kat says.

'Don't.' I shake my head. 'I trusted you.'

'I'm your best friend,' she pleads.

'Not any more.'

'I was just trying to look after the village. Barton St Martin is such a peaceful, safe village. I didn't want anything to happen to it.'

I look at her in disgust. 'The only thing any of you were doing was looking after yourselves.'

Kat disappears into the night and I sit with shaking legs on a stack of wood pallets by the door. Adrenaline rushes through my body, bumping against the realization that it's over.

Rob holds out his hand to me. 'Let's go home.'

I let him pull me into the crook of his arm, but when we're in the dark and the cold is all around us, I stop. I can't walk another step. I can't go home with Rob, back to our house together, and let the girls see him. Not until I understand his lies.

'Anna? What is it?' he asks.

'Tell me everything,' I say. 'Don't lie and don't leave anything out. Start with where you've been going when you've left us.'

'I've been in Nigeria. You know that. I wouldn't lie to you.'

'I was worried when you didn't call on Sunday. I called Artax and spoke to someone in their HR department. They didn't have a clue who you were.'

He nods but says nothing for a moment. 'I was working on an oil rig in Nigeria, exactly like I said I was, but I wasn't working through Artax. They'd take a cut of my wages—'

'To provide extra security. To keep you safe.'

'That's true, but I spoke with the oil company and took a job directly with them. I arranged my own transport to and from the airport, using the same security teams as Artax use, but paying a fraction of the cost.'

'So why didn't you tell me? Why does it always feel like you're lying to me? Like I have to dig through all your shit to find the truth and only then do you tell me?'

'It wasn't like that, Anna. I was trying to protect you. I didn't want you to spend all of the time I was away worrying.'

'Well, you failed, because I did worry and now I find out you were putting your life in even more danger. Do you know how hard it's been for the kids? It would destroy them if you were killed. Do you get that?'

'I'm here, aren't I? I'm fine.'

'For how long though?'

'For good.'

His words wind me. 'What? How? We still have another year as we are before the debts are paid. Or have you lied about that too?' I picture Molly's bright beaming eyes when she hears her daddy won't be going away again. I hear the squeals of delight as he collects our girls one by one into his arms and spins them round.

'I was earning better money so I've paid off the last of the debts. We're free. We can start again. Anthony's offered me a job, but—'

'At Stockton's? You can't be serious.'

'I know.' He shakes his head. 'Let me finish. After tonight there is no way I can work for Anthony or have anything to do with Stockton's or this village. I don't know how much Anthony and the others were involved in what Jack did to Dean, but it's clear that nobody in that stable was innocent. I'll find something else. I don't care if it's engineering or sitting at a desk. As long as I'm home every night. I promised you I'd fix this, I promised you a fresh start.'

'Away from the village?'

'Yes. Definitely.' He smiles, tentative and unsure, and it almost melts my heart. Almost.

A silence settles over us as we walk back to the house. Emotions mixing like a dozen fragrances at the perfume counter, clogging the air and making my head pound.

'I thought you'd changed,' I say after a pause. 'After what happened with your business in London I thought you'd never risk our family again.'

'I would never risk us. Not ever. That's why I've done all this. It wasn't fun for me, you know. Sleeping in a single bunk night after night, working relentlessly, eating shit food, and thinking constantly, every second, I was about to get killed. I did it for you and the girls. I got us into such a mess with money and I've got us out of it too. I did it all for you. I want to give you back the life you had, the one you deserve.'

I shake my head. 'I don't want that life any more. I thought I did, but I was wrong. I just want . . .' I shrug. 'To feel safe. To not feel worried every minute of the day. For the girls to feel safe and happy. Nothing else matters.'

'We can't live without money, Anna. Kindness and love don't pay the bills, in case you haven't noticed.'

'Of course I've noticed,' I snap. 'What do you think I've been doing while you've been away? I've been raising our family on scraps, and do you know what, they're happy – or they were until Harrie got dragged into this shit show. Do you have the first clue what this has done to her? She tried to run away tonight. I found her on the bridge over the river and I thought ... I thought she might jump. Our baby girl. I don't even know how to begin processing what she's been through or how I am going to help her.

'And those bastards have the audacity to tell me that everything they do is for the good of the community. It's bullshit. It's about money and greed and power.'

'I didn't have anything to do with that. I might've been on the Parish Council, but I was just a chair filler. Anthony didn't want a village busybody joining, and now we know why,' he says, giving a long sigh. 'You're right though, I lied about which company I was working for. Everything else was true. I just didn't want you to worry, that's all. You never used to worry so much.'

'And look where that got us.' The fight seeps out of me. 'No more lying. I know you think you're trying to protect me, but you have to be honest.'

'I promise.' He leans down and kisses me, soft and tender, and I know I'll forgive him. He's lied to protect me from my own what-if demons and I can't hate him for that. But will he forgive me so easily?

Chapter 60

Anna

'I need to get back to the girls. June is with them.' It feels late, like I've been in this field for days, but as we walk towards the road, the cold air kisses my face and I glance at my watch and see only an hour has passed, two since I ran out of my front door to find Harrie. I think about all that has happened and all that I know and it cloaks me in a heavy exhaustion I will never lift myself out of.

'I have to tell you something before we go in,' I say.

'OK.'

'While you were away, Dean and I became ... friends.'

'Friends?' The single word is laced with accusation and hurt.

'Just friends, Rob. I needed someone to talk to and it was him. He's been there for me. I didn't have an affair. The first time we hugged was two days before he went missing and that was only because I was upset. It wasn't an affair, but ...' I shrug. 'It didn't feel right either. I was relying on him for the emotional support that I should have been getting from you.'

344

Rob tightens his arm around me. 'I get it, and I'm here now. I love you, Anna.'

I take a shaking breath. 'There's something else – I'm pregnant.'

'What?' Rob's voice rings with surprise. 'But you're on the pill.'

'I know. It happens though.'

We reach the gate. The padlock is still open and we slip through and shut it behind us. Tomorrow, in the grey wintry daylight, this field will look exactly the same. There will be no sign of the horrors that Dean has been through. His face tonight was sunken, half starved, broken. He was nothing like the man who knocked on my door on that Monday with two apple turnovers from the bakery, just as I'd taken the test and found out I was pregnant.

I was a mess. Shaken. Horrified. Everything was already so hard. An uphill struggle. A sewer of shit and I'd cried and cried. Dean had taken me in his arms and hugged me tight. It was the first time we'd ever touched each other, crossed that line, and I told him everything, about London, the debts, the shitty little flat, and the baby.

A baby we couldn't afford. Another set of clothes, shoes, nappies. Another set of classes. Another everything. I didn't know how I was going to tell Rob. We'd worked out the money so meticulously. Almost every penny had been accounted for. Where were we going to find the money for a baby? And how could I have a baby with Rob away? It couldn't work. Dean told me everything would be OK, but I didn't see how it could.

'I wasn't expecting this, but it's good news,' Rob says. 'I'm happy. Anna, truly I am. I've always wanted more children. You have too. You've been worrying about it, haven't you? My little worrywart.'

'Don't call me that any more.'

'I'm sorry. You know I'm only teasing. I won't say it again, but you have to try and relax more. Deal? The debts are all gone. You're pregnant. You need to start taking care of yourself.'

I nod as I open the front door, too tired to talk any more. There is more that needs to be said, but right now I just want to see the girls.

June is at the kitchen table with a cup of tea and her knitting when I walk in. The ball of baby-blue wool is by her feet and the colour makes my chest ache as I think about the tiny human growing inside me.

The kitchen is spotless. The mess of dinner has been cleaned away and the Halloween items stacked neatly to one side.

'June, I can't thank you enough for helping me tonight. You didn't need to tidy up.'

'Oh, I didn't, dear.' June looks from me to Rob. If she's surprised to see him home, she doesn't show it. She offers him a polite smile, before turning her warmth back to me. 'Molly and Elise did.'

'Is Harrie OK?' I watch June's face. I see the worry on the deep lines of her forehead and a fear rears up inside me.

What if she's run away again?

What if . . . ? I stop myself from finishing the thought.

'She was quiet and rather cold. I suggested she have a bath and get into bed. Elise went with her and Molly is upstairs reading.'

The relief hits me with another wave of exhaustion. 'Thank you, June. Thank you so much.'

June rises to her feet. 'I've told you, my dear girl, I'm here any time you need me. I'm glad to help. I don't have grandchildren, sadly, but spending time with the girls is close enough for me.'

'We're lucky to have you in our lives, June,' I say, touching her arm as we walk to the front door. I feel a pang of guilt as I hug June goodbye. I came to the village desperate to keep to myself, to keep our dirty little secret safe, locked inside our walls. I was ashamed and shallow and I thought people would look down on us for having so little. And when I felt the eyes of the likes of Sandra and Bev on me it only made me more certain to keep myself shut away. But it has closed me off to friendships and support. I've relied on no one but Kat and then Dean, and look where that got me.

There's a soft thud from upstairs. Feet out of bed.

Rob grins and leaps up the stairs, two then three steps at a time. A second later I hear Molly's excited squeals.

Chapter 61

Anna

As Rob scoops Elise into his arms, I duck into the twins' bedroom and find Harrie. She's in bed, her breathing deep and rhythmic. I step into the room and lie down beside her, wrapping her in my arms as she stirs.

'Harrie?' I whisper.

'Is Dean dead?'

'No, baby. Dean is OK.'

'Is he . . . is he still there?' Her eyes fly open. They are filled with more horror than I can bear to see.

I shake my head. 'No. He's gone home. Your dad is here. Do you want to say hello now?'

She pauses to think and then shakes her head. 'In a minute. What will happen now?'

'I don't know.'

'I'm sorry I didn't tell June. I wanted to but I . . .' Harrie starts to tremble in my arms and I tighten my hold and kiss the top of her head.

'It's OK. I know Jack scared you and made you think he'd hurt us if you said anything, but he doesn't control the police though, Harrie. We'll go tomorrow and talk to them.'

She nods and buries her head in my shoulder and I rub her back as she cries.

We stay like that for a long time, wrapped in each other's arms while Molly and Elise's excited voices and Rob's laughter carry through the walls. I don't know if my words of comfort to Harrie are true or wishful thinking, but I do know that when we all walked out of that stable tonight, it wasn't the end.

The next morning Rob takes Elise and Molly to the park, and Harrie and I drive to the police station. A female officer with dark hair and bright inquisitive eyes guides us into an interview room and I sit beside Harrie with weak tea in a Styrofoam cup as she tells the officer everything that happened. PC Quinn makes notes, only interrupting Harrie's story to clarify a date or a time. She doesn't raise an eyebrow or scoff in disbelief when Harrie tells her about Dean trapped in the cage.

Afterwards, Harrie sits in the waiting room and I fill in the gaps with my own story. I watch PC Quinn scrawl down the names I give her. Anthony and Tracy Campbell. Mike and Bev Pritchett. Sandra and Jack Briggs. Kat Morris. I think of the other members of the Parish Council – Barry Glebe and Mary Swanson. Martin Walker and Rob. It all happened right in front of them and they had no idea. It happened right in front of all of us.

When I'm finished, I slide Dean's phone across the table. I don't know what's on it. Something that will incriminate these people, or nothing at all, but I want the police to have it.

There is no rush to the police cars when I've finished.

No flashing blue lights. PC Quinn thanks me for coming and promises me she'll be in touch soon.

We don't know until later that our trip to the police was too late. By the time we left PC Quinn they were already dead.

TWO DEAD IN MURDER-SUICIDE
1 November

The village of Barton St Martin is in shock today after two residents died in an apparent murder-suicide. Local businessman Dean Stockton shot dead decorated police officer and father-of-two Jack Briggs, before turning the gun on himself.

While the police are not looking for anyone else in connection with the murder-suicide, several residents are helping police with their inquiries, including an eleven-year-old girl.

Our chief reporter, Melissa Hart, is investigating behind the scenes of this distraught community. Pick up a copy of our weekend paper to discover the lies and secrets hidden in this idyllic village.

Village Girlies' Secret Group Chat
Sunday 1 November, 11.45

Bev Pritchett: Is it true?

Tracy Campbell: Yes.

Bev Pritchett: @SandraBriggs I'm so sorry.
Is there anything I can do?

Kat Morris: Anna and Harrie are talking
to the police. There's a reporter asking
questions. What should we say?

Bev Pritchett: OMG!!!! How the hell did
Harrie get involved in all this?

Kat Morris: She was there the night Jack
spoke to Dean. It's been a nightmare!

Bev Pritchett: What are we going to do?

Tracy Campbell: Stay calm. Talk about Harrie. Make her the story. We've been careful!!

Kat Morris: Delete this group!!

Tracy Campbell: Done.

Group chat deleted

Interview with Tracy Campbell,
member of Barton St Martin Parish
Council and member of the Parent-
Teacher Association of Barton St
Martin Primary School
Interview conducted by Melissa Hart,
The Daily Gazette, 3 November

MH: Thank you for agreeing to talk to me now.

Tracy: I've only got two minutes before I need to collect the girls from pony camp.

MH: What's the connection between Stockton's Builders and Contractors and the Parish Council?

Tracy: There is no connection.

MH: Your husband is the Chief Financial Officer for Stockton's, is he not?

Tracy: Yes.

MH: And the head of the Parish Council?

Tracy: So? What's your point?

MH: Some might consider it a conflict of interest. Mr Campbell could have swayed the Parish Council to use Stockton's over a different company?

Tracy: It had nothing to do with Anthony. Dean Stockton was the main sales force for his business. He was the one that always offered Stockton's for any repairs or work that needed doing around the village. Dean said he was giving us a fair price and rather stupidly on our parts we believed him. We thought it was a mates' rate thing. Not strictly in line with policy, but these things happen. Jack was the lead on the annual summer fete. I dread to think how much money they've stolen between them. We were all oblivious to what Dean and Jack were getting up to behind our backs. Ignorance is no excuse, but there it is.

**Interview with Martin Walker, member of
Barton St Martin Parish Council
Interview conducted by Melissa Hart,
The Daily Gazette, 3 November**

MH: Thank you for taking a few minutes to talk to me, Mr Walker.

Martin: Call me Martin. And it's no problem. No problem at all. I assume you know by now about the suspected fiddling on the Parish Council? Horrible business.

MH: What do you know about it?

Martin: Me? I know nothing. Gina and I are both in the dark. We never suspected a thing. Can you believe that? These people were our good friends. We went camping together. We spent Christmas Eve together. Countless New Years celebrating with them and we didn't have a clue what was going on.

MH: You are a member of the Parish Council though?

Martin: I know, I know, it sounds like I should have known, but I didn't, and it wasn't just me. Barry, Mary and Rob didn't know either. As for the others, I really don't know who to believe. They say they didn't know a thing about it and it was all Dean and Jack, but I'm not so sure I believe that. Look, I flipped burgers at the summer fete and voted yes when needed at the meetings. Did I think it was odd that we always used Stockton's Builders and Contractors for our repairs? No. To be honest, I thought it was a good relationship to have. They'd do what we asked and they were quick. I never saw any of the invoices or the finances. Actually, you should speak to Steve. He'll be back in an hour.

MH: Steve Morris?

Martin: Yes. He's staying here for a few days. He and Kat have had a falling out. He'll tell you everything. He's just as in the dark as we are.

Chapter 62

Seven months later

Anna

I'm painting the kitchen when the doorbell trills through the house. I jump at the noise and a drip of teal paint splats on my overstretched T-shirt. I place the roller back in the tray and wipe a cloth across my huge bump.

I glance into the garden and check on the girls. All three are still wearing the bright-red polo shirts of their new school and playing on the climbing frame Rob built for them. Molly is hanging upside down from a bar, grinning as the ends of her bunches brush against the ground. Elise is sitting on the swing laughing and Harrie is at the top, throwing a ball up in the air and catching it.

The house is a new-build on the edge of town. It is in a maze of through roads and dead ends and one identical house after another. From our living room window, I can watch Harrie and Elise kick a ball and play with their new friends in the small green park across the road. Molly and I can walk to the swings in under a minute.

Every afternoon when the weather is dry, school-children and parents spill on to the grass and the sounds of shouts and chatter carry through to the house. It's not a beauty spot, it's not quiet or tranquil, but I feel more sense of community here than I ever did in Barton St Martin.

Our fresh start at last.

Rob found a job at a local engineering firm and is home every evening just like he promised. He calls him-self Chief Taxi Driver, taking the kids to all of their clubs and trying to make up for the lost time. We're not rich and we never will be, but we earn enough to have planned a trip to France for a week at the end of the summer. It's nothing fancy – a campsite with a pool, and the beach nearby – but we're all excited. No more debts. The thought rolls across my mind – a marble that never stills.

The children have settled into their new school, their new life, faster than I could have hoped. Elise is still mourning the loss of the scholarship and there are days when I could kill Mike Pritchett for the terrible reference he gave Elise before he retired. I spoke to the admissions department at St Benedict's. I tried to explain, and while they were sympathetic, the scholar-ship had already been awarded to someone else.

And Harrie. Our sweet, funny girl. She is coming back to me. Slowly. I'm not sure she'll ever be the easy-to-smile, easy-to-joke girl she was. That was stolen from her the night of the car accident. Stolen by Jack Briggs and Kat and everything that followed. She's cautious now. Slow to trust. She sticks close to Elise at school and me at home. Even with Rob she's wary and

I can see it hurts him. Then there's the flinching, the way she jumps, hands flying out to protect herself if someone touches her unexpectedly. It breaks my heart to watch.

Tracy texted me last week. A half-hearted attempt to organize a play date for Molly and Olivia. I've not replied. Like the rest of them, she's denied knowing anything about the stealing of the village funds, pinning the blame solely on Dean and Jack. It's all lies. Molly talks about Olivia sometimes, but she has a new best friend now. His name is Ralph and he's the sweetest, kindest little boy I've ever met, and he worships the ground Molly walks on.

I push the thoughts of Barton St Martin away as I step to the front door. Some nights when I lie awake, too uncomfortable to sleep, the thoughts return and I play what happened over and over in my mind, powerless to stop the worry grabbing me by the throat, but I am getting better too. I no longer spend every waking second worrying over all the what-ifs.

My body is slow, a huge waddling vessel. Two weeks until my due date. The fluttering excitement, the mild panic, returns to my insides. Rob is waiting for the call. So is June, who visits me once a week with a cake or a casserole, and fills me in on the village gossip I don't want to hear.

Kat is moving. She and that husband of hers are divorcing.

Dean's land sold. Did you hear?

They're building seventy-eight houses on the meadow. They'll be dinky little things.

The new Parish Council are fighting the planning permission but it'll go through. The country needs more homes. People will adjust in time.

I'm grateful to June for her friendship and the support she gives us. She still babysits when I attend networking events in the town and meet Rob for dinner afterwards. I should've gone to the events years ago. There are lots of mums just like me and they're a supportive bunch. I've got more work than I can handle right now.

I open the front door and find Sue Stockton standing on my doorstep, a bunch of flowers in her hands, and Timmy hopping and dancing at her feet. There's a fragility to Sue that wasn't there on that first doorstep visit seven months ago, as though she might be blown away by a gust of late-spring wind at any moment. She's aged since I saw her at Dean's funeral. The skin on her face is sagging and her hair is now completely white.

'Hello Anna, I hope I'm not intruding,' she says, holding out the flowers.

'Not at all. I was due a break,' I say, brushing at the paint stain on my T-shirt before taking the flowers. 'These are beautiful, thank you. Come in. You'll have to forgive the mess. It's a work in progress.' I glance at the breakfast bowls still sitting by the sink and wait for the embarrassment to flush through my cheeks. Nothing happens and I almost laugh at myself. Maybe there has been one positive to come out of all of this. I've become comfortable letting things slide. I've loosened my control – my constant need to clean and tidy. There are no Excel spreadsheets pinned around the house, no routines or lists, and just in time too. In a few short weeks, we'll have two almost-teenagers, an eight-year-old and a newborn baby in our lives.

'I was just going to put the kettle on. Would you like a tea or coffee?' I ask, already filling the kettle.

'Tea would be nice, thank you.'

'Girls,' I call out the back door. 'There's a visitor here you'll want to say hello to.' Even as the words leave my mouth, Sue unclips Timmy's lead and he races into the garden, a speeding bullet of fur. I hear three delighted screams followed by cooing and excitement, a yipping bark, laughter.

Sue stands awkwardly in the kitch-ditch, as Molly calls it, a kitchen and a dining room all in one. Two walls are currently mustard-yellow and hideous, the others are a fresh teal. Rob is already talking about moving somewhere bigger. Maybe one day, but not yet. I like it here and the rent is low.

'Let's sit in the living room,' I say when the drinks are ready. 'Away from the paint fumes.'

Sue's eyes are on me as I lower myself on to the sofa in our small square living room with the bulging toy boxes and purple and yellow Lego bricks scattered across the floor.

'How long have you got?'

'Two weeks officially, but I'm painting the kitchen which is clear nesting territory so any day now I suppose.' I smile, a protective hand on my stomach for the little girl who will soon be in the world.

'How are you?' I ask.

'Oh, I'm surviving. The last few months have been hard. There are constant reminders of Dean and what happened everywhere I look. I hate that place – the house, the village. Hate it. Anthony has taken over Dean's business, you know. He hasn't even had the decency to change the name. Then there's the police investigation. Have you been following it?'

I nod. 'I've been scanning the news every day waiting for something.' Three times a day actually. I could've called PC Quinn but deep inside I know they – Anthony,

Tracy, Kat, Sandra, Mike and Bev – have got away with it and I can't bring myself to hear it.

'They all banded together and blamed the whole thing on Dean and Jack. They said it was just the two of them taking the money. Can you believe that? The police are sure the rest of them are in on it, but there is no evidence. They were smart with the money trail, I'll give them that. Throwing their little parties, pretending to sell that crap. Faking receipts. They had a forensic accountant comb through the Parish Council finances and Stockton's but it's too small-time for the police. It's not like they're looking for a murderer, is it? Dean killed Jack and then himself. Case closed.' Sue's words are matter of fact, but I catch the wobble in her tone. 'They've dumped it on HMRC but unless one of them admits it, they're all safe.'

'Mutual assured destruction,' I mumble as memories of that night in the stable fill my head.

'I'm sorry?'

'It's what Anthony said that night I found Dean. One goes down, they all go down.'

The colour drains from Sue's face.

'Are you OK?' I ask.

'Yes.' She swallows a long sip of tea before she speaks. 'Do you remember I told you about that man I saw on our driveway punching Dean? I'm sure I remember him saying that to Dean. It's such a strange expression.'

'And it wasn't Anthony?'

'I don't think so.' Sue falls silent. I see a tremble in her lower lip. Her eyes swim with tears as she looks at me. 'Why do you think Dean did it, Anna?'

I'm not sure if she means killing Jack or himself, or both, but I shake my head either way. 'He was in a bad place.'

'I should have done more to help him. I should've—'

'It's not your fault.' She smiles a little at that, but I don't think she believes it.

'I told Dean about Luke the night those beasts dropped him home, dumping him on the doorstep without even bothering to ring the doorbell. The first thing Dean asked was "Where's Luke?", and of course Dean blamed himself.

'He told me that he thought someone had hacked into his emails and knew he was planning to sell the land he owned in the village to a competitor of Stockton's. But when Kat invited him over he thought he might be able to get her on his side. I don't think he'd have gone if it had been Jack or Anthony, but he liked Kat and wanted to talk some sense into her. Then Jack turned up and Dean sensed where it was going and texted Luke asking for help, but obviously Luke never made it.

'He blamed himself for Luke's death, but he blamed Jack too. Dean was in such a bad way when he came back. You can't imagine it, Anna. I think hearing about Luke's death tipped him over the edge. I wonder sometimes, even before Jack shoved him in that cage, whether Dean was planning to kill himself. Some of the things he said, when I look back now ... Well, hindsight is a powerful thing, isn't it? But what Jack did to him – I think Dean couldn't kill himself without taking Jack with him. Some kind of warped justice for Luke's death and everything that happened. The gun belonged to his father. An old hunting rifle. I didn't even know we still had it, let alone that it worked.

'Maybe if I'd waited until the next day to tell Dean about Luke, things would be different. But I didn't and nothing will bring Dean back. Anyway, that's not why

I'm here,' she says with a weak smile. 'I've come to say goodbye. I'm finally moving to Spain.'

'I'm pleased for you.' I smile too. 'I'm sorry Dean can't be with you.'

'Me too. That man was a fool, but I loved him.' She sighs. 'There will still be reminders of Dean at the villa,' she continues. 'But they'll be good ones. He was always at his happiest there. I've sold the land. Did you know?'

'I heard.'

'It was mine, you see. Not Dean's. I didn't even know. He transferred it to me along with the house, years ago. I think he could foresee trouble ahead and wanted to keep it as separate from the company and himself as he could. I can't stop thinking about what happened. I didn't do enough while he was missing.'

'I think about it too. It wasn't your fault.'

'And it wasn't yours.'

A silence falls over us and I don't try to fill it. The baby pushes an arm out, a punch from the inside, and I mask my gasp.

'You must be wondering why I'm here and telling you all this.' Sue places her cup on the coffee table and reaches into her bag before pulling out a white A4 envelope. 'I've got something to give you.' She stands up and puts the envelope in my hands before taking her seat again.

My eyes look from Sue to the envelope and she smiles properly for the first time since she's been here. 'Open it,' she says.

I peel back the lip and pull out a single sheet of paper. *Fenwick & Wright Solicitors* is printed across the top of the letter and as my eyes glance over the words I struggle to take them in.

A single word stands out – *Trust*. Then another few – *Education of your children*.

My eyes fly back to Sue. There are tears on her face but she's smiling.

'What is this?' My voice shakes. I think . . . I think I know but I can't allow myself to believe it.

'It's an education trust for the girls, and the little one when he or she is older.'

Goosebumps prickle my skin and I shake my head. 'Why?'

'That night Dean came home, he told me about Harrie visiting him. The kindness and bravery your daughter showed meant so much to him, and to me. It kept him going knowing she would come to visit. I know that sounds stupid after . . . But, well, it mattered. Harrie explained about Elise's hard work for a scholarship and how they'd be going to different schools if she got it, but this way, they can go to the same school.'

I nod, tears forming in my eyes. 'Elise didn't get the scholarship. Mike wrote a rather damning report about her.'

'God, I've always hated that weasel,' Sue says with an exasperated huff. 'But it doesn't matter now. They can all go to the same school. I don't need much from the house sale or the land. I've got my villa and a bit of savings. That trust is the rest. It'll be enough for whatever they need, for as long as they need it. I've made sure the term "education" is flexible. It's not just school fees. It's uniforms, shoes, books, and also travel. Take them places, Anna, when you're ready. Travel with them. Maybe come to Spain for a little visit some time. It's just in your name. No offence to your husband, but I've never met him and it's you I know and you I trust. Dean told me how much your friendship meant to him. You were there for him and I'll always be so grateful for that.'

Tears are falling, streaming down my face, dripping on to the round bump of my belly. 'I can't accept this.'

'You can and you will because it's for your children. My solicitor is a nice man. He's expecting your call. He'll go through all the fine print with you. But there's one other thing I wanted to say about it. Counselling, therapy, whatever you call it these days, it's included too. For Harrie. If she needs it.'

A sob escapes my throat then and I cry and cry for this gift, this wonderful kindness. Sue moves and sits beside me on the sofa, her arm around me just as I have sat with the girls a thousand times.

'Thank you,' I whisper. 'Thank you so much.'

It's then that Timmy bounds into the living room, followed closely by Harrie, Elise and Molly – a whirlwind of excitement and noise.

'What's going on?' Elise asks. She looks at my face and then to my belly. 'Is the baby coming?'

I shake my head. 'Mrs Stockton is giving us some money.'

'Cool,' Harrie says, scooping Timmy into her arms. 'Can we buy a dog with it?'

'It's for school.' I look at Elise and her mouth drops open. 'You can go to St Benedict's. You and Harrie, and Molly when she's old enough.' I choke on the words and I know it's only a school and that the girls would find happiness anywhere, but it's what Elise so desperately wants and after the years and years of not being able to give them so much as a holiday, they deserve this. We all do.

Elise's face drains of colour. Her bottom lip

wobbles. 'Seriously?' She looks at Sue and then at me and I nod. 'And Harrie too?'

'Yes.'

'There is one more thing,' Sue says and I see the tears falling from her own eyes now. 'Timmy has always been Dean's dog, and, well, the climate in Spain will be too hot for a dog with so much fur. You can say no of course, but I wondered if Harrie would like—'

'Yes,' Harrie shouts. 'Can we, Mum? Can we look after him?' I look at the smile on Harrie's face, the hope and joy I've not seen for so long.

'Absolutely,' I laugh.

'It won't be too much with the baby?' Sue asks, looking at me.

'I'll walk him every day before school and afterwards,' Harrie jumps in. 'He can sleep on my bed.'

'And mine,' Molly shouts.

'I'm sure it will be a lovely distraction for them while I'm changing nappies and feeding.'

Sue smiles before she stands, hooking her bag over her shoulder. 'I was hoping you'd say that. I have his bed and a few things in the car. I'll send you a postcard when I'm settled. If you don't mind, I'd like to keep in touch and see how the children are getting on.'

I smile and stand too, the baby nudging at my ribs again. 'We'd love that.'

We gather around the doorstep, Timmy snuggled in Harrie's arms, and say goodbye to Sue. And then, just as she's turning to leave, I spot Rob walking down the road. My heart expands and I grin, excited to tell him about the trust. But even as the thought runs through my mind, there is something unfolding before me.

Rob is still bouncing towards us, but Sue has stopped dead. She's staring at my husband, her eyes

368

wide with recognition and fear. Rob falters, a questioning frown on his face as he looks between Sue and me. Then he smiles, his charm offensive at the ready.

Sue turns back to look at me, her mouth agape. She mouths two words. 'It's him.'

And I see it. I see it all. One split second is all it takes, like someone has thrown open the curtains and let the light pour in.

It was Rob who hit Dean that day in Sue's driveway. He must have found out that Dean wanted to sell the land.

Mutual assured destruction.

My mind races back to the night in the stable. How keen Rob was for me to go home that night. I thought it was concern for me. I hear Sandra's spiteful words. *You're involved in this too.* I thought she was looking at me, but it was Rob standing right by my side. He's been in on everything. Jack and Sandra Briggs. Mike and Bev Pritchett. Anthony and Tracy Campbell. Kat Morris. And Rob James.

I turn my gaze to Harrie – my beautiful girl – and picture the way she looks at her dad sometimes. The sideways glance. Watchful. Mistrusting. I think of the time she spent with Dean in that dark stable. She never told me what they talked about, but I think I can guess. Is that why she didn't call the police that night? It wasn't just because of Jack's threats, but because she knew her dad, her hero, was part of it.

Sue is still rooted to the spot. Her eyes flick to Rob and then back to me and I meet her gaze and nod because I know what she's seen and what she's trying to tell me.

Tears burn in my eyes and my chest rips open for the marriage I've lost, the fresh start that wasn't fresh, but rotten to its core.

Acknowledgements

When I think about the long list of thank yous I want to make, there is always one that stands out, and that is to you – the reader. Thank you for reading *Safe At Home*. I really hope you enjoyed escaping into this story. If you've got this far and can spare one more moment to write a quick review or give a rating, it really does make a big difference to authors.

To Tash Barsby, my wonderful editor, and all the Transworld team – thank you for believing in me and for making this story the best it can be.

To my fantastic agent, Tanera Simons – thank you for your unwavering support, pep talks, advice, editing notes and everything else you do behind the scenes.

To my friends and family, I'm always so grateful for your support. A special mention to Kathryn Jones for being the most amazing, eagle-eyed proofreading friend. To Saff Griffiths for always being so lovely, and to Laura, Zoe and Nikki for absolutely everything.

To my son, Tommy, who worked so hard during the months it took me to write this book and many afterwards. No matter what, we're always so proud of you. Thank you for asking me again and again why I wouldn't let you stay home while I popped to collect your sister from gymnastics. My worst case scenario answers gave me the seeds of this book. And to Lottie, my shining light of kindness and good, brave and funny, thank you for always being you and brightening every day.

I really should give a shout out to my husband Andy too. Thanks for the million ways you make every day better.

I would also like to take a moment to say that this book is dedicated to the lovely ladies in my village because they are nothing like the characters in this book!

To all the book bloggers – you lot are the bee's knees. Your dedication and support to books and authors blows my mind. Thank you!

It feels as though I can't end without a mention to the terrible year that was 2020. I may have based *Safe At Home* in a fictional year but it was written during lockdown and homeschool and endless news cycles, and it's there between the lines in Anna's anxiety and Harrie's fear. 2020 really was the year we were safest at home, and so my final thank you is to every single key worker who went to work and kept the country going. We're forever in your debt!

After the sudden death of her husband, **Tess** is
drowning in grief. All she has left is her son, **Jamie**,
and she'll do anything to protect him – but she's
struggling to cope.

When grief counsellor **Shelley** knocks on their
door, everything changes. Shelley is understanding
and kind, and promises she can help Tess through the
hardest time of her life.

But when a string of unsettling events happens and
questions arise over her husband's death, Tess starts
to suspect that Shelley may have an ulterior motive.
Tess knows she must do everything she can to keep
Jamie safe – but she's at her most vulnerable, and
that's a dangerous place to be . . .

* * * * *

'A captivating, suspenseful thriller that draws you
in – with a twist that will take your breath away.'

T. M. Logan, bestselling author of *The Holiday*

OUT NOW

If you loved *Safe At Home*, keep an eye
out for Lauren North's pulse-pounding new thriller

ALL THE WICKED GAMES

Coming in 2022